WOMEN'S VOICE
THAT MATTERS!

GREAT WOMEN'S INSPIRATIONAL SPEECHES

Dr. Gagan Jain, *D.Litt.*

MGB®
NEW DELHI (INDIA)

WOMEN'S VOICE THAT MATTERS!

GREAT WOMEN'S INSPIRATIONAL SPEECHES

This English Edition, Published in India

Published by

MG BOOKS

An Imprint of

MAANU GRAPHICS

MAANU GRAPHICS

(PUBLISHERS OF GENERAL BOOKS)

5FF, Ganpati Bhawan, 21 Ansari Road,
Darya Ganj, New Delhi-110002
Ph: 43755225, 9315898404
E-mail : maanugraphics@yahoo.com
mgbooks.maanu@yahoo.com

Printed at
Satyam Enterprises, Delhi

CONTENTS

1. **Aung San Suu Kyi** -- 7

* Opening Keynote Address, Read on video on August 31, 1995 before the NGO Forum on Women, Beijing, China

2. **Benazir Bhutto** -- 15

* Remarks At Joint Appearance With U.S. President Bill Clinton Cross Hall, The White House: April 11, 1995

* Speech To The John F. Kennedy School Of Government November 7, 1997 at the John F. Kennedy School Of Government

3. **Chandrika Bandaranike Kumaratunga** ---------- 30

* Address At The United Nations 50th Anniversary In New York on 22 October 1995

* Address To The United Nations World Summit For Social Development Sunday, 12 March 1995

4. **Condoleezza Rice** -- 38

* Republican National Convention Famous Speech Republican National Convention - Tuesday August 1, 2000

5. **Eleanor Roosevelt** -- 43

* What Libraries Mean To The Nation Famous Speech The District Of Columbia Library Association Dinner - April 1, 1936

6. **Erica Jong** -- 49

* ACLU Biennial Conference New York City - June 22,

1995

7. **Golda Meir** ---------- 56

* For the Attainment of Peace Famous Speech Address To The Israeli Knesset, Tel Aviv, Israel:26 May 1970
* Statement Before The General Assembly Of The United Nations

8. **Helen Keller** ---------- 98

* Strike Against War Famous Speech Speech at Carnegie Hall, New York City - January 5, 1916

9. **Her Majesty Queen Elizabeth II** ---------- 105

* On the Death of Princess Diana Famous Speech September 9, 1997
* On The Opening Of Parliament by Her Majesty Queen Elizabeth II Queen of the United Kingdom Wednesday, 14th May, 1997

10. **Hillary Rodham Clinton** ---------- 112

* Women's Rights Are Human Rights September 5, 1995, Beijing, China

11. **Indira Gandhi** ---------- 119

* Martin Luther King Famous Speech by Indira Gandhi New Delhi, India: January 24, 1969 Speech at the Presentation of the Jawaharial Nehru Award for International Understanding to Coretta Scott King
* At the Seventh Conference of Heads of State or Government of Non-aligned Countries, New Delhi, March 7, 1983

12. **Margaret (Hilda) Thatcher** ---------- 126

* Keynote Address to Citibank Delivered on Thursday 22 September 1994 in New Delhi, India

13. **Marie Curie** ---------- 138

* On the Discovery of Radium Famous Speech Vassar College in Poughkeepsie, NY - May 14, 1921

14. **Mary Reynolds** -- 142

* Her Days As A Slave Famous Speech, c 1925

15. **Mother Teresa** -- 151

* Nobel Lecture Speech - December 11, 1979
* The National Prayer Breakfast Famous Speech Washington, D.C. - February 4, 1994

16. **Oprah Winfrey** -- 168

* 54th Annual EMMY Awards Famous Speech Oprah Winfrey Receives the first Bob Hope Humanitarian Award - September 22, 2002

17. **Pearl Buck** -- 171

* Nobel Lecture - The Chinese Novel Famous Speech December 12, 1938 Stockholm, Sweden

18. **Princess Diana** -- 193

(Princess Of Wales and Anti-Landmine Activist)

* Responding To Landmines: A Modern Tragedy And It's Consequences Keynote Address at a one day seminar co-hosted by the Mines Advisory Group and the Landmine Survivors Network, London: June 12, 1997

19. **Sheikh Hasina** -- 198

* Address on towards Partnership between Men and Women in Politics, held in New Delhi (February 15, 1997)

20. **Shirley Chisholm** -- 205

* Equal Rights For Women Famous Speech Address To The United States House Of Representatives, Washington, DC: May 21, 1969

AUNG SAN SUU KYI
(Human Rights Leader for Burma)

INTRODUCTION

Aung San Suu Kyi was born on June 19, 1945, Rangoon, Burma [now Yangôn, Myanmar] Myanmar opposition leader, daughter of Aung San (a martyred national hero of independent Burma) and Khin Kyi (a prominent Burmese diplomat), and winner in 1991 of the Nobel Prize for Peace. She attended schools in Burma until 1960, when her mother was appointed ambassador to India.

After further study in India, she attended the University of Oxford, where she met her future husband. She had two children and lived a rather quiet life until 1988, when she returned to Burma to nurse her dying mother.

In July 1989 the military government of the newly named Union of Myanmar placed Aung San Suu Kyi under house arrest and held her incommunicado. The military offered to free her if she agreed to leave Myanmar, but she refused to do so until the country was returned to civilian government and political prisoners were freed. Aung San Sun Kyi is an honorary fellow of Oxford University. In 1991 she was awarded the Nobel Peace Prize. Aung San Suu Kyi is also author of several books, including Freedom from Fear and The Voice of Hope.

Opening Keynote Address
Read on video on August 31, 1995 before the NGO Forum on Women, Beijing, China

---

IT is a wonderful but daunting task that has fallen on me to say few words by way of opening this Forum, the greatest concourse of women (joined by a few brave men!) that has ever gathered on our planet. I want to try and voice some of the common hopes which firmly unite us in all our splendid diversity.

But first I would like to explain why I cannot be with you in person today. Last month I was released from almost six years of house arrest. The regaining of my freedom has in turn imposed a duty on me to work for the freedom of other women and men in my country who have suffered far more – and who continue to suffer far more – than I have. It is this duty which prevents me from joining you today. Even sending this message to you has not been without difficulties. But the help of those who believe in international cooperation and freedom of expression has enabled me to overcome the obstacles. They made it possible for me to make a small contribution to this great celebration of the struggle of women to mould their own destiny and to influence the fate of our global village.

The opening plenary of this Forum will be presenting an overview of the global forces affecting the quality of life of the human community and the challenges they pose for the global community as a whole and for women in particular as we approach the twenty-first century. However, with true womanly understanding, the Convener of this Forum suggested that among these global forces and challenges, I might wish to concentrate on those matters which occupy all my waking thoughts these days: peace, security, human rights and democracy. I would like to discuss these issues particularly in the context of the participation of women in politics and governance.

For millennia women have dedicated themselves almost exclusively to the task of nurturing, protecting and caring for the young and the old, striving for the conditions of peace that favour life as a whole. To this can be added the fact that, to the best of my knowledge, no war was ever started by women. But it is women and children who have always suffered most in situations of conflict. Now that we are gaining control of the primary historical role imposed on us of sustaining life in the context of the home and family, it is time to apply in the arena of the world the wisdom and experience thus gained in activities of peace over so many thousands of years. The education and empowerment of women throughout the world cannot fail to result in a more caring, tolerant, just and peaceful life for all.

If to these universal benefits of the growing emancipation of women can be added to the "peace dividend" for human development offered by the end of the Cold War, spending less on the war toys of grown men and much more on the urgent needs of humanity as a whole, then truly the next millennia will be an age the like of which has never been seen in human history. But there still remain many obstacles to be overcome before we can achieve this goal. And not least among those obstacles are intolerance and insecurity.

This year is the International Year for Tolerance. The United Nations has recognized that "tolerance, human rights, democracy and peace are closely related. Without tolerance, the foundations form democracy and respect for human rights cannot be strengthened, and the achievement of peace will remain elusive." My own experience during the years I have been engaged in the democracy movement of Burma has convinced me of the need to emphasize the positive aspect of tolerance. It is not enough simply to "live and let live": genuine tolerance requires an active effort to try to understand the point of view of others; it implies broad-mindedness and vision, as well as confidence in one's own ability to meet new challenges without resorting to intransigence or violence. In societies where men are truly confident of their own worth women are not merely "tolerated", they are valued. Their opinions are listened to with respect, they are given their rightful place in shaping the society in which they live.

There is an outmoded Burmese proverb still recited by men who wish to deny that women too can play a part in bringing necessary change and progress to their society: "The dawn rises only when the rooster crows." But Burmese people today are well aware of the scientific reasons behind the rising of dawn and the falling of dusk. And the intelligent rooster surely realizes that it is because dawn comes that it crows and not the other way round. It crows to welcome the light that has come to relieve the darkness of night. It is not the prerogative of men alone to bring light to this world: women with their capacity for compassion and self-sacrifice, their courage and perseverance, have done much to dissipate the darkness of intolerance and hate, suffering and despair.

Often the other side of the coin of intolerance is insecurity. Insecure people tend to be intolerant, and their intolerance unleashes forces that threaten the security of others. And where there is no security there can be no lasting peace. In its "Human Development Report" for last year the UNDP noted that human security "is not a concern with weapons — it is a concern with human life and dignity." The struggle for democracy and human rights in Burma is a struggle for life and dignity. It is a struggle that encompasses our political, social and economic aspirations. The people of my country want the two freedoms that spell security: freedom from want and freedom from fear. It is want that has driven so many of our young girls across our borders to a life of sexual slavery where they are subject to constant humiliation and ill-treatment. It is fear of persecution for their political beliefs that has made so many of our people feel that even in their own homes they cannot live in dignity and security.

Traditionally the home is the domain of the woman. But there has never been a guarantee that she can live out her life there safe and unmolested. There are countless women who are subjected to severe cruelty within the heart of the family which should be their haven. And in times of crisis when their menfolk are unable to give them protection, women have to face the harsh challenges of the world outside while continuing to discharge their duties within the home.

Many of my male colleagues who have suffered imprisonment for their part in the democracy movement have spoken of the great debt of gratitude they owe their womenfolk, particularly to their wives who stood by them firmly, tender as mothers nursing their newly born, brave as lionesses defending their young. These magnificent human beings who have done so much to aid their men in the struggle for justice and peace — how much more could they not achieve if given the opportunity to work in their own right for the good of their country and of the world.

Our endeavours have also been sustained by the activities of strong and principled women all over the world who have campaigned not only for my own release but, more importantly, for our cause. I cannot let this opportunity pass without speaking of the gratitude we feel towards our sisters everywhere, from heads of government to busy housewives. Their efforts have been a triumphant demonstration of female solidarity and of the power of an ideal to cross all frontiers.

In my country at present, women have no participation in the higher levels of government and none whatsoever in the judiciary. Even within the democratic movement only 14 out of the 485 MPs elected in 1990 were women – all from my own party, the National League for Democracy. These 14 women represent less than 3 percent of the total number of successful candidates. They, like their male colleagues, have not been permitted to take office since the outcome of those elections has been totally ignored. Yet the very high performance of women in our educational system and in the management of commercial enterprises proves their enormous potential to contribute to the betterment of society in general. Meanwhile our women have yet to achieve those fundamental rights of free expression, association and security of life denied also to their menfolk.

The adversities that we have had to face together have taught all of us involved in the struggle to build a truly democratic political system in Burma that there are no gender barriers that cannot be overcome. The relationship between men and women should, and can be, characterized not by patronizing behavior or exploitation, but by METTA (that is to say loving kindness), partnership and trust. We need mutual respect and understanding between men and women, instead of patriarchal domination and degradation, which are expressions of violence and engender counter-violence. We can learn from each other and help one another to moderate the "gender weaknesses" imposed upon us by traditional or biological factors.

There is an age old prejudice the world over to effect that women talk too much. But is this really a weakness? Could it not in fact be a strength? Recent scientific research on the human brain has revealed that women are better at verbal skills while men tend towards physical action. Psychological research has shown on the other hand that disinformation engendered by men has a far more damaging effect on its victims than feminine gossip. Surely these discoveries indicate that women have a most valuable contribution to make in situations of conflict, by leading the way to solutions based on dialogue rather than on viciousness or violence?

The Buddhist PAVARANA ceremony at the end of the rainy season retreat was instituted by the Lord Buddha, who did not want human beings to live in silence "like dumb animals." This ceremony, during which monks ask mutual forgiveness for any offence given during the retreat, can be said to be a council of truth and reconciliation. It might also be considered a forerunner of that most democratic of institutions, the parliament, a meeting of peoples gathered together to talk over their shared problems. All the world's great religions are dedicated to the generation of happiness and harmony. This demonstrates the fact that together with the combative instincts of man there co-exists a spiritual aspiration for mutual understanding and peace.

This forum of non-governmental organizations represents the belief in the ability of intelligent human beings to resolve conflicting interests through exchange and dialogue. It also represents the conviction that governments alone cannot resolve all the problems of their countries. The watchfulness and active cooperation of organizations outside the spheres of officialdom are necessary to ensure the four essential components of the human development paradigm as identified by the UNDP: productivity, equity, sustainability and empowerment. The last is particularly relevant: it requires that "development must be BY people, not only FOR them. People must participate fully in the decisions and processes that shape their lives." In other words people must be allowed to play a significant role in the governance of their country. And "people" include women who make up at least half of the world's population.

The last six years afforded me much time and food for thought. I came to the conclusion that the human race is not divided into two opposing camps of good and evil. It is made up of those who are capable of learning and those who are incapable of doing so. Here I am not talking of learning in the narrow sense of acquiring an academic education, but of learning as the process of absorbing those lessons of life that enable us to increase peace and happiness in our world. Women in their role as mothers have traditionally assumed the responsibility of teaching children values that will guide them throughout their lives. It is time we were given the full opportunity to use our natural teaching skills to contribute towards building a modern world that can withstand the tremendous challenges of the technological revolution which has in turn brought revolutionary changes in social values.

As we strive to teach others we must have the humility to acknowledge that we too still have much to learn. And we must have the flexibility to adapt to the changing needs of the world around us. Women who have been taught that modesty and pliancy are among the prized virtues of our gender are marvellously equipped for the learning process. But they must be given the opportunity to turn these often merely passive virtues into positive assets for the society in which they live.

These, then, are our common hopes that unite us – that as the shackles of prejudice and intolerance fall from our own limbs we can together strive to identify and remove the impediments to human development everywhere. The mechanisms by which this great task is to be achieved provide the proper focus of this great Forum. I feel sure that women throughout the world who, like me, cannot be with you join me now in sending you all our prayers and good wishes for a joyful and productive meeting.

I thank you.

BENAZIR BHUTTO

(Former Prime Minister Of Pakistan)

INTRODUCTION

Benazir Bhutto was born on June 21, 1953 at Karachi, Pakistan. Pakistani politician who became the first woman leader of a Muslim nation in modern history. She served two terms as prime minister of Pakistan, in 1988–90 and in 1993–96.

Bhutto was the daughter of the politician Zulfikar Ali Bhutto, who was the prime minister of Pakistan from 1971 until 1977. She was educated at Harvard University (B.A., 1973) and subsequently studied philosophy, political science, and economics at the University of Oxford (B.A., 1977). After her father's execution in 1979 during the rule of the military dictator Mohammad Zia-ul-Haq, Bhutto became the titular head of her father's party, the Pakistan People's Party (PPP), and endured frequent house arrest from 1979 to 1984.

In exile from 1984 to 1986, she returned to Pakistan after the lifting of martial law and soon became the foremost figure in the political opposition to Zia. She became prime minister on Dec. 1, 1988, heading a coalition government.

In elections held in October 1993 the PPP won a plurality of votes, and Bhutto again became head of a coalition government. Under renewed charges of corruption, economic mismanagement, and a decline of law and order, her government was dismissed in November 1996 by President Farooq Leghari. She had based at London, in exile, because of present situation of her country. She was assassinated on December 27, 2007 in Rawalpindi by Al-Qaeda.

Remarks At Joint Appearance With U.S. President Bill Clinton Cross Hall, The White House: April 11, 1995

MR. PRESIDENT, ladies and gentlemen: I'd like to begin by thanking the President for his kind words of support and encouragement.

Since 1989, my last visit to Washington, both the world and Pak-U.S. relations have undergone far-reaching changes. The post-Cold War era has brought into sharp focus the positive role that Pakistan, as a moderate, democratic, Islamic country of 130 million people, can play, and the fact that it is strategically located at the tri-junction of South Asia, Central Asia and the Gulf – a region of both political volatility and economic opportunity.

Globally, Pakistan is active in U.N. peacekeeping operations. We are on the forefront of the fight against international terrorism, narcotics, illegal immigration and counterfeit currency. We remain committed to the control and elimination of weapons of mass destruction, as well as the delivery systems on a regional, equitable and non-discriminatory basis.

Since 1993, concerted efforts by Pakistan and the United States to broaden the base of bilateral relations have resulted in steady progress. In September 1994, in a symbolic gesture, the United States granted Pakistan about $10 million in support for population planning. This was announced by the Vice President at the Cairo Summit on population planning. This was followed by the presidential mission, led by Energy

Secretary Hazel O'Leary, which resulted in agreement worth $4.6 billion being signed. And, now, during my visit here, we are grateful to the administration and the Cabinet secretaries for having helped us sign $6 billion more of agreements between Pakistan and the United States.

During the Defense Secretary's visit to Pakistan in January 1995, our countries decided to revive the Pakistan-United States Defense Consultative Group. And more recently, we had the First Lady and the First Daughter visit Pakistan, and we had an opportunity to discuss women's issues and children's issues with the First Lady. And we found the First Daughter very knowledgeable. We found Chelsea very knowledgeable on Islamic issues. I'm delighted to learn from the President that Chelsea is studying Islamic history and has also actually read our Holy Book, the Koran Shariah.

I'm delighted to have accepted President Clinton's invitation to Washington. This is the first visit by a Pakistani's Chief Executive in six years. President Clinton and I covered a wide range of subjects, including Kashmir, Afghanistan, Central Asia, Gulf, Pakistan-India relations, nuclear proliferation, U.N. peacekeeping, terrorism and narcotics.

I briefed him about corporate America's interest in Pakistan, which has resulted in the signing of $12 billion worth of MOUs in the last 17 months since our government too office. I urged an early resolution of the core issue of Kashmir, which poses a great threat to peace and security in our region. It has retarded progress on all issues, including nuclear and missile proliferation. A just and durable solution is the need of the hour, based on the wishes of the Kashmiri people, as envisaged in the Security Council resolutions. Pakistan remains committed to engage in a substantive dialogue with India to resolve this dispute, but not in a charade that can be used by our neighbor to mislead the international community. I am happy to note that the United States recognizes Kashmir as disputed territory and maintains that a durable solution can only be based on the will of the Kashmiri people.

Pakistan asked for a reassessment of the Pressler Amendment, which places discriminatory sanctions on Pakistan. In our view, this amendment has been a disincentive for a regional solution to the proliferation issue. Pakistan has requested the President and the administration to resolve the problem of our equipment worth $1.4 billion, which is held up. I am encouraged by my discussions with the President this morning and the understanding that he has shown for Pakistan's position. I welcome the Clinton administration's decision to work with Congress to revise the Pressler Amendment.

Thank you, Mr. President.

Speech To The John F. Kennedy School Of Government
November 7, 1997 at the John F. Kennedy School Of Government

THANK YOU. Honored guests, ladies and gentlemen. As you know, I am no stranger to America and being here at the John F. Kennedy School of Government, I'd just like you all to know how wonderful it is to come back home. I spent four of the happiest years of my life as a student at Harvard University. And those days now seem like a dream to me.

The last year has been an extraordinarily difficult period of time for me, for my family, for my country. I am well aware that many of you have been exposed to information, or should I say disinformation. I know that you have heard a negative barrage, attacking me and the record of my two administrations as the chief executive of Pakistan. That is why I am here; I still have the strength, I still have the fight—especially when it comes to the truth. I fully intend to defend myself and my record from this outrageous and sexist character assassination that is being conducted against me.

For what has happened to me, what is happening in Pakistan, may not in fact be unique; but part of a growing and disturbing trend, as the world approaches the new millennium. The attacks against me are painful and they are outright lies. But, it is only a more extreme version of what appears to be a universal deterioration of civil dialogue in politics. Not just in Pakistan, but all over the world. The search for political consensus, the main characteristic of a democratic society, has degenerated into partisan hysteria. A rule or ruin philosophy.

The breakdown of cooperation threatens the legitimacy of democratic values and norms in the modern post-Cold War international society. This is a new phenomena that blemishes the body politic. Consensus, civility and committee have been replaced with slander, prejudice and partisanship.

I would like to read you some thoughts that capture what I am saying to you today. And I quote: "Partisan politics is polluting our most important legal and ethical processes, and is damaging our political system. Proceedings, while billed as impartial, have become little more than witch hunts, designed to humiliate the opposing political party. The scandal that has developed, bankrupts individuals who are little more than pawns in larger political agendas. It threatens the ability of the political system to attract the bright, dedicated people that our nation deserves."

These are not my words; but, they may as well be. This is not written about Pakistan; but, it might as well be. For what I have quoted to you are the words of Robert Bennett, President Clinton's lawyer, from an essay attacking the subjugation of the legal and ethical process to a blatantly partisan political agenda. Right now, across the ocean in Asia, the Pakistan Peoples Party, which I lead, is being subjected to a political witch hunt, clouded in a so-called legal process.

The people of Pakistan honored me by electing me as their Prime Minister in the only two fair, free and impartial elections held in the last ten years. But, my political opponent saw to it that both governments were removed by presidential edict and not permitted to complete their full terms. Not a single member of my family has been spared. My father-in-law, my husband, and my brother-in-law have all been arrested. My mother and my sister-in-law are facing legal proceedings. Another sister-in-law had her house raided at midnight, without a search warrant or a magistrate. Yet another relative fled the country, when he was called to the Prime Minister's house, grabbed by the shirt and threatened: "You either do what we want or end up in a bed cell."

And, one of our defense lawyers was kidnapped by the regime for over two months, without a word of his whereabouts. Members of the Pakistan Peoples Party, and my political staff, including women, have faced similar treatment. I, therefore, wrote to the United Nations Secretary General, highlighting the human rights abuses. I was castigated by the regime for doing so. I was criticized for washing Pakistan's dirty linen in public. They weren't concerned that they were dirtying the linens; they were only concerned that I was washing it in public.

And, that was when the regime decided to raid my sister-in-law's house at midnight, to harass her and to harass me. That was when they decided to arrest a second defense lawyer; charging him with the kidnapping of the first. And, that was when they decided to file yet another murder case against my husband. And, that was when they falsely claimed that eight companies belonging to me had been frozen by the Swiss authorities. I had nothing to do with those companies. But, to humiliate and degrade me internationally, the regime claimed they were mine.

I know that truth and justice will eventually triumph. I know that I have the will to prove, not only for myself but for women all over, that we have the strength to stand up and defend our convictions. But, in the meantime, our family life has been affected. My young children miss their father. Not only my family, but those of my relatives, political colleagues, and supporters are being bankrupted defending charges in different courts of law. Our time and energy is depleted in reaction, rather than action, to fulfill the vindictive lust of the present regime.

However, this politics of confrontation is not limited to Pakistan, alone. All over the world, we find a greater interest in the human side of political personality. Human frailty enthralls us. This new politics of distortion and destabilization has paralyzed constructive dialogue. It has confused the public. It has led to a great cynicism across the continents about public leaders. And, it is a trend that is intensifying; not diminishing. In the United States, even a discussion of the ratification of a ban on chemical weapons takes on the character of street gang rumble.

And, while both the House and Senate spend millions upon millions of dollars in repetitive and redundant hearings, whose aim would seem to be more political than programmatic, no progress at all seems to be made on the entitlement crisis that threatens America's fiscal standing in the new century.

A ruling party, that once tried on the prerogatives of the special prosecutor during the Reagan era, now denounces exactly the same application to the Clinton era. Another party, which decried the powers of the special prosecutor in the '80s demands more and more of such appointments to investigate the opposition in the '90s. Rule or ruin.

The situation deteriorated so badly in Washington that it was thought necessary for a civility retreat to be convened. Basically to remind the members of the Congress of the United States of America the rules of common courtesy and civil dialogue. This, my friends, is in the greatest and oldest democracy on earth. Political expediency has replaced political idealism. And, political expediency has no bounds, no limits and no taste . This trend, as I said, is consistent across the continents. Four Indian prime ministers have changed within one calendar year. Governments disintegrating, not over policy, but over politics. Not over programs, but over power. Just last month in India's largest state, a riot erupted on the floor of the Assembly. Legislators hitting each other over the heads with furniture; inkwells thrown across the chamber; 14 Parliamentarians injured. This in what is often called the largest democracy on earth.

A peace process in the Middle East is allowed to be frozen, with substance often overshadowed by whispered innuendo. A decade's progress hanging in the balance. In Bangladesh, the ruling party and the opposition interchanges almost identical strategies of Parliamentary boycotts and street disruptions, as power shifts from one party to another. In Bosnia, leaders pledged to a multi-ethnic state are defeated by ethno-nationalists; threatening the very existence of the Dayton Accord.

In Pakistan, the new government elected in March almost collapsed in October when it began to undermine the judiciary, simply because the Supreme Court admitted corruption charges against the Prime Minister filed by my Party. All over the world, what do we find? All over the world, recrimination, finger-pointing and partisan condemnation are the modus operandi of the new political order. Hardly the quiet back Americana that many had predicted. We cannot afford, ladies and gentlemen, to be distracted from the real issues at hand. Building a political consensus for a new political era. I believe that our generation stands at the doorway of history. Not only the doorway of a new century, but the doorway of a new millenium. And, as we prepare ourselves to meet this new century, this new millennium, I believe we need to clearly understand the challenges that still await us and await the new century. I believe there are four simultaneous challenges that the world faces today. First, the rise of ethnic and religious hatred, prejudice and intolerance. Second, the gulf of wealth and health emerging between the developed and developing countries, and within nations themselves. Third, the growing sense of alienation by the people in a complex and fast-moving world and the ability of their governments to resolve the problem that the new technology era faces. And, fourth, the continuing gender inequity in all societies, west as well as east, that creates social division in the society as we move towards a new century.

The only good thing I can say for the forty years of the Cold War, is that it's bi-polar competition managed to suppress the ethnic and religious antagonism that had dominated the first half of the twentieth century. The simplistic dichotomy between the West and the East compartmentalized and clarified the world order. But, this also had negative consequences. During the Super Power confrontations, containing communism was paramount, even at the cost of democracy; even at the cost of human rights. Countries, like Pakistan, saw long periods of dictatorship; decades when freedom was suppressed. The press censored and billions of dollars in military and economic assistance siphoned. Similar patterns existed in South and Central America. In Portugal and Spain. In Greece and South Korea. And, in a large part of the African continent. The dawn of the new information age helped change the destiny of nations caught in the grip of dictatorship. CNN had a significant role, I believe, in bringing about the end of communism. I know many people thought it was just President Reagan; but, I think he got a lot of assistance from CNN. Because people in Eastern and Central Europe saw the beauty of freedom. They saw the consumer choices that were available and they asked a simple question: Why not here? People in South Asia and South America saw free people making free decisions, and making free choices not only in elections but in their careers and their professions. And, they, too, asked a simple question: Why not here?

With the tearing down of the Berlin Wall, many in the world

believed that our 45-year thermo-nuclear nightmare was over and a peace dividend could spread across the world. But, as T.S. Eliot once observed, between the idea and the reality falls the shadow. The twilight of the century has become Eliot's shadow. The idea, that platonic ... (inaudible) of peace that we prayed for, has eluded us. Its elusion has left people impatient, frustrated and angry. Those who believe that democracy meant instant financial progress, instant improvement in the standard of living, have lost faith in governmental systems. The frustration of newly-empowered electorates, combined with the regeneration long-suppressed ethnic and religious tensions, creates a very dangerous situation for the world as we approach the new millennium. The United States, in its extraordinary moment of international predominance, has an obligation to act as a catalyst to promote democratic values; to insure self-determination; to enforce United Nations resolutions; and to diffuse potential international conflicts before they engulf the world.

And, one of these long-simmering tensions is related to the dispute over Jamu and Kashmir. The Valley of Kashmir has been occupied by India and denied the basic right of self-determination. Tens of thousands of men, women and children have lost their lives in the quest for freedom. It is time now, consistent with President Clinton's stated policy of preemptive crisis management, to facilitate an agreement between India and Pakistan; so that the people of Kashmir and Jamu are finally allowed to determine their own future.

And, ladies and gentlemen, this is an era where we see an increasing focus on Islam and the West. The entire world community, and specifically the United States, have a fundamental strategic interest in events in the Muslim world. All across the world, in the Middle East, in Southwest Asia and Southeast Asia and Africa, one billion Muslims are at the crossroads. They must choose between progress and extremism. They must choose between education and ignorance. They must choose between the force of new technologies and the forces of old repression. Thus, one billion Muslims must choose between the past and the future.

The United States must do everything within its power to ensure that progressive, pluralistic Muslim countries like Pakistan are in a position to serve as role-models to the entire

Islamic world. And, Pakistan is also an important Asian country; at the crossroads to the strategic oil reserves of the Gulf and Central Asia. And, to the markets of South Asia and East Asia. In terms of demographics; in terms of production; in terms of consumption; in terms of markets; in terms of an expanding capital-intensive middle class, the Asian continent will surely set the tone, set the pace, and dominate the economic and geopolitical exigencies of the coming era.

I wonder how many people realize that Pakistan is the second largest Muslim state on earth. A state, as I've said, at the crossroads of the oil-rich Gulf and Central Asia. A state, as I've said, at the crossroads to the markets of South Asia and East Asia. A state that can serve as a model of moderation and modality to one billion Muslims across the planet. As a Pakistani, I wish to explore with you today the West's relationship with the Islamic world and the role that we can play to create a civil, political, economic and religious dialogue between the East and the West at this critical moment.

I believe it was only four years ago, when Harvard Professor Samuel Huntington, shocked the world with his provocative essay entitled "Clash of Civilization." As a Muslim woman, who had been educated and lived extensively in the United States and the United Kingdom, I was initially taken aback by the negative conclusion and the specter of inevitable conflict that he outlined. I particularly disagreed with Professor Huntington's unshakable pessimism about the emerging clash between the West and an increasingly self-confident and economically independent Islamic world.

But, four years later, my assessment of Professor Huntington's thesis has moderated. At the very least, I believe that his article has served a very useful purpose in bringing to the forefront of intellectual opinion significant issues that do warrant exploration, that do warrant debate. For whether we like it or not, whether it must be so or not, the world seems to be increasingly looking at the values and mores of the West and the values and traditions of Islam as mutually exclusive and confrontational.

Let's explore some of these issues today. The world is certainly a different place now than it was just ten short years ago. At that point, the nuclear threat was omnipresent. The Cold War ranged on between the West and the Soviet bloc; reaching a boiling point in the battle for the self-determination of Afghanistan. It was the alliance between the West and the Islamic world, through the fifties and the sixties, through the seventies and the eighties, that was central to the containment of communism on the Asian continent. For communism, Afghanistan became an overheated pressure cooker, that manifested the inevitable doom of a system that could not realistically address its people's political and economic needs.

Muslim resistance to the Soviets in Afghanistan proved once and for all that the Soviet Union could not, with all its military might, suppress the forces of history and the forces of justice. Afghanistan proved that might does not make right. It was the victory of the Mujahadim ; the Islamic freedom fighters supported by the Western Muslim Alliance, that proved to extinguish the fading embers of a dying system. This alliance, that of the Western Muslim Alliance, broke the back of the Soviet Union. It was our joint stand against the Soviet occupiers of Afghanistan that secured for all mankind the final victory of democracy and market-based economics.

I remember vividly my own feelings on February 15, 1989; when, as Prime Minister of Pakistan, I celebrated the final withdrawal of Soviet forces from our frontiers in Afghanistan. Little did I realize at that glorious moment that the victory in Afghanistan would be a catalyst to a curious consequence. The West's interest in, indeed need for, alliance with the Islamic world would and has steadily deteriorated over the last eight years. Interdependence during the Cold War period, gave way to indifference in the post Cold War period. Indifference has now, in many ways, been replaced with apprehension.

There are some in the West who would like to think of Muslims as terrorists and fanatics. I would like to assure you that Muslims are neither. Muslims, on the other hand, who benefited from economic and military assistance from the West for a half a century, are bewildered by the sudden turn of events where aid has totally ceased with the end of the communist threat. Muslims who consider themselves allies of the West do not comprehend the distancing of the West. For instance, a country like Pakistan was receiving $4.6 billion of military and economic assistance from the United States. Now, if somebody's earning $1,000 a month and getting an additional $500 from a friend; and, one day the friend turns around and says, Sorry. I don't have the $500; live on a $1,000. That means a drop in living standard. And, that's what it meant for many Muslim countries, including Pakistan.

Suddenly, the aid dried up. And, it coincided with the resurgence of democracy. And, instead of being better off, people were worse off; because now, we had less resources and less income. And, many could not understand why, at a time when the old resources were diminishing, the West was beginning to perceive the Muslims with a certain degree of apprehension. Because Islam is a religion that sanctifies Abraham, Moses and Jesus as prophets, it was even more bewildering for Muslims to find that the West suddenly was suspicious of them. And, Islam is, in fact, an integral part of the Judeo-Christian civilization. So, being an integral part of the Judeo-Christian civilization, it was a sudden shock for Muslims to find that the world was being perceived as being two blocs: that is, the West and Islam.

Now, Muslims do have certain problems with the way the West reacts to certain incidents. For instance, Muslims could not understand why one of the great cities of Europe was reduced to a rubble by a systematic destruction, and that this reduction of the city was captured nightly for all the world to see by CNN. Muslims could not understand why the West stood by, indifferent. This kind of event of bloodshed in a Muslim city, in the heart of Europe, with the West standing silently by, plays into the hands of extremists who say that, if it were Christian Paris on fire, and not Muslim Sarajevo, would the West have acquiesced? In the heart of Europe, a Muslim city was being destroyed and Muslims all over the world felt abandoned by the West.

So, we muse on the lessons of history and the lessons of human nature. While many in the West believe that there is no place for democracy in Islam, given the few number of democratic Muslim states, Muslims, on the other hand, believe that democracy is inherent in our faith. In Islam, dictatorship is never condoned. Dictatorship is considered a usurpation of the power of the people. Muslims are exalted to fight tyranny where ever they see it; and, indeed, Muslims are told that if you do not have the strength to fight tyranny when you see it, go into exile. But do not stand silent in the face of tyranny. For to be silent in the face of tyranny is to condone tyranny.

There are four democratic principles at the heart of Islam. The first is consultation, or Shura ; then, consensus, or Ijma ; and finally independent judgment, or Ijdaha . Instead of Islam being incompatible with democracy, our holy book makes it clear that the principle operations of the democratic process: consultation between the elected officials and the people; accountability of leaders to the people they serve, are fundamental to Islam. The holy book says that Islamic society is contingent on mutual advice, through mutual discussions, on an equal footing. Let me repeat that now: Equal footing. Ladies and gentleman, the Holy Koran is as committed to equality as it is to democracy. As committed to pluralism and tolerance as it is to order and doctrine. I know this is inconsistent with Western stereotypes. But, nevertheless, it is true. Consultation under the Holy Koran demands that public decisions are made by representative personalities. By men and by women who enjoy the confidence of the people and the integrity of their own character. Consensus provides a basis for majority rule. And, according to the Muslim scholar Luis Saffie , the legitimacy of the state depends upon the extent to which state organization and power reflect the will of the Omar , or the people.

And in the Persky element of Islamic democracy, independent judgment, we see an additional element of personal responsibility that the West, too, is trying to emulate and which lies at the heart of the Clinton administration's programmatic ideology, shaped by the writing of sociologist Amatai Edzioni . Islamic law rests on the consent of and the consultation with the people as fundamentally as British Parliamentary democracy or American separation of powers is founded on the people's will.

Western political scientists, these days, hypothesize populist strategies to create more effective forms of participatory democracy. But, Muslims do not believe they have to go back to the drawing board to conceptualize democratic order. It is right there in the holy book. Under Islam, we do not have to create a sense of community and individual responsibility. It is there in the holy book, itself. Enlightened Muslims find Western lectures on democracy condescending. Muslims need the West to acknowledge that dictatorship came out because of the strategic need to contain communism. Dictatorship did not come about because it was a part of Muslim faith or culture.

That is why, for decades, not only Muslim Asia but Spain and Portugal were governed by Fascism. Greece was ruled by military Junta. Argentina, Brazil, Paraguay, and Chile faced social and political repression. On October 21, 1997, in a lecture in Cyprus, Professor Huntington ruefully noted that non-democratic regimes, more often than not, were pro-American. The future of democracy in the post-Cold War world will remain contingent on the strategic interests of Pax Americana. The strategic interests have changed. They are no longer of an ideological nature. They are of an economic nature. Market politics, global trade and energy reserves remain the strategic interests of the West in the new political era in the post-Cold War period.

There is much that Islam and the West can do together to build a new economic and social order, as we approach the new millennium. But, the twenty-first century must be a century of moral universality; not selectivity. It is time for the West to understand that colonialism and exploitation, both of a material and spiritual kind, are over. It is also time for the Islamic world to begin to rely on ourselves and each other to address the lingering problems of the twentieth century and the unlimited opportunities of the twenty-first century.

The Muslim world needs to provide leadership in establishing the public parameters of possibilities and delineating Islam's role in the emerging political order and in the new explosion of technology and communication in the new global economy. In addressing the new exigencies of the new era, we must be prepared to work side-by-side; east and west, with other religions to improve the quality of life for all the people on this earth. And, we Muslims, must live by the true spirit of Islam. Not just by its rituals. To those who would claim to speak for Islam, but would deny to our women a place in society, I say the ethos of Islam is equality. Equality between the sexes. There is no religion that, in its writings and its teachings, is more respectful for the role of women in society than Islam.

To those in the West who would condemn Islam for being anti-women, let me as the first Muslim woman elected Prime Minister of her country recall that three Muslim countries: Pakistan, Bangladesh, and Turkey have all had democratically elected women as head of their government. In other words, my friends, there is much that we can learn from each other. Islam and the West; the West and Islam, as we cross into a new century and into a new millennium.

There are many problems that we confront simultaneously. The Islamic extremists who burn books and keep young women in purdha are really not that different from the Christian fundamentalists who attack clinics in America or the Jewish extremists who massacre worshippers in Hebron. So, let us decide to cast aside myths and stereotypes about each other. For Islam and for the West, it is time to attack the common and real enemies of our respective societies. These enemies are not people; they are ignorance and hatred. These enemies are not ethnic minorities; they are starvation and intolerance. Myopia and prejudice, whether it be religious, political, ethnic, gender or intellectual, are the common enemies of our hope for the twenty-first century. They are the fuel of the clash of civilization.

Ladies and gentlemen, we are about to cross together into a new century and into a new millennium. Whether we cross the millennium holding hands or at odds with each other is very much in our own control. The opportunities are boundless for all who believe in the blessings of the modern era, the application of technology to addressing the economic and social conditions of mankind; the end of intolerance, the flourishing of democracy and human rights. For Islam and for the West, the forces of change, the thrust of modality and technology, the strength of tolerance, the inevitability of freedom and liberty, the sanctity of human rights are all converging on this time, on our generation. On our generation; yours and mine. Providing an extraordinary opportunity for us to move the world. For in less than 800 days we will witness, for only the third time in recorded history, the momentous turning of the millennium. Where and what will we be at that extraordinary moment, when the huge ball drops and the year 2000 lights up the sky? Will we be prisoners of the mindset of the past? Or, will we be liberated to the endless possibilities of an historic future?

Our generation, yours and mine; the first in history is empowered to control our own destiny. The world has finally accepted, in the words of Robert Browning, that ignorance is not innocent; but sent. So, ladies and gentlemen, I come here to Harvard where I once studied and where you now study to tell you of my vision. For I see a third millennium where the gap between the rich and the poor states evaporates. Where illiteracy and hunger and malnutrition are conquered. I see where human rights are universal. I see a third millennium where civil dialogue is restored. I see a third millennium where people's trust in government and in themselves is restored. I see a third millennium of tolerance where religions respect other religions. I see a third millennium where every child is planned, wanted, nurtured and supported. I see a third millennium where the birth of a girl child is welcomed with the same joy as the birth of a boy. This is the third millennium I see for my country and for yours. For my children and for yours. And, I hope, together, we succeed. Thank you very much.

CHANDRIKA BANDARANIKE KUMARATUNGA

INTRODUCTION

President Chandrika Bandaranaike Kumaratunga was born to one of Sri Lanka's most distinguished families on 29th June 1945.

Her father, SWRD Bandaranaike, was a senior Minister of the Government at the time of her birth. He was later to become the Prime Minister of the country, while her mother, Sirimavo Bandaranaike, was to become the world's first woman Prime Minister in 1961.

President Kumaratunga had her early education at St. Bridget's Convent, Colombo. President Kumaratunga has been a guest lecturer at the Jawaharlal Nehru University in New Delhi and the Bradford University in U.K. She was a Research Fellow at the Institute of Commonwealth Studies, University of London from 1988 to 1991. President Kumaratunga inherited the liberal political philosophy of her father, the late SWRD Bandaranaike. In her student days in Paris, she was also greatly influenced by the radical student movement of the 1960s. The abiding element of that influence in today's vastly changed world circumstances is her deep commitment to the welfare of the deprived, the underprivileged and the disadvantaged. Her unshakable commitment to the imperatives of a plural society has been the other consistent strategy in her approach to politics. She has been a full time political activist from her early youth, establishing grass root contacts far and wide throughout the country.

Address At The United Nations 50th Anniversary In New York on 22 October 1995

MR PRESIDENT,

Your Majesties,

Excellencies and Distinguished Delegates,

Your Excellency, permit me to express my good wishes on your election as President.

I am deeply honoured to represent the people of Sri Lanka on this historic occasion.

Sri Lanka has always reposed great hopes in the United Nations for effective collective action to achieve our central aim of socio-economic development and thereby ensure social stability and peace for our people.

The transition from the Cold War era to a new world order has shifted the arena of conflict from the international to the national.

Whatever the overlay of such conflict—whether they take on religious, racial or other forms, they stem from poverty and social inequality. We believe therefore that the foundations of peace must be built on economic and social stability.

As a developing country, Sri Lanka attaches great importance to the role which the United Nations can, and must, perform in advancing the development process. Unless the principles of the Declaration on the Right to Development adopted in 1986 are applied positively with the full commitment of both developed and developing countries, the development process will not be sufficiently advanced.

We believe that the effective strengthening of the United Nations system is an essential requisite for advancing it's goals. The organisation has regrettably sometimes come to be seen by the more vulnerable States as primarily serving the interests of the more powerful States. We welcome the timely initiative of the President of last year's General Assembly to strengthen and empower the United Nations system.

Such an effective empowerment requires, in our view, that:

Firstly, development priorities should not be sacrificed in the pursuit of politico military operations which must be set at realistic, even modest levels;

Secondly, decision making by the United Nations in all areas must be based on the full engagement of all members. The Security Council in particular must become more representative and more responsive to the general membership of the United Nations;

Thirdly, commitment made for multilateral action in all fields must be honoured and diligently pursued.

In short, the revitalising process must enhance the capacity of the United Nations rather than merely effect economies and scale down its scope.

In the index of human development Sri Lanka rates high among developing countries, but we have been traumatised by ethnic tensions kept unnaturally high by the forces of terrorism and chauvinism. Nonetheless my Government is resolved to fulfill its mandate by seeking, through political negotiations, solutions to our problems which would enable our people to live in peace, security and freedom.

There are however obstacles in our way.

An armed group which claims to represent an ethnic minority has been engaged in violent acts against successive popularly elected Governments, preventing them from ensuring peace and justice for all in our land.

This group, which also operates on foreign soil, maintains an international network for fund raising based on coercion and blackmail. That network has a close nexus with powerful commercial interests engaged in narcotics trafficking, trade in illicit arms and smuggling of illegal immigrants.

Concerted international action is essential to combat terrorism and to compel the terrorists to renounce violence and enter the democratic process. Unfortunately, effective action to that has been frustrated through sterile philosophical debate about the nature of terrorism.

However, in the South Asian Association for Regional Co-operation (SAARC) we have overcome that difficulty by focusing our attention on manifestations of terrorism. The SAARC Convention on the Suppression of Terrorism provides for a collective response. This centres on a comprehensive legal regime and practical measures to combat terrorism.

I would urge similar action by the United Nations to give legal effect to the obligations arising from the Declaration on the Elimination of Terrorism adopted last year. I was happy to hear the statement of President Clinton. I hope that our common realisaton of the terrible consequences of terrorism, drug trafficking and other antisocial activities would usher in a new era of international co-operation to combat these problems.

My Government is committed to provide full opportunities in Sri Lanka for the development of the total human person. While promoting rapid economic growth, we seek to distribute its benefits equitably. This involves the maintenance of democratic institutions, and the preservation of human rights. It makes of politics the discharge of a public trust, where decision making is transparent and free of corruption, and everyone in public life is accountable for their actions.

In end, the United Nations will essentially be what we, the member States make of it, not what individual States seek to make from it.

On behalf of the Government and people of Sri Lanka, I take this opportunity to wish the United Nations success in its endeavours to transform the separate dreams of all the nations into a multifaceted yet harmonious reality.

I thank You All.

Address To The United Nations World Summit For Social Development Sunday, 12 March 1995

MR CHAIRMAN,

Your Excellencies,

Mr. Secretary-General Of The United Nations,

Ladies and Gentlemen,

Your invitation to me to address this Summit, organised on the 50th Anniversary of the United Nations is a great honour to me and to our people.

To you Mr. Chairman, to the distinguished Heads of State and Government, to the Secretary-General of the United Nations and others gathered here today, I extend my felicitations and those of my government and the people of Sri Lanka.

Poverty alleviation, the creation of employment and social Integration are critical issues that demand the immediate attention of the international community. Unless these issues are addressed urgently and effectively at national and global levels, the lofty goals of the United Nations—peace, security and economic prosperity of humankind—will continue to remain elusive; and the very existence of our societies will be drastically undermined.

Poverty and unemployment are very often the underlying causes of social conflict and violence, which undermines and erodes the social fabric upon which human prosperity and happiness rest. Our efforts at national level to overcome these problems can only succeed in a conducive international environment, in which the international community, the UN and the relevant financial institutions need to take positive steps towards assisting national economic development. It is regrettable that protective barriers on free trade, growing debt burdens, declining development assistance, worsening of terms of trade, as well as the negative effects of structural adjustment policies continue to thwart the national endeavours to achieve all round Social Development in an equitable manner. Hence the success of this Summit as embodied in the Declaration would lie in time bound, positive and concrete measures that will be taken to eliminate the adverse impacts of these trends on national economic development and the achievement of basic human needs.

We must make a collective and conscious effort to harness the positive effects of globalization. Increased trade and capital flows, development and transfer of technology, labour migration and foreign direct investment can contribute greatly towards empowering people and creating employment. Sri Lanka is proud of her enlightened social development policies pursued since independence in 1948. Relative to our per capita income of US 550 dollars, we have a life expectancy of 70 years, a literacy rate of 90 percent and population growth rate of only 1.2 percent. These are but a few of our achievements.

There are however lessons to be learnt from our past. Short-sighted economic policies which aimed at growth alone have led to: 30 percent of our households remaining below the poverty line, 14 percent of our labour force, particularly the youth, remaining unemployed, and over 30 percent of our young children being under nourished. It is hardly surprising that such widespread social exclusion was the principle factor that led to the violence of the past years.

The people's Alliance government has given the highest priority to free market policies which will combine economic growth with equity. We will carefully formulate and target our policies to ensure the equitable distribution of the fruits of development to meet the basic human needs of every sector of our society.

The alleviation of poverty will be one of our highest priorities. Towards this end we have initiated a SAMURDHI or PROSPERITY movement as the government's social safety net. By this programme we intend to broaden the horizons of those in genuine need by linking family development activities with community development projects at village, district and provincial levels. We have also taken steps to further enhance the allocation of resources in the national budget for health and education from 1995 onwards.

Mr. Chairman, the policies adopted by my government since assuming office last year, reflect a firm conviction that social development, social integration, and social justice are concepts that go beyond ensuring the physical well-being of the individual. We believe in simultaneously strengthening the democratic and legal framework within which people participate in the formulation and implementation of policy. This involves the fullest respect for human rights and fundamental freedoms and the rule of law, access to justice, elimination of discrimination as well as transparent and accountable government.

Finally, Mr. Chairman, I wish to say a few words on the peace process that my government has initiated since assuming office last year. Our experience has amply demonstrated that social development and social justice cannot be achieved in the absence of peace and security. In the context of the conflict in the North and East of Sri Lanka we have spent considerable resources and energies that could have been diverted for productive purposes. A peaceful resolution to the North East conflict arrived at through patient dialogue with all concerned, is essential for all communities in Sri Lanka to express their identities and to collectively and fully participate in national life. I am encouraged by the confidence expressed in our peace initiative by the international community and their commitment towards ensuring it success.

Mr. Chairman, in the up-hill task of achieving the objective of this summit by developing countries like Sri Lanka, the continued support of the international community would be of immense value. Countries that have effectively and efficiently utilized domestic and international resources in the realization of their social development goals would need assistance to continue their efforts at capacity building and self-reliance. Regional and sub-regional co-operation is as important as international support.

Sri Lanka fully endorses the two reports submitted to this summit by the Ministerial Conference of the Asia and Pacific Region held in the Philippines in October 1994 and the South Asian Association for Regional Co-operation (SAARC) held in Delhi in December 1994. We also have submitted the Sri Lanka National Report in which, in addition to the general trends of the conference, matters that are unique to Sri Lanka are focused upon.

These reports while highlighting the priorities of our region in the achievement of the objectives of this summit send a strong message with regard to the urgent resolution of the issues raised in them.

I wish to emphasize two aspects of the current international situation that deserve our immediate and special attention.

First, in addressing problems of global poverty, we must not be unmindful of the large populations of Asia, particularly in South Asia which suffer from poverty, malnutrition and unemployment. It will be unfortunate to presume that problems of poverty in Asia are being settled along with the rapid economic progress in some countries in Asia. Hence, the poor millions of Asia should not be forgotten in international anti-poverty initiatives.

Secondly, we are now in the Process of replenishing the resources of the International Development Association (IDA) of the World Bank, which lends on very concessional terms to the poorest countries of the world. The past soft lending by the IDA has been one of the most potent forces of poverty alleviation and I hope that this assembly can make a strong request to all donors to support the recommendation of the World Bank for the 11th Replenishment.

Mr. Chairman, we are confident that this summit will adopt a Declaration which contains practical and immediate measures that should be taken to combat the issues that we have been deliberating over the past few days. Our resolve to implement them both at national and international levels remains firm.

In conclusion Mr. Chairman, whilst thanking every one who has worked untiringly to make this Summit possible I would like to express my sincere appreciation and deep gratitude to the Government and the people of Denmark for hosting this conference and for the warm hospitality extended to me and my delegation.

Thank you.

CONDOLEEZZA RICE

INTRODUCTION

Condoleezza Rice was born November 14, 1954 in Birmingham, Alabama, she earned her bachelor's degree in political science, cum laude and Phi Beta Kappa, from the University of Denver in 1974; her master's from the University of Notre Dame in 1975; and her Ph.D. from the Graduate School of International Studies at the University of Denver in 1981. She is a Fellow of the American Academy of Arts and Sciences and has been awarded honorary doctorates from Morehouse College in 1991, the University of Alabama in 1994, the University of Notre Dame in 1995, the National Defense University in 2002, the Mississippi College School of Law in 2003, the University of Louisville and Michigan State University in 2004. She resides in Washington, D.C.

Dr. Condoleezza Rice became the Assistant to the President for National Security Affairs, commonly referred to as the National Security Advisor, on January 22, 2001. In June 1999, she completed a six year tenure as Stanford University 's Provost, during which she was the institution's chief budget and academic officer. As Provost she was responsible for a $1.5 billion annual budget and the academic program involving 1,400 faculty members and 14,000 students. As professor of political science, Dr. Rice has been on the Stanford faculty since 1981 and has won two of the highest teaching honors – the 1984 Walter J. Gores Award for Excellence in Teaching and the 1993 School of Humanities and Sciences Dean's Award for Distinguished Teaching.

Republican National Convention Famous Speech Republican National Convention - Tuesday August 1, 2000

LADIES and gentlemen, fellow delegates from the Golden State of California and fellow delegates from across this great country.

Tonight, we gather to reflect on America's unique opportunity to lead the forward march of freedom and to fortify the peace.

We offer special thanks to all those Private Ryans who served over the decades - so that tyranny would not stand.

We remember those great Republican Presidents who sustained American leadership through the decades, ended the Cold War and lifted our nuclear nightmare. Thank you - Gerald Ford, Ronald Reagan and George Herbert Walker Bush.

And we acknowledge together this remarkable truth: the future belongs to liberty - fueled by markets and trade, protected by the rule of law and propelled by the fundamental rights of the individual. Information and knowledge can no longer be bottled up by the state. Prosperity flows to those who can tap the genius of their people.

We have a presidential nominee who knows what America must do to fulfill the promise of this new century. We have a nominee who knows the power of truth and honor. We have a nominee who will be the next great President of the United States -Texas Governor George W. Bush.

It is fitting that I stand before you to talk about Governor Bush's commitment to America's principled leadership in the world, because that is the legacy and tradition of our Party - because our Party's principles made me a Republican.

The first Republican I knew was my father and he is still the Republican I most admire. He joined our party because the Democrats in Jim Crow Alabama of 1952 would not register him to vote. The Republicans did. My father has never forgotten that day, and neither have I.

I joined for different reasons. I found a party that sees me as an individual, not as part of a group. I found a party that puts family first. I found a party that has love of liberty at its core. And I found a party that believes that peace begins with strength.

George W. Bush and Dick Cheney live and breathe these Republican principles. They understand what is required for our time, and what is timeless. It all begins with integrity in the Oval Office. George W. Bush is a man of his word. Friend and foe will know that he tells the truth.

He believes that America has a special responsibility to keep the peace - that the fair cause of freedom depends on our strength and purpose. He recognizes that the magnificent men and women of America's armed forces are not a global police force. They are not the world's 911.

They are the strongest shield and surest sword in the maintenance of peace. If the time ever comes to use military force, President George W. Bush will do so to win - because for him, victory is not a dirty word.

George W. Bush will never allow America and our allies to be blackmailed. And make no mistake; blackmail is what the outlaw states seeking long-range ballistic missiles have in mind. It is time to move beyond the Cold War. It is time to have a President devoted to a new nuclear strategy and to the deployment of effective missile defenses at the earliest possible date. George W. Bush knows that America has allies and friends who share our values. As he has said, the President should call our allies when they are not needed, so that he can call upon them when they are needed. He understands the power of trade to create jobs at home and extend liberty abroad.

The George W. Bush I know is a man of uncommonly good judgment. He is focused and consistent. He believes that we Americans are at our best when we exercise power without fanfare or arrogance. He speaks plainly and with a positive spirit. In the past year, I have had a glimpse of what kind of President he will be.

I traveled with him to Mexico and saw the respect he has gained from its leaders and the affection he has won from its people. When he enters office, he will know more about our neighbor Mexico than any President in our history. He speaks to the Mexican people not just in the language of diplomacy but in their native tongue.

I have watched him explain America's interests to the Russian foreign minister, while assuring him that a peaceful Russia has nothing to fear from America.

He told the South African president of his hope for peace and prosperity in Africa.

I know that he understands the complexities of our relationship with China. He believes that conflict between our nations is not inevitable. Yet he recognizes the challenge that the Chinese government poses to our interests and values and the irresistible demand for liberty that can be unleashed by freer trade with its people.

And he has joined the bipartisan tradition of support for Israel's quest for enduring peace with its neighbors.

George W. Bush will work with Congress so that America speaks with one voice. He has demonstrated in this campaign that he will never use foreign policy for narrow partisan purposes.

The United States cannot lead unless the President inspires the American people to accept their international responsibilities. George W. Bush will inspire us, because he understands who we are. He knows that we are an innovative people who find kinship with those in other nations who are entrepreneurial in spirit. He realizes that we are a nation that has been forged not from common blood but from common purpose - that the faces of America are the faces of the world. It has not been easy for our country to make "We, the people" mean all the people. Democracy in America is a work in progress - not a finished masterpiece. But even with its flaws, this unique American experience provides a shining beacon to peoples who still suffer in places where ethnic difference is a license to kill. And George W. Bush understands that America is special among nations. That throughout our history, people everywhere have been inspired to flee tyranny and the constraints of class to gain liberty and pursue happiness in this great land.

In America, with education and hard work, it really does not matter where you came from - it matters where you are going. But that truth cannot be sustained if it is not renewed in each generation - as it was with my grandfather.

George W. Bush would have liked Granddaddy Rice. He was a poor farmer's son in rural Alabama - but he recognized the importance of education. Around 1918, he decided it was time to get book learning, so he asked, in the language of the day, where a colored man could go to college. He was told about little Stillman College, a school about 50 miles away. So Granddaddy saved his cotton for tuition and went off to Tuscaloosa.

After the first year, he ran out of cotton and needed a way to pay for college. Praise be - God gave him one. Grandfather asked how the other boys were staying in school. "They have what's called a scholarship," he was told, "and if you wanted to be a Presbyterian minister, then you could have one, too." Granddaddy Rice said, "That's just what I had in mind." And my family has been Presbyterian and college-educated ever since. This is not just my grandfather's story - it is an American story.

My friends, George W. Bush challenges us to call upon our better selves - to be compassionate toward those who are less fortunate; to cherish and educate every child, descendants of slaves and immigrants alike, and to thereby affirm the American dream for us all.

On that foundation, confident of who we are, we will extend peace, prosperity and liberty beyond our shores.

Elect George W. Bush and Dick Cheney!

God bless you and God bless America.

ELEANOR ROOSEVELT

INTRODUCTION

Eleanor Roosevelt was born in New York City on October 11, 1884, daughter of lovely Anna Hall and Elliott Roosevelt, younger brother of Theodore. When her mother died in 1892, the children went to live with Grandmother Hall; her adored father died only two years later. Attending a distinguished school in England gave her, at 15, her first chance to develop self-confidence among other girls. Tall, slender, graceful of figure but apprehensive at the thought of being a wallflower, she returned for a debut that she dreaded.

In Albany, where Franklin served in the state Senate from 1910 to 1913, Eleanor started her long career as political helpmate. She gained a knowledge of Washington and its ways while he served as Assistant Secretary of the Navy. When he was stricken with poliomyelitis in 1921, she tended him devotedly. She became active in the women's division of the State Democratic Committee to keep his interest in politics alive. From his successful campaign for governor in 1928 to the day of his death, she dedicated her life to his purposes. She became eyes and ears for him, a trusted and tireless reporter.

After the President's death in 1945 she returned to a cottage at his Hyde Park estate; she told reporters: "the story is over." Within a year, however, she began her service as American spokesman in the United Nations. She continued a vigorous career until her strength began to wane in 1962. She died in New York City that November, and was buried at Hyde Park beside her husband.

What Libraries Mean To The Nation Famous Speech
The District Of Columbia Library Association Dinner - April 1, 1936

IT has been a great pleasure to be here this evening and to hear all the things that have been said about libraries in the district and in general, and the librarians, without whom the libraries would be of little use, I am afraid. But as I sat here I fear that I have thought a good deal about the fact that there are so many places in the United States that have no libraries and that have no way of getting books.

What the libraries mean to the nation is fairly obvious to all of us, especially to those who are here this evening. We know that without libraries, without education, which is based largely on libraries, we cannot have an educated people who will carry on successfully our form of government, and it seems to me that what we really are interested in is how we can make this country more conscious of what it has not got, because we do pat ourselves on the back for the things that we have and that we do. I was looking over some maps which were sent to me and I longed to have these maps very much enlarged and put up in many, many places throughout this country, because I do not think that many people know how many states do not spend more than ten cents per capita for library books a year, and how many states have large areas, particularly rural areas, where one cannot get books.

One of the things that I have been particularly grateful for in the years of the depression—and, of course, I think, sad as it has been, we have some things to be grateful for—is that we have discovered so many things that we had not known before. These facts have come to the knowledge of a great many people who had simply passed them by before, because they did not happen to think about them, and one of these things, that we used to be able to hide, is the areas of the country which are not served in any way by libraries. I have seen photographs, for instance, of girls going out on horseback with libraries strapped on behind them, taking books to children and grown people in places that have been without libraries. We know a good deal about Mrs. Breckinridge's nursing service in Kentucky, but we know very little about the libraries that go out in the same way that her nurses do, on horseback.

I have lived a great deal in the country, in a state which prides itself in spending much money on education, and I am quite sure that son-.e people think there is no lack of education and no lack of library facilities, and sometimes I long to take people and let them see some of the back country districts that I know, in New York State. I know one place in the northern part of the state where I camped for a while in the summer, and I went to the school and talked to the teachers. They are using school books which have been passed down from one child to another. They have practically no books outside of the textbooks. The children in the district are so poor and some of them so pathetic that I suppose the struggle to live has been so great you could not think much about what you fed the mind, but I came away feeling that right there, in one of the biggest and richest states in the country, we had a big area that needed books and needed libraries to help these schools in the education of the children, and, even more, to help the whole community to learn to live through their minds.

We are doing a tremendous amount through the home economics colleges to help people to learn how to live in their homes, to better their standards of material living. We have got to think in exactly the same way about helping them to live mentally and to attain better standards, and we can do it only through the children. We can do ground work with the children; we must begin with them; but we have got to do a tremendous amount with the older people.

I had a letter the other day which was pathetic. It was from a man who said he was 74 years old. He wrote to ask me to see that the adult education classes in that particular community were not stopped, because it had meant so much to him to learn to read. He did not think that I could understand what it meant never to have been able to understand a word on the printed page. He said, "I am not the only one. My next door neighbor is 81 and he learned to read last winter, and it has just made life over for us." It gave you the feeling that there is a good deal of education that is not being done in this country, in spite of all that is done.

We have come a long way. We have done a great deal, but we still have a lot that can be done to improve our educational system, and we still have a tremendous amount to do with our libraries. We have got to make our libraries the center of a new life in the mind, because people are hungry to use their minds.

A NEW ERA AHEAD

We are facing a great change in civilization, and the responsibility, I think, for what we do with our leisure time is a very great responsibility for all of us who have intellectual interests. Somebody said to me, "I would not be so worried and I would not mind facing the fact that we are working fewer hours, if I only knew what people would do with their free time. I would not know what to do myself if I had only to work six hours a day."

That is a challenge. We, here in this country, ought to know what to do with our time, if we have it. I do not know whether we are going to have it, but if we are going to have more leisure time, it is the library, and people who live in the libraries and work in libraries, who are going to lead the way, who are going to give other people the curiosity and the vision of useful things, and pleasant things, and amusing things which can be done in those hours in which we may not have to work in the ways in which we have worked before. It is a very great responsibility, but it is also a very great interest.

Now, I think here in the city of Washington, and in nearly all big cities, the problem is a different one from the one I know so well in the country districts. I think that perhaps there are more facilities and, for that reason, there are more stimulating people engaged in solving the different problems that affect education in cities. But there is a great need, a very great need, in rural America. There is a great need for imagination in the ways used to stir the interest of old and young to use what library facilities they have, and to insist that they shall have more and to make them willing to pay for more, because, in the end, they will get something that they want out of it.

The more I have thought about the problem, the more I have felt that we do not use all our opportunities to stimulate an interest in books. Everything today in which people are interested, the radio, the movies—all of these—should, if properly used, stimulate the use of books. For instance, if there is a remarkably good movie, like The life of Pasteur, it seems to me that it should be used by people in our rural schools and rural libraries to create an interest in the life of Pasteur, the things that Pasteur did, the people around him, and all the discoveries that have come from that time on. I am sure that if we put our minds on it, there are a great many ways in which we can use the things which are coming constantly into the lives of people throughout the country to stimulate an interest in the oldest and most interesting recreation there is.

But you do have to learn to love books, you do have to learn how to read them, you do have to learn that a book is a companion, and this is done in a great many different ways. I think we can do a great deal by having more copies of the same book, perhaps less expensive books, in the libraries so that we can have a good many people reading the same books and coming together for discussion.

I know, for instance, that even in a small group, like a family, we all want to read one book at the same time, and we all want to tear each other's hair out when we can't get a copy. It seems to me that here is something we should be thinking about, to stimulate the reading of books in families and large groups of people. I think the CCC has made me realize this. One boy said to me, "Do you know about that book? I am so glad to be able to talk about it.... You know, it takes such a long time to get a book around." Now, if there had been a dozen or more copies of that book, the group would have talked about that book and it would have been a valuable contribution. It would have stimulated their intellectual thought.

I feel that the care of libraries and the use of books, and the knowledge of books, is a tremendously vital thing, and that we who deal with books and who love books have a great opportunity to bring about something in this country which is more vital here than anywhere else, because we have the chance to make a democracy that will be a real democracy, that will fulfill the vision that Senator King has just given us. It will take on our part imagination and patience and constant interest in awakening interest in other people. But, if we do, I think we shall find that our love of books will bring us a constantly widening audience and constantly more interesting contacts in whatever part of the country we may go.

ERICA JONG

INTRODUCTION

Erica Jong (born March 26, 1942) is an American author and educator. Born in New York City, Jong graduated from Barnard College in 1963. She is best known for her first novel, *Fear of Flying* (published in 1973), which created a sensation with its frank treatment of a woman's sexual desires. Jong wrote *Fear of Flying* in the first person, and her main character suffers from the fear of flying in more than one way, including the literal one. As her airline flight is taking off from New York on its way to Vienna, Austria, she says, "My fingers (and toes) turn to ice, my stomach leaps upward into my rib cage, the temperature in the tip of my nose drops to the same level as the temperature in my fingers, my nipples stand up and salute the inside of my bra (or in this case, dress—since I'm not wearing a bra)...". She created a new type of heroine, that used an affair as a means to self-discovery, breaking the boundaries of the traditional narratives that used affairs as a consequence to disaster.

Jong lived for three years, 1966-69 in Heidelberg, Germany with her second husband, while he was stationed at an army base there. She was a frequent visitor to Venice, and wrote about that city in her novel, *Shylock's Daughter*. Jong was mentioned in the

Bob Dylan song "Highlands".

In 2007, her literary archive was acquired by Columbia University in New York City.

ACLU Biennial Conference New York City - June 22, 1995

YOU know, I want to speak to you today about the creative imagination and censorship and why censorship is such a dire threat to creative people. But first I want to define some terms. I think that one of the reasons that we are embroiled in this tremendous argument about censorship and where we are vis-a-vis censorship, the so-called Communications Decency Act that is being floated in the Congress of the United States, is because we live in a time when we have a very diverse population.

And interesting enough, calls for censorship always increase when the population is extremely diverse and different standards prevail. This is almost a given: When you have an elitist or traditional society in which everybody agrees about who gets access to stuff, you don't have calls for censorship. They only occur in a society in which there are many different groups struggling for a place and trying to figure out whose word goes.

So it's very interesting. It's almost a product of the diversity of our society that we have these new calls for censorship. And I think, although it seems very depressing some days to open the paper and see so many of the things that we've fought for going down the drain, it's in a way a symbol of how much we have reached people, that there should be a worry about pornography on the internet, too free an expression of ideas and so on. So maybe there is a little bit of hope here.

Forty years ago Margaret Mead, who wrote beautifully about so many things that were not in her anthropological purview, supposedly said that censorship would always increase in a pluralistic democracy as each group warred with the other, trying to figure out who had the right to be on top and who had the right to say what other people could speak about.

I think we live in a time where the freedom to publish sexually oriented material is increasingly coming under attack. Large publishing conglomerates increasingly control all means of communication and the forces of cultural reaction are becoming extremely well organized. The brief cultural glasnost that we enjoyed in the sixties is already beginning to seem quaint. And when you think about this century and you think that it's the century that started with The Wasteland, with Prufrock, with Ulysses, and with great fights to liberate literature, which came to fruition just about 1962 when the Supreme Court liberated Tropic of Cancer.

And then, in the sixties, a time that we all remember, probably well, there was a moment when literature all over the world was changed by the release of Tropic of Cancer. Suddenly authors didn't have to shut the bedroom door when they wrote about sexuality. Suddenly, the tremendous force and passion of sexuality inspired the whole culture and created a kind of exuberance that went to other areas as well.

But that period of time was extremely narrow. I would say 20 years, 25 years. And then there was a tremendous desire for censorship again. And we come to the end of the century, and we seem to be back in 1895. It seems that we have made a complete circle.

And now the calls for censorship are coming not just from the right, but also from the left. They are coming distressingly from feminists, members of my own movement, who believe, some of them, like Andrea Dworkin and Catharine MacKinnon, that there is no danger in their joining forces with the forces of reaction. For example, Andrea Dworkin and Kitty McKinnon joined the Meese Commission in 1986, which was very strange.

So there are feminists who are saying: We don't care about the First Amendment; the First Amendment is sentimental; the First Amendment is foolish; the First Amendment is romantic and Rousseauish. We don't need that, a higher good is protecting women and protecting women against rape and protecting women against being denigrated in print, in pictures, on the internet and so on.

Well, let's look at that and what that has really accomplished in the last few years. Basically what it has accomplished, is it has given guys like Dole, like Gramm, a new vocabulary. And it's given people like Pat Robertson a new vocabulary. Instead of having to say now they are for censorship, because they want to keep all women barefoot and pregnant in Christ, they can now say: We are protecting women against denigration and abuse. And the reason that we want the Communications Decency Act is in order to protect women.

In other words, they have taken the vocabulary that Dworkin and McKinnon have given them and they've used it to drape their old barefoot and pregnant ideas. So they've become very much harder to counter. All those same old farts, the alter kockers in the Congress who sat there when Anita Hill was being pilloried and tormented, and who didn't understand anything, who didn't get it, they are getting up and saying: We are protecting women against denigration and abuse.

So basically, what Dworkin and McKinnon have done for the evangelical right, is that they've given them a new dialect that they can use to cloak their very, very ancient ideas. And that's even more terrifying, I think, than anything else that they've done and they seem not to understand that they've done this.

I'm not so interested in talking to you about why it's important to have free sexual expression in society, because I think probably many of us here agree with that. But I want to talk about why people are so interested in censoring expression when there are so many other problems in our society that need addressing.

I think that people become hysterical about expression when they feel out of control: They cannot stop rape. Children are raised in a way that they are not parented, they are not educated, they are not given values, there are too many of them, they are too poor, they are too ill, they are too hungry. Instead of addressing these problems in society, problems that come from overpopulation, problems that come from the breakdown of the family, problems that come from the severe inequity of financial access between races, between rich and poor, instead of addressing these questions, which are the real questions, it's easier to address expression and censorship. It's easier to get up and rave about how our society is being corrupted by pornographic images on the internet. Much easier to talk about that than it is to talk about the fact that there is inequality economically and that because there is inequality economically, we have people who are not socialized to be part of our society, and we don't know what to do about that problem, so let's talk about censorship and expression.

It is absolutely a red herring. It is total bullshit. It is like arresting prostitutes instead of Johns.

Do you remember last year there was a mayor, I believe it was in Miami, who decided that she was going to have the names of the Johns who frequented prostitutes read on television and printed in the newspaper? And I thought, what a sensible idea. Rather than arresting these women whose financial lack of access has put them in this profession, which is the only way they can make money, instead, expose the guys who are using the prostitutes. Don't criminalize these poor women.

It never lasted very long. It spread to a couple of other cities, but basically it didn't last very long. And we have a perfectly analogous situation, for example, in the whole debate about pornography. If criminal acts are perpetrated when pornography is made, if a child is injured, if a woman is drugged and raped during the making of a pornographic film, why not arrest these guys for rape or for child molestation. We have plenty of laws on the books that protect against rape and child molestation.

But, no, that would mean that we were going to come down on organized crime, which basically profits from pornography, and that's too hard. Perhaps it's too hard because organized crime basically contributes to the PAC funds of the people in the Congress. Who knows why? Maybe it's too hard to do that. Better to jump on expression and say that free expression is causing these problems.

So look at the underside of the problem. Look at this great debate that we've been having about censorship, free expression, the internet. It's not really about that. It's not really about whether it's good or bad to have Tropic of Cancer out there so people can read it. It is not really about any of the things that it claims to be about.

What it is really about is that people do not know how to stop the Mafia from selling pornography in which children are abused, or they don't want to do it because they profit in some way from it.

And so instead of going to the root of the problem, instead of exposing the Johns, basically it's much much easier to beat up on a bunch of fuzzy minded liberals who want to make little distinctions about what is right and what is wrong, i.e. us.

And we play right into their tendency to smokescreen the real problems, because as members of the left we're more interested in fighting each other than in fighting our real enemies. We love to fight each other. We love to make subtle distinctions and argue with each other.

And I think that we better really look at what's going on in our culture and we better look at who profits from pornography. And we better look at the laws that we already have and which ones are enforced and which ones aren't. And we better stop letting them make it an issue of censorship versus free speech, because really it's not about that. It's about economics at the bottom. It's about the fact that women and children are the lowest priority in this society. It's about the fact that women and children's rights are cut first. It's about the fact that our teenage daughters can't walk on the streets without danger of being raped. It's about a total social breakdown and it has absolutely nothing to do with expression, that is a smokescreen.

And suddenly, after having these endless conversations on TV with all kinds of people from Phyllis Schafley to Claire Short — the shadow minister of labor, in England, who is calling for censorship of pornography because it's a wonderful way for her to get elected — it suddenly occurred to me that this is not the issue at all. And I would ask you, as my colleagues, to please address the basic issue.

Rather than arguing with the people who would censor, about whether or not this is censorship. I would look at the root causes. I would look at the root causes of why people participate in pornography. I would look at the inequalities, the economic inequalities that underlie the system and I would address those and not be jollied into this whole argument about censorship. Because the truth is that anybody's political agenda, if it is not your own, is obscene.

And basically censorship, once it gets on the books, is always used in that way, to politically harass the dissenter. The reason I remain a First Amendment fundamentalist, is because I understand as a feminist, as a Jew, as a woman, as a woman who has been battered for expressing herself freely in all her books, I understand the First Amendment protects the minority, protects the dissenter, protects the woman, protects the witch.

Basically, I understand that unless you have a government of laws, rather than a government of people, you cannot protect dissent. And I understand, as a woman who probably would have been burned in the marketplace for witchcraft only about 200 years ago, that I need the First Amendment more than anybody does. And that even if I am repelled by child pornography or Bob Guccione's productions, that I have to protect those things, because essentially it's in my self-interest to do so.

So those are the terms of the debate, the way I would define it now, and I would really invite your questions.

GOLDA MEIR

(Prime Minister Of Israel)

INTRODUCTION

Golda Meir was born on May 3, 1898, Kiev and died December 8, 1978, Jerusalem. A founder and fourth prime minister (1969–74) of the State of Israel.

In 1906 Goldie Mabovitch's family emigrated to Milwaukee, Wis., where she attended the Milwaukee Normal School (now University of Wisconsin-Milwaukee) and later became a leader in the Milwaukee Labor Zionist Party. During the war, she emerged as a forceful spokesman for the Zionist cause in negotiating with the British mandatory authorities.

On May 14, 1948, Goldie Myerson was a signatory of Israel's independence declaration and that year was appointed minister to Moscow. She was elected to the Knesset (Israeli parliament) in 1949 and served in that body until 1974. Israel's lack of readiness for the war stunned the nation, and Meir formed a new coalition government only with great difficulty in March 1974 and resigned her post as prime minister on April 10.

She remained in power as head of a caretaker government until a new one was formed in June. Although in retirement thereafter, she remained an important political figure. Upon her death it was revealed that she had had leukemia for 12 years. Her autobiography, *My Life,* was published in 1975.

For the Attainment of Peace Famous Speech Address To The Israeli Knesset, Tel Aviv, Israel: 26 May 1970

AT this opening of our parliamentary session, I wish to survey the security and political conjuncture. In recent months, and in the past weeks especially, the security situation has worsened seriously on the southern front in particular, and the harmful effect of that is felt on the other fronts also.

The main feature of this escalation and tension is an advanced and dangerous stage of Soviet involvement in Egypt, at the beck and call of Egyptian aggression and infractions of the cease-fire. There is no precedent for this involvement in the history of Soviet penetration into the Middle East, and it is encouraging Egypt in its plan to renew the war of attrition and so move further along the path of its vaulting ambition to vanquish Israel.

To understand the background, we must recall Nasser's declared decision, in the spring of 1969, to abrogate the cease-fire and ignore the cease-fire lines. It is typical of Egyptian policy all along its war-mongering way. It reflects a basic doctrine—that Israel is an exception in the family of nations: the rules that civilized countries accept do not apply to Israel; an international obligation towards Israel is to be undertaken only if there is no other option, no possible alternative, and it may be renounced at the first chance. Routed on the battlefield, you acquiesce in international proposals and arrangements that enable you to rescue your regime. But should it appear that your military strength has been restored enough to let you attack, you may treat your undertaking or your signature as though it had never been. That was the end of Egypt's cease-fire undertaking of 9 June 1967, entered into at the instance of the Security Council. That was the end of Egypt's earlier regional and international undertaking on matters concerning Egypt and Israel. It is behaviour that illuminates the intentions and credibility of Cairo in all that governs its attitude to peace with Israel.

Armistice Torn to Shreds

Egypt did not do otherwise in respect of its signature of the Armistice Agreement of 1949. In the eyes of its rulers, that was no more than a temporary device to save Egypt from total collapse after its abortive aggression and afford it a breathing-space to prepare for a new campaign. Within a few years, Egypt—characteristically disavowing its international pledges—had flouted the Security Council and jettisoned the principle of freedom of navigation. With Nasser's accession to power, the Egyptians emptied the Armistice Agreement of its content altogether by despatching bands of murderers from the Gaza strip into Israel.

Nasser next started to subvert the regimes in those Arab States of which he did not approve and which would not bow to his authority. He opened up the region to Soviet penetration, he launched a plan to form a unified military command of the Arab States bordering Israel, and pressed forward with feverish preparations for a renewed assault upon us.

In 1956, his second armed threat to our existence was flung back. Once more, he evinced an interest in mediation and international settlement, for he needed them to engineer a withdrawal of Israel's forces from Sinai and, after that, from Sharm e-Sheikh and the Gaza Strip. With his knowledge and concurrence, the United Nations' Emergency Force was deployed to ensure freedom of navigation in the Gulf of Aqaba and as a guarantee that the Strip would serve no longer as a base for death-dealing incursions into Israel.

For ten years, no plaint was heard from Cairo about the Emergency Force and its functions. But Nasser was engaged all that time—with Soviet help—in building up his army anew and in subversive and adventurous activity throughout the region, culminating in the bloody war that he fought, unsuccessfully, against the Yemenite people for five years on end.

Cease-Fire: Temporary Expedient

In 1967, convinced, it seems, that he had the strength to overcome Israel in battle, he disavowed his international commitments wholesale, expelled the Emergency Force, concentrated most of his troops in eastern Sinai, re-instated his blockade of the Straits of Tiran, and prepared for a war of annihilation against Israel—a war which, in his own words, would turn back the clock to before 1948.

Up to 5 June 1967, he was entirely deaf to universal appeal to refrain from plunging the Middle East into a third maelstrom of blood and suffering. Four days later, his army undone, he was not slow to answer the Security Council's call for a cease-fire, and so, again, avert calamity for Egypt. The Council's cease-fire Resolution was not limited in time or condition. Neither did Nasser attach any limitation of time or other term to his assent.

Proof of his real designs is abundant in his subsequent declarations and deeds. The Khartoum doctrine is unchanged: no peace, no recognition, no negotiation. Israel must withdraw to the borders of 4 June 1967 and thereafter surrender its sovereignty to the "Palestinian people". Only with that twofold stipulation would the cease-fire be observed by Egypt. The logic is sound: if the stipulations are kept, Nasser's aim is won, and there will be no further cause for him to pursue aggression.

Nasser will not admit the concept of peace in its literal, humane and Jewish sense. By our definition, and in international consciousness and morality, peace means good neighbourliness and co-operation between nations. According to his thinking, to invite Egypt to make peace with Israel is to invite Egypt to accept capitulation and indignity.

That is the fount of the vortex of blood, destruction and anguish in which the peoples of the Middle East have been drowning, decade after decade.

Quiet Must Be Reciprocal

On 17 March 1969, when Egyptian artillery began to bombard our soldiers in the Canal zone, I announced, in this House, that—

The Arab States must realize that there can be quiet on the cease-fire line only if there is quiet on both sides of it, and not just on one. We want quiet, we want the cease-fire upheld. But this depends on the Arab States. The maintenance of quiet must be reciprocal.

Egypt did not hearken to my words. Its aggressiveness was redoubled. At the beginning of May, Nasser told his people that his forces had destroyed sixty per cent of the line of fortifications which Israel had built along the Canal, and would keep on until they had demolished what was left. In the ensuing years, not only have our entrenchments been reinforced, but we have hit hard at the Egyptian emplacements and foiled more than one attempt to raid across the Canal.

Toward 'Rivers of Blood and Fire'

What Nasser describes as "a war of attrition" began in March 1969. On 30 March, he could say:

The time has passed when we required any soldier at the front who opened fire on the enemy to account for his action, because we wanted to avoid complications. Now the picture is different: if a soldier at the front sees the enemy and does not open fire, he must answer for it. In December 1969, he confirmed his preparedness for war or, in his own phrase, "the advance of the Egyptian army through rivers of blood and fire".

The Israel Defence Forces have punished this vainglorious aggression. I shall not retell the tale of their courage and resource: the digging in, the daring operations of the Air Force, the power of the armor. Aggression has been repelled, the enemy's timetable upset and the pressure on our front-line eased by our striking at vital enemy military targets along the Canal and far behind it and confounding his plans for all-out war. True, to our great sorrow, we have suffered losses in killed and wounded, but our vigorous self-defence has thwarted Egypt's scheming and stultified its endeavors to wear us down and shake our southern front.

British Out—Soviets in

Thus bankrupt, the Cairo regime had only the choice between accepting Israel's constant call to return to reciprocal observance of the cease-fire, as a stepping-stone to peace, or leaning more heavily still on the Soviet Union to the point of asking it to become operationally involved, so that Egypt might carry on the war of attrition, notwithstanding the unpleasant repercussions of that involvement.

Egypt chose the second course.

In many of his speeches, Nasser claims the credit for ending British power and Egypt's subjugation to it. But the same leader who promised his people full independence of any foreign Power has preferred to renew its dependence and subservience rather than make peace with Israel, rather than honour the cease-fire. In his plight, he elects to conceal from his people the truth that, in place of the British, the Soviets are invading the area. This is the pass to which blindness and hatred have brought the Egyptian revolution.

Soviet penetration did not start yesterday or the day before. Its beginning could be seen in the mid-fifties, in a strengthening of influence by the provision of economic aid and weaponry on the easiest terms.

In May 1967, the Soviet Union provocatively spawned baseless rumours of Israeli concentrations on the Syrian border. This was a major link in the chain of developments that led to the Six-Day War. When the fighting was over, Moscow displayed no readiness to counsel the Arabs to close the chapter of violence and open one of regional cooperation – although, to extricate Nasser, it had voted for the unconditional cease-fire Resolution.

In his speech of 1 May 1970, Nasser confessed that, only three days after Egypt had submitted to that Resolution, the Soviets agreed to re-arm his forces.

His words:

On 12 June - and now I can reveal it - I received a Note from Brezhnev, Kosygin and Podgorny, in which they promised to support the Arab nation and restore Egypt's armed forces, without any payment, to their pre-war level. Thus we were able to withstand and overcome our plight and rehabilitate our armed forces anew.

The Wherewithal for War

Within the past three years, the Soviet Union has supplied Egypt, Syria and Iraq with two thousand tanks and eight hundred fighter aircraft, besides other military equipment, to an overall value of some 3.5 billion dollars, two-thirds to Egypt alone. This armament was purveyed with practically no monetary requital. Thousands of Soviet specialists are engaged in training the Egyptian forces. Soviet advisers are guiding and instructing the Egyptian forces within units and bases even during combat.

It is hard to believe that Nasser would have dared to resume aggression in March 1969 on a large scale without Russian authorization. It is harder to believe that, in May-June 1969, he would have abrogated the cease-fire without it. Not only did the Soviet Union not use its capacity to move him to comply again with the cease-fire; it even encouraged him to step up his belligerency. A conspicuous example of this disinclination to make its contribution to the restoration of quiet is Moscow's rejection of the American proposal, in mid-February 1970, for a joint appeal by the Four Powers to the parties in the region to respect the cease-fire.

It is widely assumed that the Soviet Union is not anxious for an all-out war, in which its protege, Egypt, would be worsted in battle again, but that, at the same time, it eschews a cease-fire as being a stage in progress towards peace. So it would prefer the contribution of something in-between: frontier clashes, indecisive engagements, ongoing tensions, which would allow it to exploit Egyptian dependence to the hilt, and so further its regional penetration and aims. And, by exerting military and political pressure on Israel, it seeks to satisfy Egypt's needs in a manner that will not entail the danger of another Egyptian reverse or of a "needless" peace.

Not content with bolstering Nasser's policy of aggression and war, the Soviet Union has embarked upon a campaign of antisemitic propaganda within its own borders and of venomous vilification of Israel through all its communication media and in international forums. The Soviets have gone so far in slander as to label us Nazis: without shame or compunction, they charge the Jews with taking part in pogroms organized by the Czarist regime, of collaborating with the Nazis. They represent Trotsky as a Zionist. They conduct "scientific" research which has "discovered" that there is no such thing as a Jewish people.

The purpose is twofold: to intimidate Soviet Jewry and to prepare the psychological ground for any and every mischief against Israel.

Soviet Involvement Deepens

The failure of the war of attrition, the insistence of Nasser's pleas, have persuaded the Soviets to extend their involvement. At the moment when, in New York and Washington, their representatives were meeting representatives of the Western Powers to discuss a renewal of the Jarring mission and a peace settlement, Soviet ships were sailing to Egypt, laden with SA-3 ground-to-air missiles, and thousands of Soviet experts were arriving to install, man and operate the batteries. In December 1969, signs of the entrenched bases of ground-to-air missiles could be discerned in the Canal and other zones. We estimate that there are already about twenty such bases in the heart of Egypt.

In mid-April, Soviet involvement went one step further—and the gravest so far. Soviet pilots, from bases at their disposal on Egyptian soil, began to carry out operational missions over wide areas. With that defensive coverage of their rear, the Egyptians could mount their artillery bombardment in the Canal zone on a scale unparalleled since it was started in March 1969.

Speaking on 1 May on the intensification of the war against Israel, Nasser told his audience:

In the last fifteen days a change has taken place. As we can see, our forces are taking the initiative in operations.

And in the same speech:

All this is due to the aid which the Soviet Union has furnished, and it is clear that you have heard many rumours and are destined to hear many more.
On 20 May, Nasser admitted for the first time, in an interview for the German newspaper Die Welt, that Soviet pilots were flying jet planes of the Egyptian air force and might clash with ours.

Thus the Middle East is plumbing a new depth of unease. The Soviet Union has forged an explosive link in a chain of acts that is dragging the region into an escalation of deadly warfare and foredooms any hope of peace-making.

We have informed Governments of the ominous significance of this new phase in Soviet involvement. We have explained that a situation has developed which ought to perturb not only Israel, but every state in the free world. The lesson of Czechoslovakia must not be forgotten. If the free world—and particularly the United States, its leader—can pass on to the next item on its agenda without any effort to deter the Soviet Union from selfishly involving itself so largely in a quarrel with which it has no concern, then it is not Israel alone that is imperilled, but no small nation, no minor nation, can any longer dwell in safety within its frontiers.

The Government of Israel has made it plain, as part of its basic policy to defend the State's being and sovereignty whatever betide, that the Israel Defence Forces will continue to hold the cease-fire line on the southern as on other fronts, and not permit it to be sapped or breached.

For that purpose, it is essential to stop the deployment of the ground-to-air missile pads which the Egyptians are trying to set up adjacent to the cease-fire line; the protection of our forces entrenched there to prevent the breaching of the front depends on that. No serious person will suspect Israel of wanting to provoke, or being interested in provoking, Soviet pilots integrated into the Egyptian apparatus of war, but neither will anyone in his senses expect us to allow the Egyptian army to carry through its aggressive plans without the Israel Defence Forces using all their strength and skill to defeat them, even if outside factors are helping to carry them through.

Arms Balance Must Be Restored

All this means that our search for the arms indispensable for our defence has become more urgent, more vital. When we asked to be allowed to buy more aircraft from the United States, we based ourselves on the reality that the balance of power had been shaken by the enormous arsenals flowing from the Soviet Union to Egypt free of charge. Since the President of the United States announced deferment of his decision on that critical point, it has, as I have said, become known that SA-3 batteries, with Soviet crews, have been set up in Egypt and Soviet pilots activated in operational flights. This adds a new and portentous dimension of imbalance, and the need to redress the equilibrium becomes more pressing and crucial.

We have emphasized to peace-loving Governments the necessity to bring their influence to bear and make their protests heard against a Soviet involvement which so dangerously aggravates tension in the Middle East. I have heard what the President of the United States said in his press conference on 8 May about the alarming situation, in the light of reports that Soviet pilots had been integrated into Egypt's air force. He went on to say that the United States was watching the situation, and, if it became clear that the reports were true and the escalation continued, this would drastically shift the balance of power and make it necessary for the United States to re-appraise its decision as to the supply of jets to Israel. He also said that the United States had already made it perfectly plain that it was in the interests of peace in the Middle East that no change be permitted in the balance of forces, and that the United States would abide by that obligation.

On 24 March of this year, the Secretary of State, in the President's name, declared that the United States would not allow the security of Israel to be jeopardised, and that, if steps were taken that might shake the present balance of power or if, in his view, international developments justified it, the President would not hesitate to reconsider the matter.

I do not have to tell you that I attach great importance to these statements. But, I must say, with the utmost gravity, that delay in granting our wish hardly rectifies the change for the worse in the balance of power that the new phase in Soviet involvement, with all its attendant perils, has entailed.

There is close and continuous contact between ourselves and the US authorities in the matter. Last week, the Foreign Minister had talks with the President and the Secretary of State: he was told that the urgent and detailed survey mentioned by the President four weeks ago is not yet complete, but was assured that the official United States declarations of 24 March and 8 May on the balance of power held entirely good.

In all our contacts, we have stressed how important the time factor is, for any lag in meeting our requirements can harm our interests and is likely to be interpreted by our enemies as encouraging their aggression and by the Soviet Union as condoning its intensified involvement. I find it inconceivable that the United States will not carry out its declared undertaking.

Other Fronts: Rampant Terrorism

Of late, there has been a rise in aggressive activity on the other fronts as well. Nasser is trying to step up the effectiveness of the eastern front, and Egypt's military policy has undoubtedly affected the situation on the other fronts. This destructive consequence is visible not only in terrorist operations against Israel from Jordan, Syria and Lebanon, but also in the strategy of neighbouring Governments and in domestic upheavals in Jordan and Lebanon.

The terrorist organization in Syria is a section of the Syrian army, acting under Government directives. In Jordan and Lebanon, terrorist domination has so expanded as to become a threat to the existence and authority of the Governments. In both countries, the Governments have vainly sought to reconcile opposites: their own authority and the presence and activity of the terrorist organizations. Such attempts could meet with no more than a semblance of success. More than once, the Governments seemed about to confront the organizations but each time recoiled from the encounter.

In Jordan as in Lebanon, the terrorists have taken heart from Nasser. Through his support, direct and indirect, they have strengthened their position. The authorities have compromised with them at Israel's expense, allowing them no little latitude – against Israel. They have been accorded a recognized status, which guarantees them freedom of action. The entire world knows of "the Cairo Agreement" between the terrorists and the Lebanese Government, achieved through the mediation and under the auspices of Egypt: It allows them to pursue their activities openly, in areas allotted to them, in coordination with the Lebanese authorities and army, as well as elsewhere along the border.

Between the beginning of January and 20 May, there were eleven hundred enemy operations along the Jordanian front. The Fatah and other organizations dug themselves in along the length of the Israel-Lebanon frontier, and it has become a focus of murder and sabotage: terrorists were responsible for a hundred and forty inroads along that frontier.

After a series of such acts, among them Katyusha fire on inoffensive civilians in Kiryat Shmona and other places, terrorism reached a climax on 22 May in the calculated murder, from ambush, of schoolchildren, teachers and other passengers in a school-bus.

There is no viler example of the vicious mentality and lethal policy of the terrorist organizations and their instructors in the Arab capitals than the development along the Lebanese front. Until the Six-Day War, it had been the most tranquil of all the frontiers. Even afterwards, the tension which marked the cease-fire lines and borders with Egypt and Jordan was absent there, until the Fatah and their backers entrenched themselves and decided that the Lebanese border, too, must be set aflame. And there is another aim—common to Cairo and Damascus for a number of years—which has not been wanting in terrorist policy: to prejudice Lebanon's independence and disturb the delicate equipoise between its two communities. By accepting the Cairo Agreement in November 1969, and allowing the establishment of terrorist bases in its territory, Lebanon has been progressively endangering its independence, as Jordan did before.

Endlessly provoked by terrorists from Lebanon, we retaliated a number of times against Fatah bases. The ever closer cooperation between Beirut and the terrorist organizations makes more and more evident the responsibility of the Lebanese Government. It cannot be shrugged off. We shall keep on demanding that Beirut use its power to halt aggression from its territory and do its bounden duty in restoring tranquillity.

Israel is interested in the stability of democracy in Lebanon, in its progress, integrity and peace. On 22 May, radio Beirut announced that "Lebanon has often stated that it is not prepared on any account to act as a policeman guarding Israel". So long as Lebanon evades its answerability and allows the terrorists to indulge in aggression and murder, the Government of Israel will do its bounden duty and, by all necessary measures, defend the welfare of Israel's citizens, its highways, towns and villages.

The Aspiration to Peace

We must view recent happenings against the whole background of our struggle, since the Six-Day War, to realize Israel's highest aspiration, the aspiration to peace.

To our intense disappointment, we learnt on the morrow of the Six-Day War that the rulers of the Arab States and the Soviet Union were not prepared to put an end to the conflict. Witness authoritative fulminations by the Arab Governments, the resolutions of Khartoum, the Soviet Union's identification with that policy, its assiduous efforts to rehabilitate the Arab armies with lavish and unstinted aid. We learnt that our struggle for peace would be prolonged, full of pain and sacrifice. We decided – and the nation was with us, to a man – resolutely to defend the cease-fire lines against all aggression and simultaneously press on with our strivings to attain peace.

It is our way not to glorify ourselves but to render a sober and restrained account of our policy, not hiding the hard truth from the people, even if it be grievous. The people and the world know that there is no word of truth in Egypt's fabrication of resounding victories. The main efforts of the Egyptian army have been repelled by the Israel Defence Forces. All claims of success in breaking our line are false. Most attempted sorties by Egyptian planes into our air-space have been undone, and the Egyptians are paying a heavy price for every venture to clash with our Air Force. We control the area all along the Canal cease-fire line more firmly and strongly than ever.

Soviet involvement has not deterred, and will not deter, Israel from exercising its recognized right to defend the cease-fire lines until secure boundaries are agreed upon within the compass of the peace we so much desire.

Had its aggression gained the political objectives set, Egypt could by now have celebrated victory. But Nasser and the Soviets have not realized those aims.

Three years after the Six-Day War, we can affirm that two fundamental principles have become a permanent part of the international consciousness: Israel's right to stand fast on the cease-fire lines, not budging until the conclusion of peace that will fix secure and recognized boundaries; and its right to self-defence and to acquire the equipment essential to defence and deterrence.

I have, on several occasions, explained the differences in appraisal and approach between ourselves and friendly States and Powers. I have no intention of claiming that they have entirely disappeared. Nevertheless, we cannot allow them to overshadow the recognition of those twin principles, any more than we may overlook the systematic plotting of our enemies to weaken that international consciousness and isolate Israel.

The Economic Front

Another front that will test our power to hold out is the economic. How we hold out militarily and politically is contingent on the degree of our success in surmounting economic troubles.

Our victories in three wars, our robust military stance in the interim periods of what, by comparison, has been tranquillity, as well as through these present difficult days, could never have been won without a solidly-based economy, a high educational standard of soldier and civilian, a high technological level of worker in every branch. We owe it to an unprecedentedly rapid economic development and expansion that the national income of tiny Israel almost equals that of Egypt, with a population tenfold ours and more. We must, by all necessary measures, maintain that advantage.

The central problem of the moment arises from an unfavourable balance of payments and the resultant shortage of foreign currency. The deficit in our balance of payments may be attributed, primarily, to the vastly greater defence imports: if those has stayed at their pre-Six-Day-War level, we would by now be nearing economic independence.

Until 1968, capital imports, which pay for any excess of imports over exports, had sufficed not only to cover the deficit but also to amass considerable reserves of foreign currency. Since then, they are no longer enough. There is a risk of a drop in foreign currency reserves which might prevent our sustaining the level of imports imperative for the smooth working of the economy under conditions of full employment and meeting at the same time our defence requirements.

We must, therefore, in the national interest, make every endeavour and be prepared for every sacrifice demanded for the solving of this problem. Which means that we must also restrict the growth of imports, especially of imports destined for private and public consumption and not for security. The standard of living has risen in the last three years by more than twenty-five per cent: in this period of emergency, our efforts to economize must be mirrored in pegging a standard of living that may have climbed too steeply.

One of the "unavoidables" is to cut down the State Budget and saddle the public with taxes, charges and compulsory loans on no small scale. This action was taken only in the last few weeks, and we hope that it will have the desired and sufficient effect. If it does not, if we find that imports have not been curbed enough or exports have not risen enough, that consumption keeps expanding and the deficit swelling, we will not shrink from further action.

Let me add that this implies no change in our determination, even in an emergency that tightens all belts, not to neglect the advancement of the lower-income strata; this year, too, we have adopted a number of significant measures to better their lot, and we shall continue to do so.

The policy is no easy one for those who have to discharge it, nor is it a light burden that it places on the public's shoulders. The understanding and maturity with which the man-in-the-street has accepted these stern dispositions are most commendable: only a negligible minority has tried to circumvent them.

Our economic targets are far from simple of attainment. The ongoing development of the economy, the absorption of newcomers and enormous defence expenditure present a challenge greater than we could face alone. We are deeply grateful, therefore, for the staunch cooperation of world Jewry and the assistance of friendly nations. I believe that we can continue to rely on that help, but, for moral and practical reasons alike, we cannot make demands on others if we do not first do our own share. So we must adjust our way of life, in everything that concerns wages, incomes, consumption, savings, productivity, personal effort and outlay, each of us playing his full part, to what the overriding national purpose dictates.

Pursuit of an Elusive Peace

The aspiration to peace is not only the central plank in our platform, it is the cornerstone of our pioneering life and labour. Ever since renewal of independence, we have based all our undertakings of settlement and creativity on the fundamental credo that we did not come to dispossess the Arabs of the Land but to work together with them in peace and prosperity, for the good of all.

It is worth remembering, in Israel and beyond, that at the solemn proclamation of statehood, under savage onslaught still, we called upon the Arabs dwelling in Israel.

To keep the peace and to play their part in building the State on the basis of full and equal citizenship and due representation in all its institutions, provisional and permanent.

We extended "the hand of peace and good neighbourliness to all the States around us and to their peoples", and we appealed to them "to cooperate in mutual helpfulness with the independent Jewish nation in its Land and in a concerted effort for the advancement of the entire Middle East".

On 23 July 1952, when King Farouk was deposed and the young officers, led by General Naguib, seized power in Egypt, hope sprang up in Israel that a new leaf had been turned in the neighbourly relations between Egypt and ourselves, that we were entering an age of peace and cooperation. Prime Minister David Ben-Gurion, addressing the Knesset on 18 August 1952, said:

The State of Israel would like to see a free, independent and progressive Egypt, and we bear Egypt no grudge for what it did to our forefathers in Pharoah's days, or even for what it did to us four years ago. Our goodwill towards Egypt—despite the Farouk Government's foolish behaviour towards us—has been demonstrated throughout the months of Egypt's involvement in a difficult conflict with a world Power. And it never occurred to us to exploit those difficulties and to attack Egypt or take revenge, as Egypt did to us upon the establishment of the State. And insofar as Egypt's present rulers are trying to uproot internal corruption and move their country forward to cultural and social progress, we extend to them our sincerest wishes for the success of their venture.

The answer came soon. Asked about Ben-Gurion's call for peace, Egypt's Prime Minister evaded the question, claiming that he knew no more than what he had read in the newspapers. Azzam, Secretary-General of the Arab League, said: "Ben-Gurion gave free flight to his imagination, which saw the invisible" [Al-Misri, 20 August 1952]. On 23 August 1952, Al-Ahram explained that Israel had been forced to seek peace by a tottering economy, and proceeded:

In the past, on a number of occasions, Israel tried, at sessions of the Conciliation Commission, to sit with the Arabs around the table, so as to settle existing problems. The Arabs refused, because they did not recognize the existence of the Jews, which is based on extortion.

We have never wearied of offering our neighbours an end to the bloody conflict and the opening of a chapter of peace and cooperation. All our calls have gone unheeded. Our proposals have been rejected in mockery and hatred. The policy of warring against us has persisted, with brief pauses, and thrice in a single generation forced hostilities upon us.

On 1 March 1957, in the name of the Government of Israel, I announced in the United Nations the withdrawal of our forces from the territories occupied in the Sinai Campaign. I concluded with these words:

Can we, from now on—all of us—turn over a new leaf, and, instead of fighting with each other, can we all, united, fight poverty and disease and illiteracy? Is it possible for us to put all our efforts and all our energy into one single purpose, the betterment and progress and development of all our lands and all our peoples? I can here pledge the Government and the people of Israel to do their part in this united effort. There is no limit to what we are prepared to contribute so that all of us, together, can live to see a day of happiness for our peoples and see again a great contribution from our region to peace and happiness for all humanity.
Ten years went by, of fedayun activity, and once again we were confronted with the hazard of a surprise attack by Egypt, which had assembled powerful columns in eastern Sinai. The Six-Day War was fought, but, when its battles ended, we did not behave as men drunk with victory, we did not call for vengeance, we did not demand the humiliation of the conquered. We knew that our real celebration would be on the day that peace comes. Instantly, we turned to our neighbours, saying:

Our region is now at a crossroads: let us sit down together, not as victors and conquered, but as equals; let us negotiate, let us determine secure and agreed boundaries, let us write a new page of peace, goodneighbourliness and cooperation for the profit of all the nations of the Middle East.

The call was sounded over and again in Government statements, in declarations by the Prime Minister, the Deputy Prime Minister, the Foreign Minister, the Minister of Defence and other Ministers – in the Knesset and in the United Nations, through all communication media. It was borne by emissaries, statesmen, authors, journalists, educators and by every means – public or covert – which seemed likely to bring it to our neighbours' ears.

The Knesset will not expect me to review the manifold efforts and attempts to establish any kind of contact with statesmen and competent authorities in the Arab countries. The people with whom we have tried, and shall again try, to open a dialogue do not want publicity. In this sensitive field, a hint of publication can be enough to extinguish a spark of hope. Imagination and a broad outlook are required, but imagination must not be allowed to become blindness. Patience and close attention are needed if seeds that have yet to germinate are to yield fruit in the course of time and not be sterilized by the glare of publicity.

At all events, the Government of Israel will neglect no opportunity to develop and foster soundings and contacts that may be of value in blazing a trail, always with scrupulous regard for the secrecy of the contacts, if our interlocutors so prefer.

But what have been the reactions of Arab leaders, so far, to our public proposals for peace? Here are some outstanding examples:

* On 26 July 1967, Hussein declared: "The battle which began on 5 June is only one battle in what will become a long war."

* On 1 November 1967, the Prime Minister of Israel, the late Levi Eshkol, enumerated five principles of peace, and Nasser's reply on 23 November was: "The Arabs hold steadfastly to the Khartoum decision – no peace, no recognition and no negotiation with Israel."

* From November 1967 until July 1968, Israel sent forth its calls for peace again and again, and on 16 July the Egyptian Foreign Minister replied:

With regard to Arab policy, I have always reiterated what was agreed upon at Khartoum, that we are not prepared to recognize Israel, to negotiate with it or to sign a peace with it.

* On 8 November 1968, Foreign Minister Abba Eban presented to the General Assembly of the United Nations a detailed peace

programme in nine clauses:

- The establishment of a just and lasting peace;
- The determination of secure and recognized borders;
- Security agreements, including non-aggression pacts;
- Borders open to travel and trade;
- Freedom of navigation in international waterways;
- A solution to the refugee problem through a conference of representatives of the countries of the Middle East, the countries contributing to refugee upkeep, and the United Nations Specialized Agencies to draw up a five-year plan; the conference could be convened even before general peace negotiations began;
- The Holy Places of Christianity and Islam in Jerusalem to be placed under the responsibility of the respective faiths, with the aim of formulating agreements which will give force to their universal character;
- Mutual recognition of sovereignty;
- Regional cooperation in development projects for the good of the whole region.

The Arab leaders disregarded the programme and did not even favour it with reply or comment.

* On 17 March 1969—the day on which I assumed my present office—I re-emphasized the principles of peace, saying:

We are prepared to discuss peace with our neighbours any day and on all matters. Nasser's reply, three days later, was:

There is no voice transcending the sounds of war, and there must not be such a voice—nor is there any call holier than the call to war.

* In the Knesset - on 5 May 1969, on 8 May and on 30 June—I re-enunciated our readiness—

To enter immediately into negotiations, without prior conditions, with every one of our neighbours, to reach a peace settlement.

The retort of the Arab States was swift. The commentators of Damascus, Amman and Cairo stigmatized peace as "surrender" and heaped scorn on Israel's proposals. Take, for example, this from Al-Destour, a leading Jordanian newspaper, of 15 June 1969:

Mrs. Meir is prepared to go to Cairo to hold discussions with President Abdul Nasser but, to her sorrow, has not been invited. She believes that one fine day a world without guns will emerge in the Middle East. Golda Meir is behaving like a grandmother telling bedtime stories to her grandchildren. And that was the moment for Nasser to announce abrogation of the cease-fire agreements and non-recognition of the cease-fire lines.

* On 19 September 1969, the Foreign Minister of Israel appealed in the United Nations to the Arab States—

To declare their intention to establish a lasting peace, to eliminate the twenty-one-year-old conflict, to hold negotiations for detailed agreement on all the problems with which we are faced.

He referred to Israel's affirmation to Ambassador Jarring on 2 April:

Israel accepts the Security Council Resolution (242) calling for the promotion of agreement for the establishment of a just and lasting peace, reached through negotiation and agreement between the Governments concerned. Implementation of the agreement will commence when accord has been reached on all its provisions.

* On 24 September 1969, during my visit to the United States, I was happy to hear that a statement had been made on behalf of the Egyptian Foreign Minister, then in New York, that Egypt was prepared to enter into Rhodes-style peace talks with Israel. I responded forthwith that Israel was willing and, as previously recorded, was prepared to discuss the establishment of a true peace with Egypt at any time and without prior conditions.

Within a few hours, an authoritative dementi came from Cairo. Any Egyptian readiness to enter into Rhodes-style talks was officially denied. The spokesman of the Egyptian Government termed the statement to that effect an "imperialist lie."

* On 18 December 1969, the Knesset approved the present Government's basic principles. I quote the following passages:

The Government will steadfastly strive to achieve a durable

peace with Israel's neighbours, founded on peace treaties achieved by direct negotiations between the parties. Agreed, secure and recognized borders will be laid down in the treaties. The treaties will assure cooperation and mutual aid, the solution of any problem that may be a stumbling-block on the path to peace, and the avoidance of all aggression, direct and indirect. Israel will continue to be willing to negotiate—without prior conditions from either side—with any of the neighbouring States for the conclusion of such a treaty ... The Government will be alert for any expression of willingness amongst the Arab nations for peace with Israel and will welcome and respond to any readiness for peace from the Arab States. Israel will persevere in manifesting its peaceful intentions and in explaining the clear advantages to all the peoples of the area of peaceful co-existence, without aggression or subversion, without territorial expansion or intervention in the freedom and internal regimes of the States in the area.

* In my address to the Knesset on 26 December 1969, in the Foreign Minister's address to the Knesset on 7 April 1970, and in a series of local press interviews on the eve of Passover and on the eve of Independence Day, that resolve was reaffirmed:

Day or night, if any sign whatever were to be seen, we would have responded to it.

* Ambassador Jarring came and asked what Israel's response would be if he were to invite the Foreign Ministers to Cyprus or Geneva—and there was no hesitation on our part. He asked about Rhodes, and we said—let it be Rhodes.

* In an interview published in Ma'ariv on 20 April I said:

We have no direct contacts with Egypt, but there are friends who travel around the world, to this place or that, statesmen who hate neither Israel nor Egypt. They tried to find a bridge, but could not.

On the contrary, there have been echoes of Nasser's speech of 1 May 1970, making even the resumption of the cease-fire conditional on our total withdrawal and the return of the Palestinians to Israel.

Stop the Killing!

These are but a few of our recurring solicitations for peace. We have not retracted one of them: we have not wearied of reiterating, day in, day out, our preparedness for peace: we have not abandoned hopes of finding a way into the hearts of our neighbours, though they yet dismiss our appeals with open animosity.

Today again, as the guns thunder, I address myself to our neighbours: Stop the killing, end the fire and bloodshed which bring tribulation and torment to all the peoples of the region! End rejection of the cease-fire, end bombardment and raids, end terror and sabotage!

Even Russian pilots will not contrive to destroy the cease-fire lines, and certainly they will not bring peace. The only way to permanent peace and the establishment of secure and recognized boundaries is through negotiations between the Arab States and ourselves, as all sovereign States treat one another, as is the manner of States which recognize each other's right to existence and equality, as is the manner of free peoples, not protectorates enslaved to foreign Powers or in thrall to the dark instincts of war, destruction and ruin.

To attain peace, I am ready to go at any hour to any place, to meet any authorized leader of any Arab State—to conduct negotiations with mutual respect, in parity and without pre-conditions, and with a clear recognition that the problems under controversy can be solved. For there is room to fulfill the national aspirations of all the Arab States and of Israel as well in the Middle East, and progress, development and cooperation can be hastened among all its nations, in place of barren bloodshed and war without end.

If peace does not yet reign, it is from no lack of willingness on our part: it is the inevitable outcome of the refusal of the Arab leadership to make peace with us. That refusal is still a projection of reluctance to be reconciled to the living presence of Israel within secure and recognized boundaries, still a product of the hope, which flickers on in their hearts, that they will accomplish its destruction. And this has been the state of things since 1948, long before the issue of the territories arose in the aftermath of the Six-Day War.

Moreover, if peace does not yet reign, it is equally not because of any lack of "flexibility" on our part, or because of the so-called "rigidity" of our position.

That position is: cease-fire, agreement and peace. The Arab Governments preach and practise no cease-fire, no negotiation, no agreement and no peace. Which of the two attitudes is stubborn and unyielding? The Arab Governments' or ours?

The November 1967 UN Resolution

There are some, the Arabs included, who claim that we have not accepted the United Nations Resolution of 22 November 1967, and that the Arabs have. In truth, the Arabs only accepted it in a distorted and mutilated interpretation of their own, as meaning an instant and absolute withdrawal of our forces, with no commitment to peace. They were ready to agree to an absolute Israeli withdrawal, but the Resolution stipulates nothing of the kind. According to its text and the exegesis of its compilers, the Resolution is not self-implementing. The operative clause calls for the appointment of an envoy, acting on behalf of the Secretary-General, whose task would be to "establish and maintain contact with the States concerned in order to promote agreement and assist efforts to achieve a peaceful and accepted settlement in accordance with the provisions and principles in this Resolution." On 1 May 1968, Israel's Ambassador at the United Nations announced as follows:

In declarations and statements made publicly and to Ambassador Jarring, the Government of Israel has indicated its acceptance of the Security Council's Resolution for the promotion of an agreement to establish a just and durable peace. I am authorised to reaffirm that we are willing to seek an agreement with each Arab State, on all the matters included in that Resolution. More recently, we accepted Ambassador Jarring's proposal to arrange meetings between Israel and each of its neighbours, under his auspices, and in fulfillment of his mandate under the guide-lines of the Resolution to advance a peace agreement. No Arab State has yet accepted that proposal.

This announcement of our Ambassador was reported to the House by the Foreign Minister on 29 May 1968 and to the General Assembly in September 1969. It opened the way for Ambassador Jarring to invite the parties to discuss any topic which any of them saw fit to raise, including issues mentioned in the Resolution. The Arabs and those others who assert that we are preventing progress towards peace in terms of the Resolution have no factual basis for so asserting. They seek merely to throw dust in the world's eyes, to cover up their guilt and deceive the world into thinking that we are the ones who are retarding peace.

Talks Without Pre-Conditions

It is also argued that, by creating facts on the ground, we are laying down irrevocable conditions which render negotiations superfluous or make it more difficult to enter into them. This contention, too, is wholly mistaken and unfounded. The refusal of the Arab States to enter into negotiations with us is simply an extension of their long-drawn-out intransigence. It goes back to before the Six-Day War, before there were any settlements in the administered territories.

After that fighting, we said—and we left no room for doubt—that we were willing to enter into negotiations with our neighbours with no pre-conditions on either side. This willingness does not signify that we have no opinions, thoughts or demands, or that we shall not exercise our right to articulate them in the discussions, as our neighbours are entitled to no less.

Nasser and Hussein, for example, in their official replies to Dr. Jarring, said that they saw the partition borders of 1947 as constituting definitive frontiers. I do not have to explain our attitude to that answer, but we do not insist that, in negotiating with us, the Arab States forfeit their equal right to make any proposal that they think fit, just as they cannot annul from the outset our right to express, in the discussions, any ideas or proposals which we may form. And there assuredly is no moral or political ground for demanding that we refrain from any constructive act in the territories, even though the Arab Governments reject the call for peace and make ready for war.

There is yet another argument touching on our insistence on direct negotiations: it is as devoid as are the others of any least foundation in the annals of international relations or of those between our neighbours and ourselves. For we did sit down face-to-face with the representatives of the Arab States at the time of the negotiations in Rhodes, and no one dare profess that Arab honour was thereby affronted.

There is no precedent of a conflict between nations being brought to finality without direct negotiations. In the conflict between the Arabs and Israel, the issue of direct negotiations goes to the very crux of the matter. For the objective is to achieve peace and co-existence, and how will our neighbours ever be able to live with us in peace if they refuse to speak with us at all?

From the start of the conversations with Ambassador Jarring, we agreed that the face-to-face discussions should take place under the auspices of the Secretary-General's envoy. During 1968, Dr. Jarring sought to bring the parties together under his chairmanship in a neutral place. In March 1968, he proposed that we meet Egypt and Jordan in Nicosia. We agreed, but the Arabs did not. In the same year, and again in September 1969, we expressed our consent to his proposal that the meetings be held in the manner of the Rhodes talks, which comprised both face-to-face and indirect talks; a number of times it seemed that the Arabs and the Soviets would also fall in with that proposal, but, in the end, they went back on it.

Only those who deny the right of another State to exist, or who want to avoid recognizing the fact of its sovereignty, can develop the refusal to talk to it into an inculcated philosophy of life which the pupil swears to adhere to as to a political, national principle. The refusal to talk to us directly is damning evidence that the unwillingness of the Arab leaders to be reconciled with the very being of Israel is the basic reason why peace is still to seek.

I am convinced that it is unreal and utopian to think that using the word "withdrawal" will pave the way to peace. True, those among us who do believe that the magic of that word is likely to bring us nearer to peace only mean withdrawal after peace is achieved and then only to secure and agreed boundaries demarcated in a peace treaty. On the other hand, when Arab and Soviet leaders talk of "withdrawal", they mean complete and outright retreat from all the administered territories, and from Jerusalem, without the making of a genuine peace and without any agreement on new permanent borders, but with an addendum calling for Israel's consent to the return of all the refugees.

Israel's policy is clear, and we shall continue to clarify it at every suitable opportunity, as we have done in the United Nations and elsewhere. No person dedicated to truth could misinterpret our policy: when we speak of secure and recognized boundaries, we do not mean that, after peace is made, the Israel Defence Forces should be deployed beyond the boundaries agreed upon in negotiations with our neighbours. No one could be misled—Israel desires secure and recognized boundaries with its neighbours.

Israel's Defence Forces have never crossed its borders in search of conquest, but only when the safeguarding of the existence and bounds of our State demanded it. Nasser's claim that Israel wishes to maintain the cease-fire only so as to freeze the cease-fire lines is preposterous. The cease-fire is necessary not to perpetuate the lines, but to prevent death and destruction, to make progress easier towards a peace resting upon secure and recognized boundaries. It is necessary as a step upwards on the ladder to peace. Incessant gunfire is a step downward on the ladder to war.

The question is crystal-clear, and there is no point in clouding it with semantics—or in trying to escape from reality. There is not a single article in Israel's policy which prevents the making of peace. Nothing is lacking for the making of peace but the Arab persistence in denying Israel's very right to exist. Arab refusal to acquiesce in our existence in the Middle East, alongside the Arab States, abides. The only way to peace is through a change in that recalcitrance.

When it changes, there will no longer be any obstacle to peace negotiations. Otherwise, no formulae, sophistry or definitions will avail. Those in the world who seek peace would do well to heed this basic fact and help to bring about a change in the obdurate Arab approach, which is the real impediment to peace. Any display of "understanding" and forgiveness, however unwitting, is bound to harden the Arabs in their obstinacy and hearten them in their gainsaying of Israel's right to exist, and will, besides, be exploited by Arab leaders to justify ideologically the continuance of the war against Israel.

Nothing unites our people more than the desire for peace. There is no stronger urge in Israel, and on joyful occasions and in hours of mourning alike it is expressed. Nothing can wrench out of our hearts or out of our policy this wish for peace, this hope of peace—not even our indignation over the killing of our loved ones, not even the enmity of the rulers of the Arab world.

The victories that we have won have never intoxicated us, or filled us with such complacency as to relinquish the wish and call for peace—a peace that means goodneighbourly relations, cooperation and an end to slaughter. Peace and co-existence with the Arab peoples have been, and are, among the fundamentals of Jewish renaissance. Generations of the Zionist movement were brought up on them. The desire for peace has charted the policy of all Israel's Governments, of whatever membership. No Government of Israel in power, however constituted, has ever blocked the way to peace.

With all my heart, I am convinced that in Israel, in the future as in the past, there could be no Government which would not bespeak the people's cardinal and steadfast aspiration to bring about a true and enduring peace.

Statement Before The General Assembly Of The United Nations

NEW YORK, New York: January 17, 1957

I rise to make a statement on the problems of the Sinai Desert, the Gulf of Aqaba and the Gaza Strip.

On 3 December 1956 Israeli forces withdrew from the Suez Canal area along the length of the Canal to a distance of some 50 kilometers. This action enabled the United Nations Emergency Force to take up its position for the first time along the Suez Canal, and to create conditions in which the work of clearance might begin. The Secretary-General in his discussions with Israel representatives had indicated that the clearing of the Suez Canal was the most urgent and immediate problem, after which one could deal with the general problem of withdrawal in the Sinai Desert and finally with the particular problem of the Sharm el-Sheikh area.

Subsequent phases of withdrawal carried out during December and January followed this scheme of priorities.

On 8 January 1957 Israeli forces withdrew to a more easterly line, leaving no Israeli forces west of El Arish. As a result of this action, the major part of the Sinai Desert was evacuated.

Thus the undertaking of the Israel Government transmitted by the Secretary-General to the General Assembly on 24 December had been precisely fulfilled.

On 8 January, as soon as the previous phase of withdrawal had been completed, the Israel Government informed the Secretary-General of its decision to withdraw another 25 to 30 kilometers throughout the Sinai Desert except in the area of Sharm el-Sheikh. This action enabled the entry of United Nations Emergency Forces into El Arish and the St. Catherine's Monastery.

On 14 January, one day before the previous phase of withdrawal was due for completion, the Israel Government communicated its decision to have the Sinai Desert entirely evacuated by Israel forces on 22 January with the exception of the Sharm el-Sheikh area; that is the strip on the west coast of the Gulf of Aqaba which at present ensures freedom of navigation through the Straits of Tiran and in the Gulf of Aqaba. At the same time my Government informed the Secretary-General of its willingness to enter forthwith into conversations with him in connection with the evacuation of this strip. At the meeting of 14 January the Israel representative also indicated the desire of my Government to begin discussions at an early date on the arrangements envisaged for the Gaza area.

From this narrative the General Assembly will observe that the withdrawals in the Sinai Desert have followed an orderly system of phasing, in coordination with the eastward movement of United Nations Emergency Forces following closely behind. By 22 January Israel will have evacuated approximately 30,000 sq. miles of territory which it had held at the end of November, when the United Nations Emergency Force first became capable of following up the Israeli withdrawals in force as envisaged in the General Assembly's resolution of 7 November.

It is evident, therefore, that my Government cannot accept—nor can any objective mind sustain—any criticism of Israel's action in carrying out its undertaking of 8 November "to withdraw its forces from Egyptian territory as soon as satisfactory arrangements can be made with the United Nations in connection with the United Nations Emergency Force."

On the basis of the discussions which its representatives have had during this phased withdrawal,my Government understands that there will not be any joint occupation in the area between Egyptian forces and UNEF forces; we believe that it should be the policy of the United Nations to maintain separation between Egyptian and Israeli forces.

Before I discuss the complex problems which now confront us I wish to comment on the circumstances which have attended these efforts by Israel to fulfil the objectives of the General Assembly. The position can be briefly stated. Throughout these weeks during which Israel has co-operated actively with the United Nations on the withdrawal of troops, there has not been one single act of compliance by Egypt with the recommendations or policies of the international organisation, to which she has looked for protection against the consequences of her own belligerency.

While the General Assembly's resolution of 2 November established special priority for an immediate cease-fire, it also contained other recommendations, not one of which the Egyptian Government has shown any intention to fulfil.

The 2 November resolution urged that "upon the cease-fire being effective, steps be taken to reopen the Suez Canal and restore secure freedom of navigation." This objective, so vital for the security and economic welfare of many countries, has been subjected by Egypt to every kind of obstruction and delay; conditions and provisos have been attached to every phase of its implementation. No action has been spared which might slow the process down; steps essential for the clearance of the Canal have been made conditional on the policies and preferences of the territorial power. Negotiations aiming at establishing international law in the operation of the Suez Canal have been delayed, at Egypt's behest. Above all, the Egyptian Government has given no indication that when the Canal is open it will not again be exposed to the illegality and discrimination which Egypt has maintained for the past six years, in defiance of a decision by the Security Council.

A similar fate has befallen the injunction of the General Assembly in its 2 November resolution "to desist from raids across the armistice lines in the neighbouring territory." Fedayeen gangs, operating in neighbouring countries under Egyptian direction, continue to spread death and havoc throughout our countryside. Since 3 December when the Cairo radio announced the intention of the Nasser regime to conduct raids into Israel throughout the winter, some 30 assaults have been committed. The official media of information in Egypt have reported these attacks in boastful communiques. It is evident that in this respect, too, Egypt claims the fulfillment of Assembly resolutions by others, without any parallel acts of compliance on her part.

Moreover, during a period in which the United Nations has used its full influence on Egypt's behalf for the withdrawal of troops, Egyptian policy has been masked by a grave violation of Charter principles and of fundamental human rights. Foreign nationals have been expropriated and deported. The Jewish community has been subjected to a persecution recalling some of the excesses of totalitarianism before and during the Second World War. 7,000 Egyptian Jews have been driven out by this organised cruelty, and all the conditions for a panic-stricken exodus have been wilfully created by the Nasser regime. Thousands of victims have reached Israel's welcoming shores. Some member Governments, in their direct relationships with Egypt, have been moved to express mounting indignation and concern.

World opinion has been quick to perceive the disparity between the assistance which Egypt has received of the United Nations, and the complete absence of any Egyptian response to the legitimate interests of other States and of the organised international community. The question whether Israel is not withdrawing into a position of exposure to renewed Egyptian belligerency, by land and sea, arises in our mind with increasing anxiety and concern.

The acuteness of this question will be easily perceived if we recall that twelve weeks have elapsed since my Government addressed four questions to the Egyptian Government which have still not been answered:

1. Does Egypt still adhere to the position declared and maintained by her over years that she is in a state of war with Israel?

2. Is Egypt prepared to enter into immediate negotiations with Israel with a view to the establishment of peace between the two countries as indicated in paragraph 3 of the aide-memoire

of the Government of Israel of 4 November 1956 to the Secretary-General of the United Nations?

3. Does Egypt agree to cease economic boycott against Israel and lift the blockade of Israel shipping in the Suez Canal?

4. Does Egypt undertake to recall Fedayeen gangs under her control in other Arab countries?

In our talks with the Secretary-General on withdrawal it was mutually understood at all times that the Sharm el Sheikh and Gaza areas were reserved for discussions at a later stage in the withdrawal process. Thus, if the reservation of these problems to this later stage were now made a source of criticism or blame, a serious injustice would be incurred, to the grave prejudice of future discussions. These problems are of special complexity; they touch the question of Israel's security at its most sensitive point. They cannot be treated lightly, without danger to international peace and security. In each case, a change in the existing situation without simultaneous measures to prevent the renewal of belligerency would lead to a possibility, nay, even a certainty, of tension and hostility.

I now come to explain why these problems have this special character, and why we must all work with care and precision at the stage which we have now reached in our deliberations.

THE STRAITS OF TIRAN

The strip of territory in the Sharm el Sheikh area commands the entrance to the Gulf of Aqaba through the Straits of Tiran. The only channel leading from the Red Sea to the Gulf passes between the Island of Tiran and the southeast extremity of the Sinai coast.

This channel is three miles in width, but its navigable part is only some 500 metres broad. Thus any ship passing to or from the Gulf of Aqaba must come very close to the Sinai coast.

At a point in the Sharm el Sheikh area known as Ras Nasrani, Egypt set up gun emplacements six years ago for the sole purpose of preventing ships from sailing freely in the Gulf of Aqaba to and from the port of Elath. Two of these were 6-inch guns and four 3-inch guns. They were trained on the only lane usable by ships as they sail through the Straits. These guns have blockaded the Gulf of Aqaba for the past six years.

Sharm el Sheikh, Ras Nasrani and the neighbouring islands are uninhabited, waterless and desolate. The only purpose of any human presence in those places until 3 November was to prevent free access to an international waterway. The purpose of our presence since then has been to ensure free access. It is astonishing to observe the elaborate installations; the ammunition depots; the airstrip; the spacious accommodations which the Egyptians had established, with the sole aim of obstructing the free passage of commerce between two parts of the high seas.

These installations were established towards the end of 1949. In reply to a query addressed to it by the American Embassy in Cairo, the Egyptian Government, on 28 January 1950, gave assurances that it had no intention of interfering with peaceful shipping, and that passage through the Straits would "as in the past remain free in conformity with international practice and with recognised principles of international law." This Egyptian document has been recorded in full in the verbatim records of the Security Council (SPV/659 par. 103).

In spite of this assurance, and of the fact that the Gulf of Aqaba is a recognised waterway, Egypt has used its gun emplacements to blockade the passage of ships bound for Elath through the Straits of Tiran. The blockade in the Suez Canal, which was condemned by the Security Council in 1951, has been carried out by Egypt with equal stringency—and illegality—in the Gulf of Aqaba.

The blockade works primarily through its deterrent effect, but many acts of force have been committed against ships exercising innocent passage in this international waterway. Fire has been opened on British, American and Italian ships; interference and obstruction have been offered to vessels of Norwegian, Danish and other flags. These acts of piracy had almost eliminated commerce and navigation in the Gulf of Aqaba; slowed down the development of the Port of Elath; inflicted illicit injury on Israel's economy and trade, and denied other countries an alternative route to the Suez Canal, as a link between the Red Sea and the Mediterranean.

On 3 November, when Israel forces entered the Sharm el Sheikh area to assure Israel's self-defence against wanton belligerency, these guns were silenced. To-day, for the first time, ships of all nations are free to move north and south through the Straits of Tiran to and from Elath. An alternative link to Suez joining the Red Sea and Mediterranean is now open to all shipping without distinction of flag.

In his Note to the General Assembly the Secretary-General refers to "the international significance of the Gulf of Aqaba" which justifies "the right of innocent passage through the Straits of Tiran and the Gulf in accordance with rules of international law." In 1949 the International Court of Justice ruled that when straits are geographically part of a highway used for international navigation, the vessels of all nations enjoy the right of free passage therein, whether or not the straits are entirely or partly within the territorial waters of one or more states. In the words of the Court, they belong to the class of international highways through which passage cannot be prohibited by a coastal state.

The international character of the Gulf of Aqaba and the Straits of Tiran is fully confirmed by the jurisprudence of the United Nations. In 1951, the Security Council denounced the Egyptian blockade against Israel, as inconsistent with Egypt's international obligations. In particular, the Security Council denied Egypt the right to exercise visit, search or seizure or to apply restrictions against shipping on the grounds of "belligerent rights". Egypt was called upon to cease all such practices. While the Council's decision was prompted by the Egyptian illegalities in the Suez Canal, its judgments against visit, search or seizure are couched in broader terms, so as to be of general application.

In March 1954 the Security Council discussed an Israeli complaint against Egyptian restrictions both in the Suez Canal and the Gulf of Aqaba. The majority voted for a resolution condemning these restrictions, wherever applied, and calling for their immediate cessation. This resolution was presented by New Zealand and supported by the United States, the United Kingdom, France, Brazil, Colombia, Turkey and Denmark. Interpreting the majority view, the New Zealand representative said:

"The final paragraph of the draft resolution (para. 6) refers only to the complaint of interference with ships in the Gulf of Aqaba... The arguments advanced by the representatives of Egypt in justification of that interference cannot be sustained and in fact have already been rejected by the Council."

Thus the illegal character of Egypt's restrictions is established by recognised principles of international law, by the jurisprudence of the Security Council and of the International Court of Justice; by the consensus of the Maritime Powers; and even by Egypt's own admission in its assurance to the United States on 28 January 1950.

Israel is the only country in the world, except Egypt, with a coastline both on the Mediterranean and on the Red Sea. The fact that its territory unites the Eastern and Western oceans across a land bridge of less than 150 miles constitutes Israel's most important geographical advantage; to have had this facility denied by illegal action for many years is an outrage which should no longer be suffered. Indeed, having in recent weeks experienced the use of this open international waterway, Israel can surely not be asked to acquiesce in its ever being closed again. The development of the southern part of our country; the expansion of our port facilities at Elath; our right of free commerce with friendly nations in Africa and Asia; the vision of our country as a bridge between the traffic and ideas of the Eastern and Western worlds; the liberation of countries in Europe and Asia from exclusive dependence on a single Canal at Suez, exploited by Egypt to hold other states up to injury and extortion; the consequent denial to Egypt of a position of monopoly and domination, unhealthy both for itself and for the maritime nations—all these great issues are bound up in the problem of ensuring free passage through the Gulf of Aqaba and the Straits of Tiran. The more this problem is contemplated the bigger it becomes. It is an issue of broad international scope.

Israel is not alone in having a vital interest in the permanent maintenance of free navigation in the Gulf of Aqaba. Countries whose economy depends upon the flow of trade between the Red Sea and the Mediterranean have already suffered loss through the Egyptian blockade in this international waterway. The Gulf, freed from the illegal Egyptian blockade, can become a pivotal point of international commerce. The port facilities at Elath are being constantly improved. Communications of all kinds across the relatively short land-link between the two seas are under active improvement; and other projects are in a planning stage. If this position is not impaired, then no single state, and therefore no state at all, will have a stranglehold on the jugular vein of other nations.

The relevance of this consideration is already shown by an item appearing in this morning's New York Times.

The avoidance of any renewed blockade in the Gulf of Aqaba and the Straits of Tiran is an objective which the Government of Israel is resolved to pursue with the utmost tenacity. We have no national interests superior to this. We cannot take the responsibility of allowing this interest to be endangered, and of seeing Egyptian guns ever again set up to obstruct the commerce of nations in this international waterway.

Nor, I believe, will the United Nations wish to assume that responsibility. It is unthinkable that our Organisation should, for whatever motive, be instrumental in restoring an illicit blockade. What would history say of the United Nations which for the past five years has not been able to keep the Suez Canal open without discrimination, if it should now be instrumental in obstructing the alternative route between the Red Sea and the Mediterranean? Is it not sufficient that Egypt's policies have denied the world the use of the Suez Canal? Must the blockade also be brought back to the only alternative route? For nine years Egypt has refused to maintain a legal situation in the Suez Canal. Is it conceivable that similar discrimination should be brought back to the Gulf of Aqaba and the Straits of Tiran?

But this result, shocking as it seems, would certainly occur if the United Nations were to press for Israel's withdrawal, without, at the same time, establishing effective arrangements for ensuring permanent freedom of navigation through the Straits and the Gulf.

Unless special measures are now instituted, Israel's withdrawal, after an uncertain interlude of United Nations Emergency Force occupation, would be succeeded by the establishment of Egyptian guns. The open waterway would again become a closed lake. Ships would be detained and assaulted. Since Israel can never again allow her legitimate commerce to be intercepted in the Gulf, Egyptian belligerency would have dire effects. That this prospect is very real is proved by an Egyptian broadcast a few days ago:

"The Arabs will pursue every Israeli ship which tries to pass into the Gulf of Aqaba until they destroy her."

In August 1951, in discussing Egypt's maritime blockade, the representative of Brazil uttered a grave warning. He said:

"Should we accept the Egyptian thesis, we would be bound to recognize any measures of reprisal adopted by the Israel Government. It is obvious that in the exchange of hostile acts that would follow we could hardly expect to lay the foundations of a definite solution to the Palestine question."

Thus, the establishment of effective guarantees for permanent freedom of navigation in the Gulf and the Straits is essential not only for the defense of international and Israeli interests, but also for the preservation of peace. If conflict were to break out, who can be sure to what it might lead?

Because the problem of the Sharm el Sheikh area raises such grave issues it has been reserved for discussion to this late stage. It was no doubt for this reason that in conversations between the Israeli delegate and the Secretary-General it was mutually understood that the very complication of the problems, and the international interest involved, implied a need for negotiation in order to safeguard that international interest and that therefore this belonged to a later state of the general withdrawal.

Surely no delegate who studies this problem can doubt its gravity. Our sole aim and interest in the Sharm el Sheikh area is to ensure that we take no action now which would leave even the smallest chance of such a tragic result as the restoration of the blockade and the consequent renewal of regional conflict and of international tension.

On the other hand, a solution is not impossible. My delegation has variant proposals in mind which it will be prepared to explore in the continuing course of its discussions on the problems of withdrawal. Ways can be sought of simultaneously reconciling two objectives—the withdrawal of Israeli forces, and the effective guaranteeing of permanent freedom of navigation in this international waterway.

The mere entry into this area of United Nations Emergency Force, even with the specific aim of preventing belligerency, would not in itself be a solution. For, there is yet no clarity about the functions of the United Nations Emergency Force or about the duration of its tenure. Any temporary measure for preventing belligerency and securing free navigation would not be effective unless it were ensured in advance that it would operate until a peace settlement were achieved, or until some other effective measure were established by international guarantees for ensuring permanent freedom of navigation. Such guarantees could, perhaps, be furnished either by the principal Maritime Powers; or by an agreement between the four coastal states; or by some combination of the two forms of guarantee. But, if the United Nations Emergency Force were to be regarded as a key to the solution of this problem, greater clarity and precision would be needed in defining its functions and the conditions and duration of its tenure.

THE GAZA STRIP

In his Note to the General Assembly the Secretary-General states that "further discussions with the representatives of Israel are required" on the question of the Gaza strip. On 14 January, Israel representatives stated that they were ready for such discussions at an early date. At this stage I wish only to describe the general background of our thinking on the Gaza question.

When the State of Israel was established in 1948, the Egyptian army crossed the Sinai Desert into the Negev, in defiance of the cease-fire resolution of the Security Council, in an attempt to destroy Israel's new-born independence by force of arms. The attack was held by the Israel settlements in the Negev. The Egyptians were driven back across the international frontier into Sinai. They succeeded, however, in clinging to a narrow rectangular strip 6 miles wide extending north from the Egyptian frontier for 26 miles along the Mediterranean coast to a point within 35 miles of Tel Aviv.

The Gaza strip was an integral part of the mandated territory of Palestine, and is geographically and economically part of the Negev.

For the eight years of its occupation by Egypt, this strip served as a base to spread terror and wreak havoc against Israel.

The bulk of the area is rural, with urban centers at Gaza, with a population of 45,000; Khan Unis with a population of 14,000 and Rafa with a population of 5,000. The resident population of the entire strip is estimated at 80,000. Only about a third of the population manages to support itself on citriculture, date growing and some small industry.

Within the Gaza strip there live some 200,000 refugees who are fed, clad and generally provided for by United Nations Relief and Works Agency, and other international relief agencies. Throughout the Egyptian occupation of Gaza, Egypt did not annex the Gaza strip, but treated it as occupied territory provisionally administered by the Egyptian military authorities. In a ruling given by the Cairo Court of Administrative Jurisdiction in September 1955, it was stated that the Gaza strip was outside Egyptian territory and that the Egyptian authorities were exercising "a kind of control over part of the territory of Palestine."

Throughout their occupation of the strip, which ended in November 1956, Egypt acted in Gaza as a foreign conqueror. There was no democratic local representation in Government councils. No action was taken to improve the impoverished condition of the area. Restrictions were placed on the passage of persons and goods from the Gaza strip to Egypt.

As a result of these conditions, many Gaza inhabitants fled to Jordan and to other Arab countries.

The only purpose which the Gaza strip served during the Egyptian occupation was that of providing a convenient base for aggression against Israel. Extending deep into the heart of Israeli territory, the Gaza area was excellently situated as a springboard for this purpose. Over the years, attacks were launched week by week and month by month against the land and people of Israel, and against Israel property and vital installations. Egypt established a closely knit chain of gun positions along the entire demarcation line, subjecting Israel villages to intermittent fire, making life unbearable across large areas of the Northern Negev and the southern coastal plain. Israeli casualties in killed and wounded as a result of Egyptian attacks, nearly all of which emanated from the strip, totalled no less than 573. This was in addition to innumerable cases of sabotage, mine-laying, robbery and theft.

In the summer of 1955 the Nasser regime launched a new form of aggression against Israel from the Gaza strip. Amongst the destitute elements of the local population and refugee camps, the Egyptian High Command organised fedayeen units as military formations of the Egyptian army. In the past eighteen months, these units carried out an intensified campaign of attack upon Israel. They ambushed road traffic, killed men, women and children, blew up wells and water installations, mined roads at night, demolished houses in which farmers and their families were peacefully asleep. These outrages culminated in major outbreaks during August and September 1955, April 1956 and October 1956.

In the ominous build-up of Egyptian forces, with offensive weapons obtained during the first half of 1956, the Gaza strip had an essential role both as a centre for fedayeen groups, and as the forward base of an Egyptian Army division which was stationed there within and hour's drive from Tel Aviv.

Since the expulsion of Egyptian forces from Gaza fedayeen have ceased to infest the countryside. When the tensions and hostilities had died down in early November, the refugee camps became calm. Israel farmers and their families in the Negev had at last attained physical security. Since 3 November no house, no school, no baby home in their villages has been shelled from across the border.

The report submitted by the representative of the Secretary-General, Colonel Nelson, who visited the Gaza strip at the end of November lies before the General Assembly as Document A/3491. According to this report "the Israel authorities have methodically established a program to stabilise life in Gaza." "They have established law and order." "The execution of civic responsibilities is being worked out progressively with the local officials." "The Israel Administration allows the United Nations Relief and Works Agency complete freedom throughout the area." "A plan to make available basic foodstuffs at subsidised prices from Israel Government stocks to the local non-refugee population is being worked out." "Measures were being introduced to facilitate the marketing of agricultural produce, citrus and dates for export from the Gaza area. In speaking to several farmers there was evidence that arrangements were being made through the Israeli Citrus Board to actually export the agricultural produce."

Colonel Nelson reports on the opening of banks and credit facilities. He certifies that "there was relatively small physical damage caused in the area due to the events of the 2nd and 3rd of November." "On 25 November the Israel civilian police reporting to Israel Central Police Headquarters was established in the area, and is being coordinated with the local police. Throughout the area one could see both Israeli civil police and the local police patrolling." On the other hand "there were few troops evident in the area as compared to the concentration of Egyptian troop units prior to 2 November."

Colonel Nelson goes on to report that "water installations are functioning throughout the area;" that "power stations in the area are back to normal;" that telephone communication is being restored progressively;" that "requisitioned cars and trucks are being progressively returned to their owners;" that "hospitals are in full operation;" that "Israel Health Ministry representatives have been in the area to coordinate and assist."

Religious institutions in the area are pursuing their activities without interruption. In a letter addressed on 18 November to the Israel Ministry of Religious Affairs, Monseigneur Antonio Vergani, Vicar General in Israel of the Latin Patriarchate, stated "I have found that everything has gone for the best and that as soon as the occupation of the town by Israel forces had started an officer came immediately to the Latin Church where some 1,500 persons sought refuge, and having ascertained that no harm occurred, posted another officer and guard." Similar tributes to a growing stability and peace in the Gaza area have been recorded by the Senior Vicar of the Armenian Patriarchate and by the representatives of the International Red Cross Committee.

The future status of the Gaza strip remains to be determined. It must be recalled that Gaza is separated from Egypt by scores of miles of desert. The Egyptian military regime during the past eight years was provisional in character, and of undefined legal status; and it resulted in the decay of the area and in the impoverishment of its population. No contribution whatever had been made by Egypt to the solution of any part of the refugee problem, despite the fact that this problem had been created through the invasion of Israel by Egypt and other Arab states in 1948. It is inconceivable to my Government that the nightmare of the previous eight years should be reestablished in Gaza with international sanction. Shall Egypt be allowed once more to organise murder and sabotage in this strip? Shall Egypt be allowed to condemn the local population to permanent impoverishment and to block any solution of the refugee problem?

My Government believes that a solution of Gaza's problems, and especially of the problem of Arab refugees can be found. On the other hand, it must be admitted that any international force would be powerless to prevent the return of elements which would incite and intimidate the local population and the refugees, and the recrudescence of fedayeen activities. Nor is it possible to maintain an area such as the Gaza strip almost entirely devoid of economic resources in a state of economic isolation from any adjoining territory.

It will be seen that the issues which arise are complex, and offer no easy solution. There are difficult political and security problems in which 80,000 residents and some 200,000 refugees are involved. It is clear that some time is needed to work out a permanent solution of all these problems. They cannot be solved overnight. The Government of Israel is prepared immediately to enter into discussions in a quest for a solution. But we must not ignore the report of the representative of the Secretary-General who writes that "the removal of any effective authority from the area would cause an eruption either by the refugees or the local inhabitants in the form of looting or destruction of property." It is not difficult to envisage what suffering and dislocation would come upon this sorely tried region, if there were to be an uprooting of all those elements of social, economic and municipal stability which have now been established. Opportunities must be nourished for bringing about radical improvement in the economic and social condition of the inhabitants and for working out a solution of the refugee problem. We believe that all this can be guaranteed by the continuance of the present administrative processes, working in cooperation with representatives of the local population and of the United Nations Relief and Works Agency, and in suitable contact and relationship with the United Nations. While we are not yet ready with final proposals, we hope shortly to present detailed plans to the international community whereby the Gaza strip would achieve peace and stability; whereby the economic future of the population will be assured, and whereby the United Nations with Israel's fullest cooperation, will be enabled to proceed effectively towards a solution of the refugee problem. The withdrawal of Israeli military forces from the Gaza strip can well be one of the elements in the arrangements which we envisage.

We are ready at an early date to pursue our thinking along these lines with the Secretary-General in accordance with paragraph 9 of his note to the General Assembly. In this case, as in that of the entrance to the Gulf of Aqaba, the desire to proceed speedily with the fulfilment of the General Assembly's objectives on the withdrawal of troops should be tempered by a prudent concern for the avoidance of disruptions and dislocations and above all for the prevention of any risk of resuming the deadly conditions of belligerency which made Gaza a focus of international conflict during the previous eight years.

Mr. President, the General Assembly will surely have no difficulty in concluding that the problem of the Gulf of Aqaba with its broad international perspectives ; and the question of the Gaza strip, with its almost unparalleled complexity, require further clarification in a cooperative spirit. I do not doubt that if the General Assembly leaves room for that consideration the progress already recorded in the Secretary-General's note can be crowned by arrangements which will eliminate the prospect of the renewal of belligerency by land and by sea. In the pursuit of such arrangements my delegation will bend every resource of heart and mind in the days that lie ahead.

HELEN KELLER

INTRODUCTION

Helen was born in Tuscumbia, Alabama on June 27, 1880. However, her real life began one day in March of 1887, when she was almost seven years old.

She was always to call that the most important day I can remember in my life. It was the day when Annie Sullivan, a 20-year-old graduate of the Perkins School for the Blind, came to be her teacher. They were inseparable until Annie's death in 1936.

Even as a little girl Helen expressed a desire to go to college. In 1900, she entered Radcliffe College and graduated from there cum laude in 1904. She thus became the first deaf-blind person to graduate from college. Throughout these years, Annie Sullivan laboriously spelled books and lectures into her pupil's hand.

In 1936, Helen Keller moved to Westport, Connecticut, where she lived until her death on June 1, 1968, at the age of 87. In his eulogy at her funeral, Senator Lister Hill said of her, "She will live on, one of the few, immortal names not born to die. Her spirit will endure as long as man can read and stories can be told of the woman who showed the world there are no boundaries to courage and faith."

Strike Against War Famous Speech
Speech at Carnegie Hall, New York City - January 5, 1916

TO begin with, I have a word to say to my good friends, the editors, and others who are moved to pity me. Some people are grieved because they imagine I am in the hands of unscrupulous persons who lead me astray and persuade me to espouse unpoplular causes and make me the mouthpiece of their propaganda. Now, let it be understood once and for all that I do not want their pity; I would not change places withone of them. I know what I am talking about. My sources of information are as good and reliable as anybody else's. I have papers and magazines from England, France, Germany and Austria that I can read myself. Not all the editors I have met can do that. Quite a number of them have to take their French and German second hand. No, I will not disparage the editors. They are an overworked, misunderstood class. Let them remember, though, that if I cannot see the fire at the end of their cigarettes, neither can they thread a needle in the dark. All I ask, gentlemen, is a fair field and no favor. I have entered the fight against preparedness and against the economic system under which we live. It is to be a fight to the finish, and I ask no quarter.

The future of the world rests in the hands of America. The future of America rests on the backs of 80,000,000 working men and women and their children. We are facing a grave crisis in our national life. The few who profit from the labor of the masses want to organize the workers into an army which will protect the interests of the capitalists. You are urged to add to the heavy burdens you already bear the burden of a larger army and many additional warships. It is in your power to refuse to carry the artillery and the dread-noughts and to shake off some of the burdens, too, such as limousines, steam yachts and country estates. You do not neet to make a great noise about it. With the silence and dignity of creators you can end wars and the system of selfishness and exploitation that causes wars. All you need to do to bring about this stupendous revolution is to straighten up and fold your arms.

We are not preparing to defend our country. Even if we were as helpless as Congressman Gardner says we are, we have no enemies foolhardy enough to attempt to invade the United States. The talk about attack from Germany and Japan is absurd. Germany has its hands full and will be busy with its own affairs for some generations after the European war is over.

With full control of the Atlantic Ocean and the Mediterranean Sea, the allies failed to land enough men to defeat the Turks at Gallipoli; and then they failed again to land an army at Salonica in time to check the Bulgarian invasion of Serbia. The conquest of America by water is a nightmare confined exclusively to ignorant persons and members of the Navy League.

Yet, everywhere, we hear fear advanced as argument for armament. It reminds me of a fable I read. A certain man found a horseshoe. His neighbor began to weep and wail because, as he justly pointed out, the man who found the horseshoe might someday find a horse. Having found the shoe, he might shoe him. The neighbor's child might some day go so near the horse's hells as to be kicked, and die. Undoubtedly the two families would quarrel and fight, and several valuable lives would be lost through the finding of the horseshoe. You know the last war we had we quite accidentally picked up some islands in the Pacific Ocean which may some day be the cause of a quarrel between ourselves and Japan. I'd rather drop those islands right now and foret about them than go to war to keep them. Wouldn't you?

Congress is not preparing to defend the people of the United States. It is planning to protect the capital of American speculators and investors in Mexico, South America, China, and teh Philippine Islands. Incidentally this preparation will benefit the manufacturers of munitions and war machines.

Until recently there were uses in the United States for the money taken from the workers. But American labor is exploited almost to the limit now, and our national resources have all been appropriated. Still the profits keep piling up new capital. Our flourishing industry in implements of murder is filling the vaults of New York's banks with gold. And a dollar that is not being used to make a slave of some human being is not fulfilling its purpose in the capitalistic scheme. That dollar must be invested in South America, Mexico, China, or the Philippines.

It was no accident that the Navy League came into prominence at the same time that the National City Bank of New York established a branch in Buenos Aires. It is not a mere coincidence that six business associates of J.P. Morgan are officials of defense leagues. And chance did not dictate that Mayor Mitchel chould appoint to his Committee of Safety a thousand men that represent a fifth of the wealth of the United States. These men want their foreign investments protected.

Every modern war has had its root in exploitation. The Civil War was fought to decide whether to slaveholders of the South or the capitalists of the North should exploit the West. The Spanish-American War decided that the United States should exploit Cuba and the Philippines. The South African War decided that the British should exploit the diamond mines. The Russo-Japanese War decided that Japan should exploit Korea. The present war is to decide who shall exploit the Balkans, Turkey, Persia, Egypt, India, China, Africa. And we are whetting our sword to scare the victors into sharing the spoils with us. Now, the workers are not interested in the spoils; they will not get any of them anyway.

The preparedness propagandists have still another object, and a very important one. They want to give the people something to think about besides their won unhappy condition. They know the cost of living is high, wages are low, employment is uncertain and will be much more so when the European call for munitions stops. No matter how hard and incessantly the people work, they often cannot afford the comforts of life; many cannot obtain the necessities.

Every few days we are given a new war scare to lend realism to their propaganda. They have had us on the verge of war over the Lusitania, the Gulflight, the Ancona, and now they want the workingmen to become excited over the sinking of the Persia. The workingman has no interest in any of these ships. The Germans might sink every vessel on the Atlantic Ocean and the Mediterranean Sea, and kill Americans with every one—the American workingman would still have no reason to go to war.

All the machinery of the system has been set in motion. Above the complaint and din of the protest from the workers is heard the voice of authority.

"Friends," it says, "fellow workmen, patriots; your country is in danger! There are foes on all sides of us. There is nothing between us and our enemies except the Pacific Ocean and the Atlantic Ocean. Look at what has happened to Belgium. Consider the fate of Serbia. Will you murmur about low wages when your country, your very liberties, are in jeopardy? What are the miseries you endure compared to the humiliation of having a victorious German army sail up the East River? Quit your whining, get busy and prepare to defend your firesides and your flag. Get an army, get a navy; be ready to meet the invaders like the loyal-hearted freemen you are."

Will the workers walk into this trap? Will they be fooled again? I am afraid so. The people have always been amenable to oratory of this sort. The workers know they have no enemies except their masters. They know that their citizenship papers are no warrant for the safety of themselves or their wives and children. They know that honest sweat, persistent toil and years of struggle bring them nothing worth holding on to, worth fighting for. Yet, deep down in their foolish hearts they believe they have a country. Oh blind vanity of slaves!

The clever ones, up in the high places know how childish and silly the workers are. They know that if the government dresses them up in khaki and gives them a rifle and starts them off with a brass band and waving banners, they will go forth to fight valiantly for their own enemies. They are taught that brave men die for their country's honor. What a price to pay for an abstraction—the lives of millions of young men; other millions crippled and blinded for life; existence made hideous for still more millions of human being; the achievement and inheritance of generations swept away in a moment—and nobody better off for all the misery! This terrible sacrifice would be comprehensible if the thing you die for and call country fed, clothed, housed and warmed you, educated and cherished your children. I thinkthe workers are the most unselfish of the children of men; they toil and live and die for other people's country, other people's sentiments, other people's liberties and other people's happiness! The workers have no liberties of their own; they are not free when they are compelled to work twelve or ten or eight hours a day. they are not free when they are ill paid for their exhausting toil. They are not free when their children must labor in mines, mills and factories or starve, and when their women may be driven by poverty to lives of shame. They are not free when they are clubbed and imprisoned because they go on strike for a raise of wages and for the elemental justice that is their right as human beings.

We are not free unless the men who frame and execute the laws represent the interests of the lives of the people and no other interest. The ballot does not make a free man out of a wage slave. there has never existed a truly free and democratic nation in the world. From time immemorial men have followed with blind loyalty the strong men who had the power of money and of armies. Even while battlefields were piled high with their own dead they have tilled the lands of the rulers and have been robbed of the fruits of their labor. They have built palaces and pyramids, temples and cathedrals that held no real shrine of liberty.

As civilization has grown more complex the workers have become more and more enslaved, until today they are little more than parts of the machines they operate. Daily they face the dangers of railroad, bridge, skyscraper, frieght train, stokehold, stockyard, lumber raft and min. Panting and training at the docks, on the railroads and underground and on the seas, they move the traffic and pass from land to land the precious commodities that make it possible for us to live. And what is their reward? A scanty wage, often poverty, rents, taxes, tributes and war indemnities.

The kind of preparedness the workers want is reorganization and reconstruction of their whole life, such as has never been attempted by statesmen or governments. The Germans found out years ago that they could not raise good soldiers in the slums so they abolished the slums. They saw to it that all the people had at least a few of the essentials of civilization—decent lodging, clean streets, wholesome if scanty food, proper medical care and proper safeguards for the workers in their ocupations. That is only a small part of what should be done, but what wonders that one step toward the right sort of preparedness has wrought for Germany! For eighteen months it has kept itself free from invasion while carrying on an extended war of conquest, and its armies are still pressing on with unabated vigor. It is your business to force these reforms on the Administration. Let there be no more talk about what a government can or cannot do. All these theings have been done by all the belligerent nations in the hurly-burly of war. Every fundamental industry has been managed better by the governments than by private corporations.

It is your duty to insist upon still more radical measure. It is your business to see that no child is employed in an industrial establishment or mine or store, and that no worker in needlessly exposed to accident or disease. It is your business to make them give you clean cities, free from smoke, dirt and congestion. It is your business to make them pay you a living wage. It is your business to see that this kind of preparedness is carried into every department on the nation, until everyone has a chance to be well born, well nourished, rightly educated, intelligent and serviceable to the country at all times.

Strike against all ordinances and laws and institutions that continue the slaughter of peace and the butcheries of war. Srike against war, for without you no battles can be fought. Strike against manufacturing scrapnel and gas bombs and all other tools of murder. Strike against preparedness that means death and misery to millions of human being. Be not dumb, obedient slaves in an army of destruction. Be heroes in an army of construction.

HER MAJESTY QUEEN ELIZABETH II

INTRODUCTION

Her Majesty The Queen was born in London on April 21, 1926 and later christened Elizabeth Alexandra Mary. She was the first child of The Duke and Duchess of York, who later became King George VI and Queen Elizabeth. The Princess Elizabeth, along with her sister the Princess Margaret (born four years later), had her early education at home and, after her father succeeded to the Throne in 1936, became heiress presumptive. Shortly after her eighteenth birthday, she was appointed Counsellor of State during the King's absence and, for the first time, exercised certain functions of the Crown.

After the Second World War, The Princess Elizabeth's public engagements grew in number and frequency. On November 20, 1947, The Princess Elizabeth married Lieutenant Philip Mountbatten, now His Royal Highness The Prince Philip Duke of Edinburgh.

The couple first toured Canada as Their Royal Highnesses The Princess Elizabeth and The Duke of Edinburgh in the autumn of 1951, travelling from coast to coast.

On numerous fronts, The Queen's relationship with Canada and Canadians continues to grow stronger with each passing year. She has given Her patronage to many Canadian organizations and retains a special relationship with the Canadian Forces.

On the Death of Princess Diana Famous Speech
September 9, 1997

SINCE last Sunday's dreadful news we have seen, throughout Britain and around the world, an overwhelming expression of sadness at Diana's death.

We have all been trying in our different ways to cope. It is not easy to express a sense of loss, since the initial shock is often succeeded by a mixture of other feelings: disbelief, incomprehension, anger – and concern for those who remain.

We have all felt those emotions in these last few days. So what I say to you now, as your queen and as a grandmother, I say from my heart.First, I want to pay tribute to Diana myself.

She was an exceptional and gifted human being. In good times and bad, she never lost her capacity to smile and laugh, nor to inspire others with her warmth and kindness.

I admired and respected her – for her energy and commitment to others, and especially for her devotion to her two boys.

This week at Balmoral, we have all been trying to help William and Harry come to terms with the devastating loss that they and the rest of us have suffered.

No one who knew Diana will ever forget her. Millions of others who never met her, but felt they knew her, will remember her.

I for one believe that there are lessons to be drawn from her life and from the extraordinary and moving reaction to her death.

I share in your determination to cherish her memory.This is also an opportunity for me, on behalf of my family, and especially Prince Charles and William and Harry, to thank all of you who have brought flowers, sent messages, and paid your respects in so many ways to a remarkable person.

These acts of kindness have been a huge source of help and comfort. Our thoughts are also with Diana's family and the families of those who died with her.

I know that they too have drawn strength from what has happened since last weekend, as they seek to heal their sorrow and then to face the future without a loved one.

I hope that tomorrow we can all, wherever we are, join in expressing our grief at Diana's loss, and gratitude for her all-too-short life. It is a chance to show to the whole world the British nation united in grief and respect.

On The Opening Of Parliament by Her Majesty Queen Elizabeth II Queen of the United Kingdom Wednesday, 14th May, 1997

MY Lords And Members Of The House Of Commons;

The Duke of Edinburgh and I look forward to receiving State Visits by His Excellency the President of Brazil in December and by Their Majesties the Emperor and Empress of Japan next year. We also look forward to our visit to Canada and to our State Visits to Pakistan and India.

My Government intends to govern for the benefit of the whole nation.

The education of young people will be my Government's first priority. They will work to raise standards in schools, colleges and universities and to promote lifelong learning at the workplace. They will cut class sizes using money saved as a result of legislation phasing out the assisted places scheme. A further Bill will contain measures to raise educational standards, develop a new role for local education authorities and parents, establish a new framework for the decentralised and equitable organisation of schools, propose reforms to the teaching profession, and respond positively to recommendations from the National Committee of Inquiry into the future of higher education.

The central economic objectives of my Government are high and stable levels of economic growth and employment, to be achieved by ensuring opportunity for all. The essential platform for achieving these objectives is economic stability.

To that end a Bill will be introduced to give the Bank of England operational responsibility for setting interest rates, in order to deliver price stability and support the Government's overall economic policy, within a framework of enhanced accountability. My Government will also ensure that public borrowing is controlled through tough fiscal rules and that the burden of public debt is kept at a stable and prudent level. They will aim to deliver high and sustainable levels of growth and employment by encouraging investment in industry, skills, infrastructure and new technologies; by reducing long-term unemployment, especially among young people; by promoting competition; and by helping to create successful and profitable business. These policies will enhance Britain's position as a leading industrial nation.

My Government have pledged to mount a fundamental attack upon youth and long-term unemployment and will take early steps to implement a welfare-to- work programme to tackle unemployment, financed by a levy on the excess profits of the privatised utilities which will be brought forward in an early Budget.

A new partnership with business will be at the heart of my Government's plans to build a modern and dynamic economy to improve the competitiveness of British industry. They will bring forward legislation to reform and strengthen competition law and introduce a statutory right to interest on late payment of debts. My Government is committed to fairness at work and will introduce a national minimum wage.

Legislation will be brought forward to amend criminal law and to combat crime, including reform of the youth justice system and measures against anti-social behaviour. A Bill will be introduced to prohibit the private possession of handguns.

My Government will improve the National Health Service, as a service providing care on the basis of need to the whole population. They will bring forward new arrangements for decentralisation and co-operation within the service and for ending the internal market. Legislation will be introduced to clarify the existing powers of NHS Trusts to enter into partnerships with the private sector. A White Paper will be published on measures to reduce tobacco consumption, including legislation to ban tobacco advertising.

My Government will contribute to the achievement of high standards of food safety and protection of public health throughout the food chain, will ensure openness and transparency of information to consumers, and will consult widely on recommendations for a Food Standards Agency.

A Bill will be introduced to ensure that as many people as possible have access to the benefits of the National Lottery including for health and education projects.

Measures will be introduced to enable capital receipts from the sale of council houses to be invested in housebuilding and renovation as part of my Government's determination to deal with homelessness and unemployment.

My Government is committed to open and transparent Government. They will introduce a Bill to strengthen data protection controls. They will enhance people's aspirations for better, more accessible and accountable public services, using Information Technology to the full. A White Paper will be published on proposals for a Freedom of Information Bill.

A Bill will be introduced to incorporate into United Kingdom law the main provisions of the European Convention on Human Rights.

Decentralisation is essential to my Government's vision of a modern nation. Legislation will be introduced to allow the people of Scotland and Wales to vote in referendums on my Government's proposals for a devolved Scottish Parliament and the establishment of a Welsh Assembly. If these proposals are approved in the referendums, my Government will bring forward legislation to implement them. Legislation will be introduced to provide for a referendum on a directly elected strategic authority and a directly elected mayor for London. A Bill will be brought forward to establish Regional Development Agencies in England outside London.

In Northern Ireland my Government will seek reconciliation and a political settlement which has broad support, working in co-operation with the Irish Government. They will work to build trust and confidence in Northern Ireland by bringing forward legislation to deal with terrorism and to reduce tension over parades, and other measures to protect human rights, combat discrimination in the workplace, increase confidence in policing and foster economic development.

Members of the House of Commons, Estimates for the public service will be laid before you. My Lords and Members of the house of Commons,

In the European Union, my Government will take a leading role. They will seek to promote employment, improve competitiveness, complete the Single Market and opt into the Social Chapter. They will seek further reform of the Common Agricultural Policy to secure lower food prices for consumers and save money, support the rural economy and enhance the environment. They will seek changes to the Common Fisheries Policy to conserve fish stocks in the long-term interest of the UK fishing industry. They will play a full part in the debate about Economic and Monetary Union.

My Government will work for the early and successful enlargement of the European Union. They will pursue an outcome to the Intergovernmental Conference and use their Presidency in the first half of 1998 to strengthen European co-operation while advancing the United Kingdom's interests and to make the Union more open, democratic and efficient. A Bill will be introduced to amend the European Communities Act if necessary.

My Government will ensure a strong defence based on the North Atlantic Treaty Organisation, and promote international peace and security. They will play a major role in decisions to shape NATO's future, including enlargement, and to include Russia in a wider security framework. To ensure that the United Kingdom's defence capabilities are matched to the changing strategic setting, my Government will reassess our essential security interests and defence needs.

My Government will retain strong armed forces, including the nuclear deterrent. Preventing the proliferation of weapons of mass destruction will be a priority.

My Government will work for reforms to make the United Nations more effective and for an early resolution of its funding crisis. My Government will continue to support peace in Bosnia and Herzegovina. They will work for a settlement in Cyprus. They will promote efforts for a durable peace in the Middle East.

My Government will work on behalf of Hong Kong's people to achieve a successful transition which preserves their way of life and promotes their continued stability and prosperity.

Preparations will continue for the G7 Summit to be held in Birmingham and the second Asia-Europe Meeting in London in 1998. My Government will host the meeting of the Commonwealth Heads of Government in October 1997 and seize the opportunity to increase co-operation between the United Kingdom and other members of the Commonwealth.

My Government have established a Department for International Development. They will publish a White Paper setting out how, through more coherent policies, they will tackle global poverty and promote sustainable development. They will rejoin the United Nations Educational, Scientific and Cultural Organisation.

My Government will promote open markets around the world, while ensuring that the interests of developing countries and the global environment are fairly reflected.

The promotion of human rights worldwide will be a priority, as will the fight against terrorism, organised crime, money laundering and drug misuse and trafficking at home and abroad.

My Government will seek to restore confidence in the integrity of the nation's political system by upholding the highest standards of honesty and propriety in public life. They will consider how the funding of political parties should be regulated and reformed.

They will programme House of Commons business to ensure more effective scrutiny of Bills and better use of the time of Members of the House of Commons. During the course of the session, my Government will also publish in draft for public consultation a number of Bills, which it intends to introduce in subsequent sessions of this Parliament. They will propose the establishment of a new Select Committee of the House of Commons to look at ways of making Parliamentary procedure more effective and efficient.

Other measures will be laid before you.

My Lords and Members of the House of Commons,

I pray that the blessing of Almighty God may rest upon your counsels.

HILLARY RODHAM CLINTON

INTRODUCTION

Hillary Rodham Clinton was born on October 26, 1947, Chicago, Illinois, U.S.A., U.S. senator (2001-), American first lady (1993-2001)—the wife of Bill Clinton, 42nd president of the United States—and an accomplished lawyer and children's rights advocate.

She campaigned for Republican presidential candidate Barry Goldwater in 1964 and chaired the local chapter of the Young Republicans. A year later, after she enrolled at Wellesley College, her political views began to change. Influenced by the assassinations of Malcolm X, Robert F. Kennedy, and Martin Luther King, Jr., she joined the Democratic Party and volunteered in the presidential campaign of antiwar candidate Eugene McCarthy.

After Bill was elected governor of Arkansas in 1978, she continued to pursue her career and retained her maiden name (until 1982), bringing considerable criticism from voters who felt that her failure to change her name indicated a lack of commitment to her husband. Their only child, Chelsea Victoria, was born in 1980.

In 2003 Hillary's much-anticipated memoir of her White House years, *Living History*, was published and set sales records; she had received an advance of about $8 million for the book. In 2006 she was easily reelected to the Senate. The following year Hillary announced that she would seek the Democratic Party's presidential nomination for 2008, for which was she is a strong contender.

Women's Rights Are Human Rights
September 5, 1995, Beijing, China

THIS speech was given during the United Nations Fourth World Conference on Women.

Thank you very much Gertrude Mongella, for your dedicated work that has brought us to this point.

Distinguished delegates and guests, I would like to thank the Secretary General of the United Nations for inviting me to be part of this important United Nations Fourth World Conference on Women. This is truly a celebration – a celebration of the contributions women make in every aspect of life: in the home, on the job, in the community, as mothers, wives, sisters, daughters, learners, workers, citizens and leaders.

It is also a coming together, much the way women come together every day in every country.

We come together in fields and in factories. In village markets and supermarkets. In living rooms and board rooms.

Whether it is while playing with our children in the park, or washing clothes in a river, or taking a break at the office water cooler, we come together and talk about our aspirations and concerns. And time and again, our talk turns to our children and our families.

However different we may appear, there is far more that unites us than divides us. We share a common future. And we are here to find common ground so that we may help bring new dignity and respect to women and girls all over the world – and in so doing, bring new strength and stability to families as well.

By gathering in Beijing, we are focusing world attention on issues that matter most in the lives of women and their families: access to education, health care, jobs, and credit, the chance to enjoy basic legal and human rights and to participate fully in the political life of their countries.

There are some who question the reason for this conference. Let them listen to the voices of women in their homes, neighborhoods, and workplaces.

There are some who wonder whether the lives of women and girls matter to economic and political progress around the globe. ... Let them look at the women gathered here and at Hairou.... the homemakers, nurses, teachers, lawyers, policymakers, and women who run their own businesses.

It is conferences like this that compel governments and peoples everywhere to listen, look and face the world's most pressing problems.

Wasn't it after the women's conference in Nairobi ten years ago that the world focused for the first time on the crisis of domestic violence?

Earlier today, I participated in a World Health Organization forum. In that forum we talked about ways that where government officials, NGOs, and individual citizens are working on ways to address the health problems of women and girls.

Tomorrow, I will attend a gathering of the United Nations Development Fund for Women. There, the discussion will focus on local – and highly successful – programs that give hard_working women access to credit so they can improve their own lives and the lives of their families.

What we are learning around the world is that, if women are healthy and educated, their families will flourish. If women are free from violence, their families will flourish. If women have a chance to work and earn as full and equal partners in society, their families will flourish.

And when families flourish, communities and nations will flourish.

That is why every woman, every man, every child, every family, and every nation on our planet does have a stake in the discussion that takes place here.

Over the past 25 years, I have worked persistently on issues relating to women, children and families. Over the past two and a half years, I have had the opportunity to learn more about the challenges facing women in my own country and around the world.

I have met new mothers in Indonesia, who come together regularly in their village to discuss nutrition, family planning, and baby care.

I have met working parents in Denmark who talk about the comfort they feel in knowing that their children can be cared for in creative, safe, and nurturing after school centers.

I have met women in South Africa who helped lead the struggle to end apartheid and are now helping build a new democracy.

I have met with the leading women of my own hemisphere who are working every day to promote literacy and better health care for the children in their countries.

I have met women in India and Bangladesh who are taking out small loans to buy milk cows, rickshaws, thread and other materials to create a livelihood for themselves and their families.

I have met doctors and nurses in Belarus and Ukraine who are trying to keep children alive in the aftermath of Chernobyl.

The great challenge of this conference is to give voice to women everywhere whose experiences go unnoticed, whose words go unheard.

Women comprise more than half the world's population. Women are 70% percent of the world's poor, and two thirds of those who are not taught to read and write.

Women are the primary caretakers for most of the world's children and elderly. Yet much of the work we do is not valued – not by economists, not by historians, not by popular culture, not by government leaders.

At this very moment, as we sit here, women around the world are giving birth, raising children, cooking meals, washing clothes, cleaning houses, planting crops, working on assembly lines, running companies, and running countries.

Women also are dying from diseases that should have been

prevented or treated; they are watching their children succumb to malnutrition caused by poverty and economic deprivation; they are being denied the right to go to school by their own fathers and brothers; they are being forced into prostitution, and they are being barred from the bank lending office and banned from the ballot box.

Those of us who have the opportunity to be here have the responsibility to speak for those who could not.

As an American, I want to speak up for women in my own country – women who are raising children on the minimum wage, women who can't afford health care or child care, women whose lives are threatened by violence, including violence in their own homes.

I want to speak up for mothers who are fighting for good schools, safe neighborhoods, clean air and clean airwaves.....for older women, some of them widows, who have raised their families and now find that their skills and life experiences are not valued in the workplace... for women who are working all night as nurses, hotel clerks, and fast food chefs so that they can be at home during the day with their kids... and for women everywhere who simply don't have time to do everything they are called upon to do each day.

Speaking to you today, I speak for them, just as each of us speaks for women around the world who are denied the chance to go to school, or see a doctor, or own property, or have a say about the direction of their lives, simply because they are women.

The truth is that most women around the world work both inside and outside the home, usually by necessity.

We need to understand that there is no one formula for how women should lead their lives.

That is why we must respect the choices that each woman makes for herself and her family. Every woman deserves the chance to realize her God given potential.

We also must recognize that women will never gain full dignity until their human rights are respected and protected.

Our goals for this conference, to strengthen families and societies by empowering women to take greater control over their own destinies, cannot be fully achieved unless all governments – here and around the world – accept their responsibility to protect and promote internationally recognized human rights.

The international community has long acknowledged – and recently affirmed at Vienna – that both women and men are entitled to a range of protections and personal freedoms, from the right of personal security to the right to determine freely the number and spacing of the children they bear.

No one should be forced to remain silent for fear of religious or political persecution, arrest, abuse or torture.

Tragically, women are most often the ones whose human rights are violated.

Even in the late 20th century, the rape of women continues to be used as an instrument of armed conflict. Women and children make up a large majority of the world's refugees. And when women are excluded from the political process, they become even more vulnerable to abuse.

I believe that, on the eve of a new millennium, it is time to break our silence. It is time for us to say here in Beijing, and the world to hear, that it is no longer acceptable to discuss women's rights as separate from human rights.

These abuses have continued because, for too long, the history of women has been a history of silence. Even today, there are those who are trying to silence our words.

The voices of this conference and of the women at Hairou must be heard loud and clear:

It is a violation of human rights when babies are denied food, or drowned, or suffocated, or their spines broken, simply because they are born girls.

It is a violation of human rights when women and girls are sold into the slavery of prostitution.

It is a violation of human rights when women are doused with gasoline, set on fire and burned to death because their marriage dowries are deemed too small.

It is a violation of human rights when individual women are raped in their own communities and when thousands of women are subjected to rape as a tactic or prize of war.

It is a violation of human rights when a leading cause of death worldwide among women ages 14 to 44 is the violence they are subjected to in their own homes by their own relatives.

It is a violation of human rights when young girls are brutalized by the painful and degrading practice of genital mutilation.

It is a violation of human rights when women are denied the right to plan their own families, and that includes being forced to have abortions or being sterilized against their will.

If there is one message that echoes forth from this conference, let it be that human rights are women's rights.... And women's rights are human rights, once and for all.

Let us not forget that among those rights are the right to speak freely. And the right to be heard.

Women must enjoy the right to participate fully in the social and political lives of their countries if we want freedom and democracy to thrive and endure.

It is indefensible that many women in non_governmental organizations who wished to participate in this conference have not been able to attend – or have been prohibited from fully taking part.

Let me be clear. Freedom means the right of people to assemble, organize, and debate openly. It means respecting the views of those who may disagree with the views of their governments.

INDIRA GANDHI
(Prime Minister Of India)

INTRODUCTION

Indira Nehru Gandhi was born on November 19, 1917 and would be the only child of Jawaharlal and Kamala Nehru.

In 1938, Indira finally joined the Indian National Congress Party, something she always longed to do.

Soon afterwards in 1942, she married journalist Feroze Gandhi to whom she eventually bore two sons.

Soon after the couple was married, they were sent to prison on charges of subversion by the British. Her first and only imprisonment lasted from September 11, 1942 until May 13, 1943 at the Naini Central Jail in Allahabad.

In January 1966 the Congress party leaders chose Mrs. Gandhi to be Prime Minister. She led the country for sixteen years. Her life was part of the story of modern India. She was killed by two of her bodyguards. She was sixty-four years old.

She began to involve the armed forces in resolving violent

domestic conflicts between 1980 and 1984. She was assassinated by her own guards on October 31, 1984.

Martin Luther King Famous Speech by Indira Gandhi
New Delhi, India: January 24, 1969
Speech at the Presentation of the Jawaharial Nehru Award for International Understanding to Coretta Scott King

THIS is a poignant moment for all of us. We remember vividly your last visit to our country. We had hoped that on this occasion, Dr. King and you would be standing side by side on this platform. That was not to be. He is not with us but we feel his spirit. We admired Dr. King. We felt his loss as our own. The tragedy rekindled memories of the great martyrs of all time who gave their lives so that men might live and grow. We thought of the great men in your own country who fell to the assassin's bullet and of Mahatma Gandhi's martyrdom here in this city, this very month, twenty-one years ago. Such events remain as wounds in the human consciousness, reminding us of battles, yet to be fought and tasks still to be accomplished. We should not mourn for men of high ideals. Rather we should rejoice that we had the privilege of having had them with us, to inspire us by their radiant personalities. So today we are gathered not to offer you grief, but to salute a man who achieved so much in so short a time. It is befitting, Madam, that you whom he called the "courage by my side", you who gave him strength and encouragement in his historic mission, should be with us to receive this award.

You and your husband both had foreseen that death might come to him violently. It was perhaps inherent in the situation. Dr. King chose death for the theme of a sermon, remarking that he would like to be remembered as a drum major for justice, for peace and for righteousness. When you were once asked what you would do if your husband were assassinated, you were courage personified, replying that you might weep but the work would go on. Your face of sorrow, so beautiful in its dignity coupled with infinite compassion, will forever be engraved in our hearts.

Mahatma Gandhi also had foreseen his end and had prepared himself for it. Just as training for violence included learning to kill, the training for non-violence, he said, included learning how to die. The true badge of the satyagrahi is to be unafraid.

As if he too had envisaged the martyrdoms of Mahatma Gandhi and Martin Luther King, Rabindranath Tagore once sang:

In anger we slew him,

With love let us embrace him now,

For in death he lives again amongst us,

The mighty conqueror of death.

This award, Madam, is the highest tribute our nation can bestow on work for understanding and brotherhood among men. It is named after a man who himself was a peace-maker and who all his life laboured passionately for freedom, justice and peace in India and throughout the world. Dr. Martin Luther King's struggle was for these same values. He paid for his ideals with his blood, forging a new bond among the brave and the conscientious of all races and all nations.

Dr. King's dream embraced the poor and the oppressed of all lands. His work ennobled us. He spoke of the right of man to survive and recognized three threats to the survival of man—racial injustice, poverty and war. He realised that even under the lamp of affluence which was held aloft by science, lay the shadow of poverty, compelling two-thirds of the peoples of the world to exist in hunger and want. He proclaimed that mankind could be saved from war only if we cared enough for peace to sacrifice for it.

Dr. Martin Luther King drew his inspiration from Christ, and his method of action from Mahatma Gandhi. Only through truth can untruth be vanquished. Only through love can hatred be quenched. This is the path of the Buddha and of Christ, and in our own times, that of Mahatma Gandhi and of Martin Luther King.

They believed in the equality of all men. No more false doctrine has been spread than that of the superiority of one race over another. It is ironical that there should still be people in this world who judge men not by their moral worth and intellectual merit but by the pigment of their skin or other physical characteristics.

Some governments still rest on the theory of racist superiority—such as the governments of South Africa and the lawless regime in Rhodesia. Unregenerate groups in other countries consider one colour superior to another. Our own battle is not yet over. Caste and other prejudices still survive, but most of us are ashamed of them and recognise them as evils to be combated. We are trying hard to eradicate them.

While there is bondage anywhere, we ourselves cannot be fully free. While there is oppression anywhere, we ourselves cannot soar high. Martin Luther King was convinced that one day the misguided people who believed in racial superiority would realise the error of their ways. His dream was that white and black, brown and yellow would live and grow together as flowers in a garden with their faces turned towards the sun. As you yourself said, "All of us who believe in what Martin Luther King stood for, must see to it that his spirit never dies". That spirit can never die. There may be setbacks in our fight for the equality of all men. There may be moments of gloom. But victory must and will be ours. Let us not rest until the equality of all races and religions becomes a living fact. That is the most effective and lasting tribute that we can pay to Dr. King.

At the Seventh Conference of Heads of State or Government of Non-aligned Countries, New Delhi, March 7, 1983

WHEN assuming the reins of government in 1946, my father, Jawaharlal Nehru, declared India's determination "to keep away from the power blocs or groups, aligned against one another, which have led in the past to world wars and which may again lead to disasters on an even vaster scale." Later, he explained that once "foreign relations go out of your hands into the charge of somebody else, to that extent and in that measure you are not independent... So our policy will continue to be not only to keep away from alignments, but also to try to make friendly co-operation possible. We approach the whole world on a friendly basis."

As more countries became free, the number of those who believed in peaceful coexistence and wished to keep out of military alliances increased steadily. It was natural for these nonaligned countries to come together, not to form another bloc but to raise the voices of the exploited millions through a moral and political movement.

The very growth in the membership of our Movement -twenty-five in Belgrade, a hundred now - proves that nonalignment meets a felt need of vast numbers of people In various continents.

Its significance is not to be measured by the number of divisions or the megatons of destructive power we command but by the intensity with which we desire peace and freedom, development and international justice.

Other governments may have conflicting opinions on right and wrong. We, the nonaligned have chosen peace, which surely is the right and inevitable choice. We have sought and continue to seek friendship with all, except governments which are racist or threaten the hard-earned freedom of others. Nonalignment is not vague, not negative, not neutral.

Nonalignment is national Independence and freedom. It stands for peace and the avoidance of confrontation. It aims at keeping away from military alliances. it means equality among nations and the democratization of international relations, economic and political. It wants global co-operation for development on the basis of mutual benefit. It is a strategy for the recognition and preservation of the world's diversity.

... Humankind is balancing on the brink of the collapse of the world economic system and annihilation through nuclear war. Should these tragedies occur, can anyone of us, large, small. rich or poor, from North or South, West or East, hope to escape? Let us analyze the economic crisis. We of the developing world have no margin of safety. We shall be the first and worst sufferers in any economic background. In this interdependent world, where you cannot "stir a flower without troubling a star," even the most affluent are not immune to such disturbances.

... Development, independence, disarmament and peace are closely related. Can there be peace alongside nuclear weapons? Without peace, my father said, all our dreams of development turn to ashes. It has been pointed out that global military expenditure is 20 times the total official development assistance. Each day, each hour, the size and the lethality of nuclear weapons increase. A nuclear aircraft carrier costs $ 4 billion, which is more than the GNP of 53 countries. The hood of the cobra is spread. Humankind watches in frozen fear, hoping against hope that it will not strike. Never before has the earth faced so much death and danger.

The destructive power contained in nuclear stockpiles can kill human life, indeed all life, many times over and might well prevent its reappearance for ages to come. Terrifying is the vividness of such descriptions by scientists. Yet, some statesmen and strategists art as though there is not much difference between these and the earlier artillery pieces. The arms race continues because of the pursuit of power and desire for one upmanship, and also because many industries and interests flourish on it. More recently, the notion has been propagated that tactial nuclear weapons are usable in "limited wars." Powerful States propagate the untenable doctrine of deterrence. New areas are being brought into the scope of strategic groupings, military blocs and alliances. New bases and facilities are being established. That is why our responses must be surer, swifter and sharper.

The desire for peace is universal even within countries which themselves produce nuclear weapons and in those where they are deployed. The Nonaligned Movement is history's biggest peace movement. It welcomes these spontaneous upsurges of peoples. But Governments persist in propounding, practicing and pursuing the self-same strategic interests, spheres of influence, balance of power, and tutelary relations reminiscent of the earlier theory of divine right.

The paradox of our age is that while weapons become increasingly sophisticated, minds remain imprisoned in ideas of simpler times. Technically, the colonial age has ended. But the wish to dominate persists. Neo-colonialism comes wrapped in all types of packages-in technology and communications, commerce and culture. It takes boldness and integrity to resist it. There are intense political and economic pressures. The limited economic viability, indeed the very survival of many of the nonaligned, especially those with small populations, is threatened through artificial barriers In trade, technology transfer and access to resources. It should be within our ability to devise measures to help these small nations to maintain their independence and nonalignment.

Only with coexistence can there be any existence. We regard non-interference and non-intervention as basic laws of international behavior. Yet different types of interventions, open or covert, do take place in Asia, in Africa, in Latin America. They are all intolerable and unacceptable. Interference leads to intervention and one intervention often attracts another. No single power or group of powers has the justification or moral authority to so interfere or intervene. You cannot condemn one instance but condone another. Each situation has its own origins. Whatever they be, solutions must be political and peaceful. All States must abide by the principle that force or the threat of force will not be used against the territorial integrity or political independence of another state.

... Our plans for a better life for each of our peoples depend on world peace and the reversal of the arms race. Negotiations confined to a closed circle of nuclear-weapon powers have made little progress. We are non-nuclear States, who want nuclear energy used only for peace. But we too have a right to live and be heard. In the name of humanity and on behalf of us all, I call upon nuclear -weapon powers to give up the use of nuclear weapons in any circumstances; suspend all nuclear weapons: and resume disarmament negotiations with determination to reach agreement.

...Nationalism does not detach us from our common humanity. What a marvelous opportunity is ours with the immense knowledge and Increasing capability. Let us grasp it, though it be in the midst of dangers. Faith in the future has brought so many across the continents and the oceans to meet here. We are here because we do believe that minds and attitudes can and must be changed and the injustice and suffering can and must be diminished. Our world is small but it has room for all of us to live together and to improve the quality of the lives for our peoples in peace and beauty.

MARGARET (HILDA) THATCHER

INTRODUCTION

British Conservative Prime Minister (1979-90), Educated at Oxford, worked as a research chemist.

The only British prime minister in the 20th century to win three consecutive terms and, at the time of her resignation, Britain's longest continuously serving prime minister since 1827, she accelerated the evolution of the British economy from statism to liberalism and became, by personality as much as achievement, the most renowned British political leader since Winston Churchill.

Margaret Thatcher was born on Oct. 13, 1925, Grantham, Lincolnshire, England. British Conservative Party politician and prime minister (1979–90), Europe's first woman prime minister. Following her marriage called to the Bar in 1954.

Elected MP in 1959 and after holding junior offices became Minister of Education (1970-74). In 1975 replaced Edward Heath as leader of the Conservative Party to become the first woman leader in British politics and society. Under her leadership er party moved more to the 'right'. She advocated privatization of Nationalised industries. She was elected P.M. for third time in 1987. She resigned in Nov. 1990 owing her stiff opposition to Britain's monetary and economic union with Europe.

Keynote Address to Citibank Delivered on Thursday 22 September 1994 in New Delhi, India

INDIA has a deep fascination for me, as it does for so many English people. I gleaned my first knowledge of it from the marvellous poems and stories of Rudyard Kipling, with their vivid descriptions of real life, and he remains to this day my favourite source of quotations. From his poems we learned that essential wisdom and insight into human nature which is still relevant in today's world. But I remember something else as well when I was young; and that is the pride we all felt in India: in her splendour, her mystery, her colour and the indefinable affinity we felt with her people. And perhaps that is not so surprising because each of our countries has a strong tradition and a long history, which gives us both a confidence and a sense of continuity.

So strongly was this felt in my family that when, like most children, I was asked the question "What would you like to do when you grow up?" my reply was "To become part of the Indian Civil Service". To which my father had the foresight to reply (remember this was the mid-1930s) "There probably won't be one by the time you are qualified".

It was only much later that I had my first direct experience of India and that was when I visited your country as Secretary of State for Education and Science in the 1970s when I saw a very different side of India : the huge reservoir of talented people, your ancient prowess in mathematics and science, as later described so vividly in the Festival of India in 1982, the advances in medicine, in computing skills and in civil nuclear power.

I came to India several times as Prime Minister and had the privilege then and subsequently of getting to know three of your own Prime Ministers. The first was Indira Gandhi with whom I instinctively felt a very special personal affinity. Even though we certainly didn't agree on everything, we were able to talk things through with a frankness and understanding which was matchless. Both of us knew and understood the loneliness of office. Later I made the sad journey to Delhi for her funeral, the victim of an assassination. It was a particularly poignant occasion, for only three weeks before I myself had so narrowly escaped injury in the bomb blast in Brighton and Mrs. Gandhi had sent me a note of sympathy for those who had been killed in which she expressed her horror that such things should happen in a civilised society.

Then of course I knew Rajiv Gandhi well. He fearlessly took up the challenge of terrorism and eventually paid with his life, but only after he had infused Indians with a renewed pride in their country and enthusiasm for India's future opportunities.

Lastly and most recently, Prime Minister Rao who, together with Finance Minister Dr. Singh, is courageously carrying through the difficult task of reforming and liberalising India's economy within an established framework of democratic politics.

I have some experience of that myself! In the Eighties in Britain we had to rein in the power of the trade unions and make them democratically accountable to their members. We had to get government out of running business, for which it has no talent or qualifications, and give management the power to manage, through our programme of privatisation. We had to cut regulations and cut public expenditure, to reduce the overburdening apparatus of central government, and we cut tax to increase the incentives to effort. All these changes were vital for Britain's future and for ending our nation's decline. They were steps which had not been attempted before because somehow the people and politicians had come to see the advance of socialism as inevitable. Well we proved them wrong—but it was tough going. So I know both how difficult the tasks facing Prime Minister Rao are and how vital it is for India's future that he should succeed just as it was vital for Brtitian's future that I did.

India and Britain : The destinies of our two countries began to flow together through trade and then were linked politically for well over a century. Neither of us should be self-conscious about the contribution each made to the other during that time. I hope you will agree that we contributed quite a lot: a highly professional civil service, a rule of law with independent courts of justice, and a strong, non-political military tradition. They were ours and they became yours: you took them on and built on them in your own inimitable way. From the time when history thrust our two countries together we have developed a close understanding—*between the world's oldest democracy and the world's largest democracy.* It is a relationship based on deep and instinctive friendship, something which Mahatma Gandhi himself recognised when he said while visiting London in 1931 "I am carrying with me thousands upon thousands of English friendships. I do not know them, but I read the affection in their eyes...."

Here in New Delhi we can see the physical embodiment of the British legacy. Lutyens's magnificent "new" city was built to reflect the greatness of India. These buildings stand as a reminder of the past and a symbol of the present—the stones of empire became the home of democracy. I was fortunate enough to have Lutyens's grandson, Nicholas Ridley, in my own cabinet and I often remarked to him that it was a great tragedy that Britain had not had the common sense to invite his grandfather to redesign some of *our own* Cities! As so often we exported our best.

We are just as proud of India's contribution to Britain, both through history and in contemporary times. We came to know your great wisdom and philosophy, your art and science. The Indian Empire gave us *both* a stature and self-confidence that enabled us to play the role in the world which the instincts and traditions of our peoples demanded. That desire for an influential voice in world affairs is just as characteristics of India as it is of Britain. When the call of duty came to defend freedom against the tyrannies of this century, India recruited on a voluntary basis more than two million men—*the largest voluntary recruitment ever recorded throughout history.* Later, India was to become a powerful advocate on behalf of the Non-Aligned movement which it led.

Today we hear much talk of expanding the Permanent Membership of the United Nations Security Council. Personally, I would say leave well alone, but if there is to be a change, *no country has a better claim than India as the world's largest democracy, its second most populous country and the greatest regional power in South Asia* : a stronger claim, surely, than that of any other candidate. And I do not say that *because* I am in India—I first said it in Japan.

May I also pay tribute to the exceptional contribution which the Indian community in Britain makes to *our* national life. Their strong sense of family, their instinct for commerce and their passionate desire for education are an example to other groups, and so is their capacity for hard work and their success. And in my own constituency most of them also had the good sense to vote Conservative!

Democracy - a Universal cause : India derives unique authority from her unwavering commitment to democracy. Your experience makes nonsense of the argument which one occasionally hears, that democracy and human rights are somehow not suitable or practical for large and populous countries nor for Asia.

India's message to the world is that democracy is not just a Western concept. It is a vibrant, living force drawing on beliefs and traditions which are centuries old and which have their origins in varied civilisations across the globe. Of course in recent history it has been moulded by Western thought and Western practice but perhaps in some of its most basic characteristics it shares a great deal with the village assemblies which dominated Indian life thousands of years ago.

Moreover *all* human beings have certain things in common. We are all born into a family and into a community. We all have a sense of good and evil, a natural moral sense and a conscience. We all recognise and admire bravery and heroism. The child instinctively wants to please its parents and the parent naturally wants to protect the child. Surely this is what we call human nature. *what makes men human is common to them all and acts as a bridge between them.*

The fundamental rights—freedom of speech, freedom of worship, freedom of movement, freedom of association and liberty under the law—are not the property of any group of countries, nor the hallmark of one culture as opposed to others. They apply universally. Combined with representative government they are the core of democracy.

And democracy is gaining ground. In 1993 Freedom House, an organisation which monitors these things, found that there were 75 democratic countries, up from 55 a decade earlier; but 31% of the world's population, the greater part in China, still lived under repressive regimes, this is down from 44% a decade ago. 1994 has seen an important addition to these figures as South Africa has been brought to full democracy. I hope before long that Cuba will join them.

The Great Experiment : Political and personal freedom are only part of the equation. They are inseparable from economic freedom. Whichever one you start with you will find that you finish with them all. *That* was how our forefathers expected liberty to progress. They could not possibly have foreseen that this century would witness the two worst tyrannies and the two worst wars the world has ever known. Nazism and fascism were defeated in battle but Stalin's Russia continued to pursue its ambition of world hegemony. As Winston Churchill observed, an Iron Curtain was brought down dividing the world in two.

On the one side, the way of freedom. On the other, communism, the way of coercion. For 70 years they coexisted, indeed it seemed as though the world had unwittingly entered into a great experiment to decide which was the better way of life for our peoples. Then the Communist system collapsed and *its cruelties and poverty of spirit became clear to all.*

The Free World could point to the failings of Communism to deliver material progress or human rights as proof positive that the diametrically opposite system—of *free* institutions, *free* enterprise and a *free* people—was the key to the success of the democratic world.

Some 36 million people have been killed in battle this century—an enormous sacrifice. But recent statistics now tell the horrific story of what really happened under Communism and other tyrannies. At least 119 million people have been killed by government genocide, massacres and other mass killings. And about 115 million of these were killed by totalitarian governments *as many as 95 million by Communist ones.*

And yet there were still those who were taken in by Communism's propaganda. But the Battle Doesn't End. The defeat of tyranny—in this case Marxist/Leninism—without a shot being fired was a new experience. At the end of world War Two because our enemies were *totally defeated* we were able to go in and put in place all the right institutions.

But when it came to the end of the Cold War we had not defeated the communist regimes from *without,* they had collapsed from *within.* So it has been mainly for the people of the communist countries *themselves* to bring about change.

Perhaps we underestimated the tremendous difficulty they would have in managing the transition from a tyranny to a free and responsible society.

I believe that we could, and should, have done far more through the international institutions to help. Ten years ago we would have given almost *anything* for the Cold War to end. When it did, we were too absorbed in our own affairs to understand the nature of their problems or to formulate a fitting response.

Russian Roulette and Chinese Chequers : Russia has always been an important country, and always will be. There is a tendency to regard her only as a European country—but as Britain and India both have reason to know, she is also very much an Asian one too. Her borders extend from the Baltic to the Pacific, occupying 11 time zones. She is the largest country in the world, although her population is only 150 million, whereas India's is some 870 million. Her global status must be respected and the pride of her people taken into account.

The Russians are struggling to achieve an enterprise economy. When President Gorbachev started the reform process he began by giving personal and political freedom. He did not know how to go about introducing a successful free market reform—although in his speeches he began to talk about the need for more initiative. By giving personal and political liberty, itself an enormous step forward, doubtless he hoped that more open discussion combined with outside help would point the way forward.

China took a different approach. Since 1978, Deng Xiaoping, although refusing to give personal and political liberty, has steadily encouraged a market or *enterprise economy.* "I wish we had started that way", the Russian leaders used to say to me but historically, the Russians had little taste for enterprise and their brief experience of it was snuffed out by Lenin in 1917. Moreover, China benefited from investment from Taiwan, Hong Kong and Singapore, while Russia has no such diaspora to help her.

Perhaps the greatest difference between the Russians and the Chinese is that the Chinese are born traders as are Indian people *wherever* they dwell in the world. Today, in world trade terms, the "Chinese Trio" of China, Taiwan and Honk Kong, is behind only the United States and Germany. The World Bank estimates that the East Asia region as a whole imports $800 billion of goods annually—more than all the imports into the US and growing at a rate of 15% per annum. Viewed from the outside China appears to be a large but single market. In fact China is a union of many, possibly as many as forty, economic units. As in India's case, a good number of its cities are larger than many countries and the average sized province had a population of between 50 and 60 million people. Of course with a total population of 1.1 billion there are bound to be variations in the rate of growth but with willingness to *devolve economic power I do not share the opinion of some commentators who see China, like the USSR, breaking up. Her people have a cohesive political will* which should hold the country together through the turbulence ahead.

Asia—Great Expectations : The transformations in Russia and China are part of a hurricane of change which has swept across Asia, carrying millions out of poverty and bringing new hope. The world has never seen such a rapid economic expansion as it is witnessing today in these areas. The age of automation has been even more radical than the age of mechanisation. "Smart" machines now transfer technology instantaneously from one country to another. Development which used to take years can be achieved in months.

Today the Asia Pacific region has the highest growth rates in the world, in spite of the recession.

— Across Asia output is doubling every ten years.

— Savings ratios are running at over 30% of GDP—providing ample resources for investment.

— Asian banks hold over one third of the world's foreign currency reserves.

The Tiger" nations, as they are called, have thrived on international competition and have demonstrated that they have the will ana enterprise to present a formidable challenge to the United States and Europe. There are some who fear that the growth in Asia will place an unbearable burden on both investment and natural resources. But they ignore the fact that this new economic dynamism will in itself generate new wealth, which in turn can be invested. They ignore the high savings ratios in these countries and they forget that the pace of technological change, as you know in India, is providing us with new ways to unlock resources all the time. Therefore we should not see either East or Southern Asia as challengers for ever fewer resources but generators of new ones. Just as the scene shifts in a play, so I think the next Act in world history will be played out *more in Asia than in Europe, more in the Pacific than the Atlantic.* This will heighten India's role in world affairs in the future— especially as she has both a full democracy and an enterprise economy.

But there are yet dangers which could upset this story of success. Even now, when we have just signed the GATT Round—which still remains to be fully ratified—the pressures between open trade and protection continue to be finely balanced.

But free trade is *more* than just a set of dry statistics it has much wider benefits.

It is a force for political co-operation—it is no mere chance that rising protectionism in the 1930s preceded global conflict.

It is a force which enables poor regions and countries to penetrate international markets generating wealth by selling goods at a competitive price bringing hope of a better standard of living to their peoples.

We still have to convince popular opinion in Europe and the United States, and in some parts of India, that opening markets to foreign goods and services *raises living standards and generates jobs.* We still have to win the argument that just as economic and political freedom go together, so too do open trade and international harmony. Trade is the lifeblood of nations, the progenitor of peace.

Warming UP?—The End of the Cold War and its Effects: The end of the Cold War has had a *great effect on how we view the world.* Having won the great ideological battle, the pseudo-intellectuals now pose a new argument : one that says that our way is too materialistic. The people who propound this view have forgotten that it was *Marx* who described religion as the opium of the people, and he and Lenin who denied freedom and regarded the people merely as cogs in their political machine. Moreover, it is our task to help people out of poverty to a more rewarding and fuller life.

Economic freedom is *real* freedom. Just as coercion exercised on economic grounds is no less *real* coercion. Countries are not rich in proportion to their natural resources; if that were so Russia would be the richest country in the world; she has everything, oil, gas, diamonds, platinum, gold, silver, the industrial metals, timber, and a rich soil. Countries are rich whose governments have policies which *encourage the essential creativity of man* who, in order to succeed, must work with others to produce goods and services which people choose to buy. So Japan, Switzerland, Hong Kong, Taiwan, Singapore and so on have no natural resources but are now among the most prosperous countries in the world.

Indeed as the Pope observed "today the decisive factor is increasingly man himself, that is his knowledge, especially his scientific knowledge, his capacity for interrelated organisation as well as his ability to perceive the needs of others and to satisfy them."

And how does man achieve this?—*through the market.* The market is not a new-fangled invention of some academic economists. The freedom to buy and sell, to trade and barter, is the oldest system of exchange known to man. It is not merely an *economic practice* but also a *vibrant social activity.* It brings people together in a community of work and in the colourful, teeming life of the market place itself.

Only a flourishing free enterprise economy can generate the higher living standards at every level and the jobs which people need if we can honestly say that they are enjoying the benefits of freedom.

In seeking to liberate people from poverty and servitude it is the business ethic in action which is the cutting edge of progress.

I am very much aware that the scale of your problem in tackling poverty is greater than anything we in modern Britain have known. But there is no point on this account in trying to slow down the necessary economic reform which will promote prosperity and generate a multitude of new small businesses. The quickest and best way to tackle poverty is by moving swiftly to create a successful market economy.

Good News/Bad News : I for my part, certainly never believed that with the end of the Cold War we would see a new world order in the sense that some optimists used the term—although we are seeing the world ordered in a very different way. One of the lessons of history which is surely least controversial, is that there is really *no limit* to the perverted creeds, aggressive ambitions and Utopian follies which politicians or religious fanatics can dream up given the chance. The potential for new dictators to arise and perpetrate new horrors is and always will be there. You have only to look around to see that *peace has not broken out.*

The good news is that :

- Israel and the Palestinians have reached agreement,
- there have been improvements in Cambodia and in Vietnam
- and in South Africa democracy now reigns. The bad news is that :
- there are still religious fanatics (a better and more accurate term than fundamentalists) who utterly distort their creed, pursuing their ambitions through violence, which as scholars point out is without sanction in the true religion.
- there are battles over boundaries and over ethnic minorities,
- countries like North Korea continue to sell weapons to areas of high tension,
- and there is the danger of "loose" nuclear weapons finding their way out of the huge inventories of the former Soviet Union.
- and in Bosnia the tragedy, ethnic cleansing and fighting continue in the heart of Europe.

We delude ourselves if we think that the United Nations can deal with these things—although we must give it credit for humanitarian aid. We are only just beginning to come to grips with the questions of what part nations and international bodies should play in our disorderly World Order.

Don't Forget the Nation State : Nothing is more insidious than a fashionable consensus about international politics. And a kind of consensus among Foreign Ministers and diplomats has recently grown up according to which the great threat to all good things can be summed up in just one word : nationalism.

Of course nationalism untamed by respect for human rights

and unchecked by democracy can be a force for evil. But that has nothing to do with nations based on liberty, justice and democracy.

In fact, it is the ideology of *race* rather than nation which has produced most of the perversions in the past, coupled with the fact that such nations are governed by tyrants and dictators.

When conflict occurs it is not enough for the UN to pass resolutions, you *need nation states* because it is *only they* who are willing to *act resolutely*. Their resources and military readiness are the only real deterrent to violence and aggression, as we saw in the Gulf. Resolutions are not enough. It required the leadership and action of the United States and Britain, joined by other *nation* states to free Kuwait and defeat the aggressor. *No System of collective security has ever proved effective on its own,* as Henry Kissinger has pointed out.

Mr Chairman, the challenges of the next century will apply whatever walk of life we are in, whatever part of the globe we inhabit. If international strains cannot be reduced, or conflicts contained, then the twenty first century could turn out to be even more unstable than the twentieth. Stability, prosperity and harmony go hand in hand. Each contributes to the others. Remove one and the others are placed in jeopardy.

At the beginning of this century the advance of science and of democracy gave cause for optimism about the future. No-one could have foreseen the events which were to happen.For India it has been a century which has brought freedom, democracy and now rising prosperity.

No statement about India can be wholly complete, for India is not one people but many—a fusion of cultures, religions and languages—a land of great beauty and timeless tradition. A land of contrasts, for you are a part of the East but you have a deep understanding of the West.

You have successfully built a strong and deliberately secular democracy, which in spite of the difficulties you have faced has never faltered and you have embarked on the road to economic freedom. All of this combined with the wisdom that is India, will surely equip you to be one of the economic and political giants of the Twenty First Century.

MARIE CURIE

INTRODUCTION

Marie Curie was born November 7, 1867 in Poland and died on July 4, 1934. Her co-discovery with her husband Pierre Curie of the radioactive elements radium and polonium represents one of the best known stories in modern science for which they were recognized in 1901 with the Nobel Prize in Physics. In 1911, Marie Curie was honored with a second Nobel prize, this time in chemistry, to honor her for successfully isolating pure radium and determining radium's atomic weight.

Maria (Marie Fr.) Sklodowska-Curie, born in Warsaw, Poland, was one of the first woman scientists to win worldwide fame, and indeed, one of the great scientists of this century.

She is best known as the discoverer of the radioactive elements polonium and radium and as the first person to win two Nobel prizes. Dr. Marie Curie is known to the world as the scientist who discovered radioactive metals i.e. Radium & Polonium.

Marie Curie was a Polish physicist and chemist who lived between 1867-1934. Together with her husband, Pierre, she discovered two new elements (radium and polonium, two radioactive elements that they extracted chemically from pitchblende ore) and studied the x-rays they emitted. She found that the harmful properties of x-rays were able to kill tumors.

On the Discovery of Radium Famous Speech Vassar College in Poughkeepsie, NY - May 14, 1921

I could tell you many things about radium and radioactivity and it would take a long time. But as we can not do that, I shall only give you a short account of my early work about radium. Radium is no more a baby, it is more than twenty years old, but the conditions of the discovery were somewhat peculiar, and so it is always of interest to remember them and to explain them.

We must go back to the year 1897. Professor Curie and I worked at that time in the laboratory of the school of Physics and Chemistry where Professor Curie held his lectures. I was engaged in some work on uranium rays which had been discovered two years before by Professor Becquerel.

I spent some time in studying the way of making good measurements of the uranium rays, and then I wanted to know if there were other elements, giving out rays of the same kind. So I took up a work about all known elements, and their compounds and found that uranium compounds are active and also all thorium compounds, but other elements were not found active, nor were their compounds. As for the uranium and thorium compounds, I found that they were active in proportion to their uranium or thorium content. The more uranium or thorium, the greater the activity, the activity being an atomic property of the elements, uranium and thorium.

Them I took up measurements of minerals and I found that several of those which contain uranium or thorium or both were active. But then the activity was not what I could expect, it was greater than for uranium or thorium compounds like the oxides which are almost entirely composed of these elements.

Then I thought that there should be in the minerals some unknown element having a much greater radioactivity than uranium or thorium. And I wanted to find and to separate that element, and I settled to that work with Professor Curie. We thought it would be done in several weeks or months, but it was not so. It took many years of hard work to finish that task. There was not one new ,lenient, there were several of them. But the most important is radium, which could be separated in a pure state.

Now, the special interest of radium is in the intensity of its rays which several million times greater than the uranium rays. And the effects of the rays make the radium so important. If we take a practical point of view, then the most important property of the rays is the production of physiological effects on the cells of the human organism. These effects may be used for the cure of several diseases. Good results have been obtained in many cases. What is considered particularly important is the treatment of cancer. The medical utilization of radium makes it necessary to get that element in sufficient quantities. And so a factory of radium was started to begin with in France, and later in America where a big quantity of ore named carnotite is available. America does produce many grams of radium every year, but the price is still very high because the quantity of radium contained in the ore is so small. The radium is more than a hundred thousand times dearer than gold.

But we must not forget that when radium was discovered no one knew that it would prove useful in hospitals. The work was one of pure science. And this is a proof that scientific work must not be considered from the point of view of the direct usefulness of it. It must be done for itself, for the beauty of science, and then there is always the chance that a scientific discovery may become like the radium a benefit for humanity.

The scientific history of radium is beautiful. The properties of the rays have been studied very closely. We know that particles are expelled from radium with a very great velocity near to that of the light. We know that the atoms of radium are destroyed by expulsion of these particles, some of which are atoms of helium. And in that way it has been proved that the radioactive elements are constantly disintegrating and that they produce at the end ordinary elements, principally helium and lead. That is, as you see, a theory of transformation of atoms which are not stable, as was believed before, but may undergo spontaneous changes.

Radium is not alone in having these properties. Many having other radio-elements are known already, the polonium, the mesothorium, the radiothorium, the actinium. We know also radioactive gases, named emanations. There is a great variety of substances and effects in radioactivity. There is always a vast field left to experimentation and I hope that we may have some beautiful progress in the following years. It is my earnest desire that some of you should carry on this scientific work and keep for your ambition the determination to make a permanent contribution to science.

MARY REYNOLDS

INTRODUCTION

Babcock, Mary Reynolds *(8 Aug. 1908-17 July 1953)*, philanthropist, was born in Winston of Scottish ancestry. On 16 Dec. 1929 she married Charles Henry Babcock, an investment banker from Philadelphia. In 1936, when Mrs. Babcock inherited $30 million from her father, she was described as one of the richest women in the world. Her primary interest was in helping others, and she contributed generously to many worthwhile causes.

In 1951 she and her husband gave three hundred acres at Reynolda to Wake Forest College, and the college moved from Wake County to Winston-Salem where a completely new campus was built. Her will provided $12 million for a charitable trust, and the Mary Reynolds Babcock Foundation was established at Reynolda with her husband as the first chairman of the board. Since 1954, the foundation has contributed generously to Wake Forest University and to other organizations, particularly those concerned with private higher education, social welfare, and the arts. Mary Reynolds Babcock was shy and retiring. She enjoyed a limited circle of friends and delighted in collecting recipes and growing flowers, but her primary interest was philanthropy.

She was the mother of Mary Katherine, Barbara, Betsy Main, and Charles Henry, Jr. One portrait of her hangs in Babcock Dormitory, Salem College, and another in the offices of the Mary Reynolds Babcock Foundation at Reynolda. She died in New York City and was buried in Winston-Salem.

Her Days As A Slave Famous Speech, c 1925

MY paw's name was Tom Vaughn and he was from the north, born free man and lived and died free to the end of his days. He wasn't no eddicated man, but he was what he calls himself a piano man. He told me once he lived in New York and Chicago and he built the insides of pianos and knew how to make them play in tune. He said some white folks from the south told he if he'd come with them to the south he'd find a lot of work to do with pianos in them parts, and he come off with them.

He saw my maw on the Kilpatrick place and her man was dead. He told Dr. Kilpatrick, my massa, he'd buy my maw and her three chillun with all the money he had, iffen he'd sell her. But Dr. Kilpatrick was never one to sell any but the old niggers who was part workin' in the fields and past their breedin' times. So my paw marries my maw and works the fields, same as any other nigger. They had six gals: Martha and Pamela and Josephine and Ellen and Katherine and me.

I was born same time as Miss Sara Kilpatrick. Dr. Kilpatrick's first wife and my maw come to their time right together. Miss Sara's maw died and they brung Miss Sara to suck with me. It's a thing we ain't never forgot. My maw's name was Sallie and Miss Sara allus looked with kindness on my maw.

We sucked till we was a fair size and played together, which wasn't no common thing. None the other li'l niggers played with the white chillun. But Miss Sara loved me so good.

I was jus' bout big nough to start playin' with a broom to go bout sweepin' up and not even half doin' it when Dr. Kilpatrick sold me. They was a old white man in Trinity and his wife died and he didn't have chick or child or slave or nothin'.

Massa sold me cheap, cause he didn't want Miss Sara to play with no nigger young'un. That old man bought me a big doll and went off and left me all day, with the door open. I jus' sot on the floor and played with that doll. I used to cry. He'd come home and give me somethin' to eat and then go to bed, and I slep' on the foot of the bed with him. I was scart all the time in the dark. He never did close the door.

Miss Sara pined and sickened. Massa done what he could, but they wasn't no peartness in her. She got sicker and sicker, and massa brung nother doctor. He say, You li'l gal is grievin' the life out her body and she sho' gwine die iffen you don't do somethin' bout it.' Miss Sara says over and over, I wants Mary.' Massa say to the doctor, That a li'l nigger young'un I done sold.' The doctor tells him he better git me back iffen he wants to save the life of his child. Dr. Kilpatrick has to give a big plenty more to git me back than what he sold me for, but Miss Sara plumps up right off and grows into fine health. "Then massa marries a rich lady from Mississippi and they has chillun for company to Miss Sara and seem like for a time she forgits me.

Massa Kilpatrick wasn't no piddlin' man. He was a man of plenty. He had a big house with no more style to it than a crib, but it could room plenty people. He was a medicine doctor and they was rooms in the second story for sick folks what come to lay in. It would take two days to go all over the land he owned. He had cattle and stock and sheep and more'n a hundred slaves and more besides. He bought the bes' of niggers near every time the spec'lators come that way. He'd make a swap of the old ones and give money for young ones what could work. "He raised corn and cotton and cane and taters and goobers, sides the peas and other feedin' for the niggers. I member I helt a hoe handle mighty onsteady when they put a old women to larn me and some other chillun to scrape the fields. That old woman would be in a frantic. She'd show me and then turn bout to show some other li'l nigger, and I'd have the young corn cut clean as the grass. She say, For the love of Gawd, you better larn it right, or Solomon will beat the breath out you body.' Old man Solomon was the nigger driver.

Slavery was the worst days was ever seed in the world. They was things past tellin', but I got the scars on my old body to show to this day. I seed worse than what happened to me. I seed them put the men and women in the stock with they hands screwed down through holes in the board and they feets tied together and they naked behinds to the world. Solomon the the [sic] overseer beat them with a big whip and massa look on. The niggers better not stop in the fields when they hear them yellin'. They cut the flesh most to the bones and some they was when they taken them out of stock and put them on the beds, they never got up again.

When a nigger died they let his folks come out the fields to see him afore he died. They buried him the same day, take a big plank and bust it with a ax in the middle nough to bend it back, and put the dead nigger in betwixt it. They'd cart them down to the graveyard on the place and not bury them deep nough that buzzards wouldn't come circlin' round. Niggers mourns now, but in them days they wasn't no time for mournin'.

The conch shell blowed afore daylight and all hands better git out for roll call or Solomon bust the door down and get them out. It was work hard, git beatin's and half fed. They brung the victuals and water to the fields on a slide pulled by a old mule. Plenty times they was only a half barrel water and it stale and hot, for all us niggers on the hottes' days. Mostly we ate pickled pork and corn bread and peas and beans and taters. They never was as much as we needed.

The times I hated most was pickin' cotton when the frost was on the bolls. My hands git sore and crack open and bleed. We'd have a li'l fire in the fields and iffen the ones with tender hands couldn't stand it no longer, we'd run and warm our hands a li'l bit. When I could steal a tater, I used to slip it in the ashes and when I'd run to the fire I'd take it out and eat it on the sly. "In the cabins it was nice and warm. They was built of pine boardin' and they was one long room of them up the hill back of the big house. Near one side of the cabins was a fireplace. They'd bring in two, three big logs and put on the fire and they'd last near a week. The beds was made out of puncheons fitted on holes bored in the wall, and planks laid cross them poles. We had tickin' mattresses filled with corn shucks. Sometimes the men build chairs at night. We didn't know much bout havin' nothin', though.

Sometimes massa let niggers have a li'l patch. They'd raise

taters or goobers. They liked to have them to help fill out on the victuals. Taters roasted in the ashes was the best tastin' eatin' I ever had. I could die better satisfied to have jus' one more tater roasted in hot ashes. The niggers had to work the patches at night and dig the taters and goobers at night. Then if they wanted to sell any in town they'd have to git a pass to go. They had to go at night, cause they couldn't ever spare a hand from the fields.

Once in a while they's give us a li'l piece of Sat'day evenin' to wash out clothes in the branch. We hanged them on the ground in the woods to dry. They was a place to wash clothes from the well, but they was so many niggers all couldn't get round to it on Sundays. When they'd git through with the clothes on Sat'day evenin's the niggers which sold they goobers and taters brung fiddles and guitars and come out and play. The others clap they hands and stomp they feet and we young'uns cut a step round. I was plenty biggity and like to cut a step.

We was scart of Solomon and his whip, though, and he didn't like frolickin'. He didn't like for us niggers to pray, either. We never heared of no church, but us have prayin' in the cabins. We'd set on the floor and pray with our heads down low and sing low, but if Solomon heared he'd come and beat on the wall with the stock of his whip. He'd say, I'll come in there and tear the hide off you backs.' But some the old niggers tell us we got to pray to Gawd that he don't think different of the blacks and the whites. I know that Solomon is burnin' in hell today, and it pleasures me to know it.

Once my maw and paw taken me and Katherine after night to slip to nother place to a prayin' and singin'. A nigger man with white beard told us a day am comin' when niggers only be slaves of Gawd.

We prays for the end of Trib'lation and the end of beatin's and for shoes that fit our feet. We prayed that us niggers could have all we wanted to eat and special for fresh meat. Some the old ones say we have to bear all, cause that all we can do. Some say they was glad to the time they's dead, cause they'd rather rot in the ground than have the beatin's. What I hated most was when they'd beat me and I didn't know what they beat me for, and I hated they strippin' me naked as the day I was born.

When we's comin' back from that prayin', I thunk I heared the nigger dogs and somebody on horseback. I say, Maw, its them nigger hounds and they'll eat us up.' You could hear them old hounds and sluts abayin'. Maw listens and say, Sho nough, them dogs am running' and Gawd help us!' Then she and paw talk and they take us to a fence corner and stands us up gainst the rails and say don't move and if anyone comes near, don't breathe loud. They went to the woods, so the hounds chase them and not git us. Me and Katherine stand there, holdin' hands, shakin' so we can hardly stand. We hears the hounds come nearer, but we don't move. They goes after paw and maw, but they circles round to the cabins and gits in. Maw say its the power of Gawd.

In them days I weared shirts, like all the young'uns. They had collars and come below the knees and was split up the sides. That's all we weared in hot weather. The men weared jeans and women gingham. Shoes was the worstes' trouble. We weared rough russets when it got cold, and it seem powerful strange they'd never git them to fit. Once when I was a young gal, they got me a new pair and all brass studs in the toes. They was too li'l for me, but I had to wear them. The trimmin's cut into my ankles and them places got mis'ble bad. I rubs tallow in them sore places and wrops rags around them and my sores got worser and worser. The scars are there to this day.

I wasn't sick much, though. Some the niggers had chills and fever a lot, but they hadn't discovered so many diseases then as now. Dr. Kilpatrick give sick niggers ipecac and asafoetide and oil and turpentine and black fever pills. "They was a cabin called the spinnin' house and two looms and two spinnin' wheels goin' all the time, and two nigger women sewing all the time. It took plenty sewin' to make all the things for a place so big. Once massa goes to Baton Rouge and brung back a yaller girl dressed in fine style. She was a seamster nigger. He builds her a house way from the quarters and she done fine sewin' for the whites. Us niggers knowed the doctor took a black woman quick as he did a white and took any on his place he wanted, and he took them often. But mostly the chillun born on the place looked like niggers. Aunt Cheyney allus say four of hers were massas, but he didn't give them no mind. But this yaller gal breeds so fast and gits a mess of white young'uns. She larnt them fine manners and combs out they hair.

Onct two of them goes down the hill to the doll house where the Kilpatrick chillun am playin'. They wants to go in the dollhouse and one the Kilpatrick boys say, That's for white chillun.' They say, "We ain't no niggers, cause we got the same daddy you has, and he comes to see us near every day and fotches us clothes and things from town.' They is fussin' and Missy Kilpatrick is listenin' out her chamber window. She heard them white niggers say, He is our daddy and we call him daddy when he comes to our house to see our mama.'

When massa come home that evenin' his wife hardly say nothin' to him, and he ask her what the matter and she tells him, Since you asks me, I'm studyin' in my mind bout them white young'uns of that yaller nigger wench from Baton Rouge. He say, Now, honey, I fotches that gal jus' for you, cause she a fine seamster.' She say, It look kind of funny they got the same kind of hair and eyes as my chillun and they got a nose looks like yours.' He say, Honey, you jus' payin' tention to talk of li'l chillun that ain't got no mind to what they say.' She say, Over in Mississippi I got a home and plenty with my daddy and I got that in my mind.'

Well, she didn't never leave and massa bought her a fine new span of surrey hosses. But she don't never have no more chillun and she ain't so cordial with the massa. Margaret, that yallow gal, has more white young'uns, but they don't never go down the hill no more to the big house.

Aunt Cheyney was jus' out of bed with a sucklin' baby one time, and she run away. Some say that was nother baby of massa's breedin'. She dont' come to the house to nurse her baby, so they misses her and old Solomon gits the nigger hounds and takes her trail. They gits near her and she grabs a limb and tries to hist herself in a tree, but them dogs grab her and pull her down. The men hollers them onto her, and the dogs tore her naked and et the breasts plumb off her body. She got well and lived to be a old woman, but nother woman has to suck her baby and she ain't got no sign of breasts no more.

They give all the niggers fresh meat on Christmas and a plug tobacco all round. The highes' cotton picker gits a suit of clothes and all the women what had twins that year gits a outfittin' of clothes for the twins and a double, warm blanket.

Seems like after I got bigger, I member' more'n more niggers run away. They's most allus cotched. Massa used to hire out his niggers for wage hands. One time he hired me and a nigger boy, Turner, to work for some ornery white trash name of Kidd. One day Turner goes off and don't come back. Old man Kidd say I knowed bout it, and he tied my wrists together and stripped me. He hanged me by the wrists from a limb on a tree and spraddled my legs around the trunk and tied my feet together. Then he beat me. He beat me worser than I ever been beat before and I faints dead away. When I come to I'm in bed. I didn't care so much iffen I died.

I didn't know bout the passin of time, but Miss Sara come to me. Some white folks done git word to her. Mr. Kidd tries to talk hisself out of it, but Miss Sara fotches me home when I'm well enough to move. She took me in a cart and my maw takes care of me. Massa looks me over good and says I'll git well, but I'm ruint for breedin' chillun.

After while I taken a notion to marry and massa and missy marries us same as all the niggers. They stands inside the house with a broom held crosswise of the door and we stands outside. Missy puts a li'l wreath on my head they kept there and we steps over the broom into the house. Now, that's all they was to the marryin'. After freedom I gits married and has it put in the book by a preacher.

One day we was workin' in the fields and hears the conch shell blow, so we all goes to the back gate of the big house. Massa am there. He say, Call the roll for every nigger big nough to walk, and I wants them to go to the river and wait there. They's gwine be a show and I wants you to see it.' They was a big boat down there, done built up on the sides with boards and holes in the boards and a bit gun barrel stickin' through every hole. We ain't never seed nothin' like that. Massa goes up the plank onto the boat and comes out on the boat porch. He say, This am a Yankee boat." He goes inside and the water wheels starts movin' and that boat goes movin' up the river and they says it goes to Natches.

The boat wasn't more'n out of sight when a big drove of sojers comes into town. They say they's Fed'rals. More'n half the niggers goes off with them sojers, but I goes on back home cause of my old mammy.

Next day them Yankees is swarmin' the place. Some the niggers wants to show them somethin'. I follows to the woods. The niggers shows them sojers a big pit in the ground, bigger'n a big house. It is got wooden doors that lifts up, but the top am sodded and grass growin' on it, so you couldn't tell it. In that pit is stock, hosses and cows and mules and money and chinaware and silver and a mess of stuff them sojers takes.

We jus' sot on the place doin' nothin' till the white folks comes home. Miss Sara come out to the cabin and say she wants to read a letter to my mammy. It come from Louis Carter, which is brother to my mammy, and he done follow the Fed'rals to Galveston. A white man done write the letter for him. It am tored in half and massa done that. The letter say Louis am workin' in Galveston and wants mammy to come with us, and he'll pay our way. Miss Sara say massa swear, Damn Louis Carter. I ain't gwine tell Sallie nothin',' and he starts to tear the letter up. but she won't let him, and she reads it to mammy.

After a time massa takes all his niggers what wants to Texas with him and mammy gits to Galveston and dies there. I goes with massa to the Tennessee Colony and then to Navasota. Miss Sara marries Mr. T. Coleman and goes to El Paso. She wrote and told me to come to her and I allus meant to go.

My husband and me farmed round for times, and then I done housework and cookin' for many years. I come to Dallas and cooked seven year for one white family. My husband died years ago. I guess Miss Sara been dead these long years. I allus kep' my years by Miss Sara's years, count we is born so close. "I been blind and mos' helpless for five year. I'm gittin' might enfeeblin' and I ain't walked outside the door for a long time back. I sets and members the times in the world. I members now clear as yesterday things I forgot for a long time. I members bout the days of slavery and I don't lieve they ever gwine have slaves no more on this earth. I think Gawd done took that burden offen his black chillun and I'm aimin' to praise him for it to his face in the days of Glory what ain't so far off.

MOTHER TERESA

INTRODUCTION

Mother Teresa was born in Yugoslavia on 26th August 1910. She became a nun at the age of 18. She came to India as a Loretto sister to teach in Loretto convents in Kolkata.

In 1950 she started the famous order of the 'Missionaries of Charity'. Soon many homes for the homeless, schools and hospitals were opened all over the country and abroad. For her great work of selfless love for the unloved she had been awarded many prizes and titles both in India and in other countries. She was too big a person for these awards.

The holy work she did could never be made small by being paid for. She worked untiringly till the day she passed away. She died on the 5th of September, 1997 in Kolkata. She was a real saint and both Kolkata and India are proud that she died as an Indian. In her death India lost an angel of mercy that day. It was indeed a black Friday for the whole world. The work she started carries on without any lack of love by her followers all over the world.

Nobel Lecture Speech - December 11, 1979

AS we have gathered here together to thank God for the Nobel Peace Prize I think it will be beautiful that we pray the prayer of St. Francis of Assisi which always surprises me very much- we pray this prayer every day after Holy Communion, because it is very fitting for each one of us, and I always wonder that 4-500 years ago as St. Francis of Assisi composed this prayer that they had the same difficulties that we have today, as we compose this prayer that fits very nicely for us also. I think some of you already have got it- so we will pray together.

Let us thank God for the opportunity that we all have together today, for this gift of peace that reminds us that we have been created to live that peace, and Jesus became man to bring that good news to the poor. He being God became man in all things like us except sin, and he proclaimed very clearly that he had come to give the good news. The news was peace to all of good will and this is something that we all want- the peace of heart- and God loved the world so much that he gave his son - it was a giving - it is as much as if to say it hurt God to give, because he loved the world so much that he gave his son, and he gave him to Virgin Mary, and what did she do with him?

As soon as he came in her life - immediately she went in haste to give that good news, and as she came into the house of her cousin, the child- the unborn child- the child in the womb of Elizabeth, leapt with joy. He was that little unborn child, was the first messenger of peace. He recognised the Prince of Peace, he recognised that Christ has come to bring the good news for you and for me. And as if that was not enough- it was not enough to become a man - he died on the cross to show that greater love, and he died for you and for me and for that leper and for that man dying of hunger and that naked person lying in the street not only of Calcutta, but of Africa, and New York, and London, and Oslo- and insisted that we love one another as he loves each one of us. And we read that in the Gospel very clearly- love as I have loved you- as I love you- as the Father has loved me, I love you- and the harder the Father loved him, he gave him to us, and how much we love one another, we, too, must give each other until it hurts. It is not enough for us to say: I love God, but I do not love my neighbour. St. John says you are a liar if you say you love God, and you don't love your neighbour. How can you love God whom you do not see, if you do not love your neighbour whom you see, whom you touch, with whom you live. And so this is very important for us to realise that love, to be true, has to hurt. It hurt Jesus to love us, it hurt him. And to make sure we remember his great love he made himself the bread of life to satisfy our hunger for his love. Our hunger for God, because we have been created for that love. We have been created in his image. We have been created to love and be loved, and then he has become man to make it possible for us to love as he loved us. He makes himself the hungry one- the naked one - the homeless one- the sick one- the one in prison- the lonely one - the unwanted one- and he says: You did it to me. Hungry for our love, and this is the hunger of our poor people. This is the hunger that you and I must find, it may be in our own home.

I never forget an opportunity I had in visiting a home where they had all these old parents of sons and daughters who had just put them in an institution and forgotten maybe. And I went there, and I saw in that home they had everything, beautiful things, but everybody was looking towards the door. And I did not see a single one with their smile on their face. And I turned to the Sister and I asked: How is that? How is it that the people they have everything here, why are they all looking towards the door, why are they not smiling? I am so used to see the smile on our people, even the dying one smile, and she said: This is nearly every day, they are expecting, they are hoping that a son or daughter will come to visit them. They are hurt because they are forgotten, and see- this is where love comes. That poverty comes right there in our own home, even neglect of love. Maybe in our own family we have somebody who is feeling lonely, who is feeling sick, who is feeling worried, and these are difficult days for everybody. Are we there, are we there to receive them, is the mother there to receive the child?

I was surprised in the West to see so many young boys and girls given into drugs, and I tried to find out why- why it is like that, and the answer was: Because there is no one in the family to receive them. Father and mother are so busy they have no time. Young parents are in some institution and the child takes back to the street and gets involved in something. We are talking of peace. These are things that break peace, but I feel the greatest destroyer of peace today is abortion, because it is a direct war, a direct killing- direct murder by the mother herself. And we read in the Scripture, for God says very clearly: Even if a mother could forget her child- I will not forget you - I have carved you in the palm of my hand. We are carved in the palm of His hand, so close to Him that unborn child has been carved in the hand of God. And that is what strikes me most, the beginning of that sentence, that even if a mother could forget something impossible - but even if she could forget - I will not forget you. And today the greatest means - the greatest destroyer of peace is abortion. And we who are standing here - our parents wanted us. We would not be here if our parents would do that to us. Our children, we want them, we love them, but what of the millions. Many people are very, very concerned with the children in India, with the children in Africa where quite a number die, maybe of malnutrition, of hunger and so on, but millions are dying deliberately by the will of the mother. And this is what is the greatest destroyer of peace today. Because if a mother can kill her own child- what is left for me to kill you and you kill me- there is nothing between. And this I appeal in India, I appeal everywhere: Let us bring the child back, and this year being the child's year: What have we done for the child? At the beginning of the year I told, I spoke everywhere and I said: Let us make this year that we make every single child born, and unborn, wanted. And today is the end of the year, have we really made the children wanted? I will give you something terrifying. We are fighting abortion by adoption, we have saved thousands of lives, we have sent words to all the clinics, to the hospitals, police stations - please don't destroy the child, we will take the child. So every hour of the day and night it is always somebody, we have quite a number of unwedded mothers- tell them come, we will take care of you, we will take the child from you, and we will get a home for the child. And we have a tremendous demand from families who have no children, that is the blessing of God for us. And also, we are doing another thing which is very beautiful- we are teaching our beggars, our leprosy patients, our slum dwellers, our people of the street, natural family planning.

And in Calcutta alone in six years- it is all in Calcutta- we have had 61,273 babies less from the families who would have had, but because they practise this natural way of abstaining, of self-control, out of love for each other. We teach them the temperature meter which is very beautiful, very simple, and our poor people understand. And you know what they have told me? Our family is healthy, our family is united, and we can have a baby whenever we want. So clear- those people in the street, those beggars- and I think that if our people can do like that how much more you and all the others who can know the ways and means without destroying the life that God has created in us.

The poor people are very great people. They can teach us so many beautiful things. The other day one of them came to thank and said: You people who have vowed chastity you are the best people to teach us family planning. Because it is nothing more than self-control out of love for each other. And I think they said a beautiful sentence. And these are people who maybe have nothing to eat, maybe they have not a home where to live, but they are great people. The poor are very wonderful people. One evening we went out and we picked up four people from the street. And one of them was in a most terrible condition- and I told the Sisters: You take care of the other three, I take of this one that looked worse. So I did for her all that my love can do. I put her in bed, and there was such a beautiful smile on her face. She took hold of my hand, as she said one word only: Thank you - and she died.

I could not help but examine my conscience before her, and I asked what would I say if I was in her place. And my answer was very simple. I would have tried to draw a little attention to myself, I would have said I am hungry, that I am dying, I am cold, I am in pain, or something, but she gave me much more - she gave me her grateful love. And she died with a smile on her face. As that man whom we picked up from the drain, half eaten with worms, and we brought him to the home. I have lived like an animal in the street, but I am going to die like an angel, loved and cared for. And it was so wonderful to see the greatness of that man who could speak like that, who could die like that without blaming anybody, without cursing anybody, without comparing anything. Like an angel- this is the greatness of our people. And that is why we believe what Jesus had said: I was hungry- I was naked- I was homeless - I was unwanted, unloved, uncared for - and you did it to me.

I believe that we are not real social workers. We may be doing social work in the eyes of the people, but we are really contemplatives in the heart of the world. For we are touching the Body Of Christ 24 hours. We have 24 hours in this presence, and so you and I. You too try to bring that presence of God in your family, for the family that prays together stays together. And I think that we in our family don't need bombs and guns, to destroy to bring peace - just get together, love one another, bring that peace, that joy, that strength of presence of each other in the home. And we will be able to overcome all the evil that is in the world.

There is so much suffering, so much hatred, so much misery, and we with our prayer, with our sacrifice are beginning at home. Love begins at home, and it is not how much we do, but how much love we put in the action that we do. It is to God Almighty- how much we do it does not matter, because He is infinite, but how much love we put in that action. How much we do to Him in the person that we are serving.

Some time ago in Calcutta we had great difficulty in getting sugar, and I don't know how the word got around to the children, and a little boy of four years old, Hindu boy, went home and told his parents: I will not eat sugar for three days, I will give my sugar to Mother Teresa for her children. After three days his father and mother brought him to our home. I had never met them before, and this little one could scarcely pronounce my name, but he knew exactly what he had come to do. He knew that he wanted to share his love.

And that is why I have received such a lot of love from you all. From the time that I have come here I have simply been surrounded with love, and with real, real understanding love. It could feel as if everyone in India, everyone in Africa is somebody very special to you. And I felt quite at home I was telling Sister today. I feel in the Convent with the Sisters as if I am in Calcutta with my own Sisters. So completely at home here, right here.

And so here I am talking with you- I want you to find the

poor here, right in your own home first. And begin love there. Be that good news to your own people. And find out about your next-door-neighbor - do you know who they are? I had the most extraordinary experience with a Hindu family who had eight children. A gentleman came to our house and said: Mother Teresa, there is a family with eight children, they had not eaten for so long- do something. So I took some rice and I went there immediately. And I saw the children- their eyes shining with hunger - I don't know if you have ever seen hunger. But I have seen it very often. And she took the rice, she divided the rice, and she went out. When she came back I asked her - where did you go, what did you do? And she gave me a very simple answer: They are hungry also. What struck me most was that she knew- and who are they, a Muslim family - and she knew. I didn't bring more rice that evening because I wanted them to enjoy the joy of sharing. But there were those children, radiating joy, sharing the joy with their mother because she had the love to give. And you see this is where love begins- at home. And I want you- and I am very grateful for what I have received. It has been a tremendous experience and I go back to India- I will be back by next week, the 15th I hope - and I will be able to bring your love.

And I know well that you have not given from your abundance, but you have given until it has hurt you. Today the little children they have- I was so surprised - there is so much joy for the children that are hungry. That the children like themselves will need love and care and tenderness, like they get so much from their parents. So let us thank God that we have had this opportunity to come to know each other, and this knowledge of each other has brought us very close. And we will be able to help not only the children of India and Africa, but will be able to help the children of the whole world, because as you know our Sisters are all over the world. And with this prize that I have received as a prize of peace, I am going to try to make the home for many people that have no home. Because I believe that love begins at home, and if we can create a home for the poor- I think that more and more love will spread. And we will be able through this understanding love to bring peace, be good news to the poor. The poor in our own family first, in our country and in the world.

To be able to do this, our Sisters, our lives have to be woven with prayer. They have to be woven with Christ to be able to understand, to be able to share. Because today there is so much suffering - and I feel that the passion of Christ is being relived all over again - are we there to share that passion, to share that suffering of people. Around the world, not only in the poor countries, but I found the poverty of the West so much more difficult to remove. When I pick up a person from the street, hungry, I give him a plate of rice, a piece of bread, I have satisfied. I have removed that hunger. But a person that is shut out, that feels unwanted, unloved, terrified, the person that has been thrown out from society - that poverty is so hurtable and so much, and I find that very difficult. Our Sisters are working amongst that kind of people in the West. So you must pray for us that we may be able to be that good news, but we cannot do that without you, you have to do that here in your country. You must come to know the poor, maybe our people here have material things, everything, but I think that if we all look into our own homes, how difficult we find it sometimes to smile at each other, and that the smile is the beginning of love.

And so let us always meet each other with a smile, for the smile is the beginning of love, and once we begin to love each other naturally we want to do something. So you pray for our Sisters and for me and for our Brothers, and for our Co-Workers that are around the world. That we may remain faithful to the gift of God, to love Him and serve Him in the poor together with you. What we have done we should not have been able to do if you did not share with your prayers, with your gifts, this continual giving. But I don't want you to give me from your abundance, I want that you give me until it hurts.

The other day I received 15 dollars from a man who has been on his back for twenty years, and the only part that he can move is his right hand. And the only companion that he enjoys is smoking. And he said to me: I do not smoke for one week, and I send you this money. It must have been a terrible sacrifice for him, but see how beautiful, how he shared, and with that money I bought bread and I gave to those who are hungry with a joy on both sides, he was giving and the poor were receiving. This is something that you and I- it is a gift of God to us to be able to share our love with others. And let it be as it was for Jesus. Let us love one another as he loved us. Let us love Him with undivided love. And the joy of loving Him and each other- let us give now - that Christmas is coming so close. Let us keep that joy of loving Jesus in our hearts. And share that joy with all that we come in touch with. And that radiating joy is real, for we have no reason not to be happy because we have no Christ with us. Christ in our hearts, Christ in the poor that we meet, Christ in the smile that we give and the smile that we receive. Let us make that one point: That no child will be unwanted, and also that we meet each other always with a smile, especially when it is difficult to smile.

I never forget some time ago about fourteen professors came from the United States from different universities. And they came to Calcutta to our house. Then we were talking about that they had been to the home for the dying. We have a home for the dying in Calcutta, where we have picked up more than 36,000 people only from the streets of Calcutta, and out of that big number more than 18,000 have died a beautiful death. They have just gone home to God; and they came to our house and we talked of love, of compassion, and then one of them asked me: Say, Mother, please tell us something that we will remember, and I said to them: Smile at each other, make time for each other in your family. Smile at each other. And then another one asked me: Are you married, and I said: Yes, and I find it sometimes very difficult to smile at Jesus because he can be very demanding sometimes. This is really something true, and there is where love comes - when it is demanding, and yet we can give it to Him with joy. Just as I have said today, I have said that if I don't go to Heaven for anything else I will be going to Heaven for all the publicity because it has purified me and sacrificed me and made me really ready to go to Heaven. I think that this is something, that we must live life beautifully, we have Jesus with us and He loves us. If we could only remember that God loves me, and I have an opportunity to love others as he loves me, not in big things, but in small things with great love, then Norway becomes a nest of love. And how beautiful it will be that from here a centre for peace has been given. That from here the joy of life of the unborn child comes out. If you become a burning light in the world of peace, then really the Nobel Peace Prize is a gift of the Norwegian people. God bless you!

The National Prayer Breakfast Famous Speech Washington, D.C. - February 4, 1994

ON the last day, Jesus will say to those at his right hand,

"Come, enter the Kingdom. For I was hungry and you gave me food, I was thirsty and you gave me drink, I was sick and you visited me."

Then Jesus will turn to those on his left hand and say,

"Depart from me because I was hungry and you did not feed me, I was thirsty and you did not give me drink, I was sick and you did not visit me."

These will ask him,

"When did we see you hungry, or thirsty, or sick, and did not come to your help?"

And Jesus will answer them,

"Whatever you neglected to do unto one of the least of these, you neglected to do unto me!"

As we have gathered here to pray together, I think it will be beautiful if we begin with a prayer that expresses very well what Jesus wants us to do for the least. St. Francis of Assisi understood very well these words of Jesus and his life is very well expressed by a prayer. And this prayer, which we say every day after Holy Communion, always surprises me very much, because it is very fitting for each one of us. And I always wonder whether eight hundred years ago when St. Francis lived, they had the same difficulties that we have today. I think that some of you already have this prayer of peace, so we will pray it together.

Let us thank God for the opportunity he has given us today to have come here to pray together. We have come here especially to pray for peace, joy, and love. We are reminded that Jesus came to bring the good news to the poor. He had told us what that good news is when he said, "My peace I leave with you, my peace I give unto you."

He came not to give the peace of the world, which is only that we don't bother each other. He came to give peace of heart which comes from loving - from doing good to others.

And God loved the world so much that he gave his son. God gave his son to the Virgin Mary, and what did she do with him? As soon as Jesus came into Mary's life, immediately she went in haste to give that good news. And as she came into the house of her cousin, Elizabeth, Scripture tells us that the unborn child - the child in the womb of Elizabeth - leapt with joy. While still in the womb of Mary, Jesus brought peace to John the Baptist, who leapt for joy in the womb of Elizabeth.

And as if that were not enough - as if it were not enough that God the Son should become one of us and bring peace and joy while still in the womb, Jesus also died on the Cross to show that greater love. He died for you and for me, and for that leper and for that man dying of hunger and that naked person lying in the street - not only of Calcutta, but of Africa, of everywhere. Our Sisters serve these poor people in 105 countries throughout the world. Jesus insisted that we love one another as he loves each one of us. Jesus gave his life to love us, and he tells us that he loves each one of us. Jesus gave his life to love us, and he tells us that we also have to give whatever it takes to do good to one another. And in the Gospel Jesus says very clearly, " Love as I have loved you."

Jesus died on the Cross because that is what it took for him to do good for us - to save us from our selfishness and sin. He gave up everything to do the Father's will, to show us that we too must be willing to give everything to do God's will, to love one another as he loves each of us. If we are not willing to give whatever it takes to do good for one another, sin is still in us. That is why we too must give to each other until it hurts.

Love always hurts

It is not enough for us to say, "I love God." But I also have to love my neighbor. St. John says that you are a liar if you say you love God and you don't love your neighbor. How can you love God whom you do not see, if you do not love your neighbor whom you see, whom you touch, with whom you live? And so it is very important for us to realize that love, to be true, has to hurt. I must be willing to give whatever it takes not to harm other people and, in fact, to do good to them. This requires that I be willing to give until it hurts. Otherwise, there is no true love in me and I bring injustice, not peace, to those around me.

It hurt Jesus to love us. We have been created in his image for greater things, to love and to be loved. We must "put on Christ," as Scripture tells us. And so we have been created to love as he loves us. Jesus makes himself the hungry one, the naked one, the homeless one, the unwanted one, and he says, "You did it to me." On the last day he will say to those on his right, "whatever you did to the least of these, you did to me," and he will also say to those on his left, "whatever you neglected to do for the least of these, you neglected to do it for me."

When he was dying on the Cross, Jesus said, "I thirst." Jesus is thirsting for our love, and this is the thirst for everyone, poor and rich alike. We all thirst for the love of others, that they go out of their way to avoid harming us and to do good to us. This is the meaning of true love, to give until it hurts.

I can never forget the experience I had in visiting a home where they kept all these old parents of sons and daughters who had just put them into an institution and, maybe, forgotten them. I saw that in that home these old people had everything: good food, comfortable place, television - everything. But everyone was looking toward the door. And I did not see a single one with a smile on his face.

I turned to Sister and I asked, "Why do these people, who have every comfort here - why are they all looking toward the door? Why are they not smiling?" (I am so used to seeing the smiles on our people." Even the dying ones smile.) And Sister said, "This is the way it is, nearly everyday. They are expecting - they are hoping - that a son or daughter will come to visit them. They are hurt because they are forgotten."

See, this neglect to love brings spiritual poverty. Maybe in our family we have somebody who is feeling lonely, who is feeling sick, who is feeling worried. Are we there? Are we willing to give until it hurts, in order to be with our families? Or do we put our own interests first? These are the questions we must ask ourselves, especially as we begin this Year of the Family. We must remember that love begins at home, and we must also remember that "the future of humanity passes through the family.

I was surprised in the West to see so many young boys and girls given to drugs. And I tried to find out why. Why is it like that, when those in the West have so many more things than those in the East? And the answer was, "Because there is no one in the family to receive them." Our children depend on us for everything: their health, their nutrition, their security, their coming to know and love God. For all of this, they look to us with trust, hope, and expectation. But often father and mother are so busy that they have no time for their children, or perhaps they are not even married, or have given up on their marriage. So the children go to the streets, and get involved in drugs, or other things. We are talking of love of the child, which is where love and peace must begin. These are the things that break peace.

But I feel that the greatest destroyer of peace today is abortion, because it is a war against the child - a direct killing of the innocent child - murder by the mother herself. And if we accept that a mother can kill even her own child, how can we tell other people not to kill one another? How do we persuade a woman not to have an abortion? As always, we must persuade her with love, and we remind ourselves that love means to be willing to give until it hurts. Jesus gave even his life to love us. So the mother who is thinking of abortion, should be helped to love - that is, to give until it hurts her plans, or her free time, to respect the life of her child. The father of that child, whoever he is, must also give until it hurts. By abortion, the mother does not learn to love, but kills even her own child to solve her problems. And by abortion, the father is told that he does not have to take any responsibility at all for the child he has brought into the world. That father is likely to put other women into the same trouble. So abortion just leads to more abortion. Any country that accepts abortion is not teaching the people to love, but to use any violence to get what they want. That is why the greatest destroyer of love and peace is abortion.

Many people are very, very concerned with the children of India, with the children of Africa, where quite a few die of hunger, and so on. Many people are also concerned about all the violence in this great country of the United States. These concerns are very good. But often these same people are not concerned with the millions who are being killed by the deliberate decision of their own mothers. And this is what is the greatest destroyer of peace today: abortion, which brings people to such blindness.

"I want this child!"

And for this I appeal in India and I appeal everywhere: "Let us bring the child back." The child is God's gift to the family. Each child is created in the special image and likeness of God for greater things - to love and to be loved. In this Year of the Family we must bring the child back to the center of our care and concern. This is the only way that our world can survive, because our children are the only hope for the future. As other people are called to God, only their children can take their places.

But what does God say to us? He says, "Even if a mother could forget her child, I will not forget you. I have carved you in the palm of my hand." We are carved in the palm of his hand; that unborn child has been carved in the hand of God from conception, and is called by God to love and to be loved, not only now in this life, out forever. God can never forget us.

I will tell you something beautiful. We are fighting abortion by adoption - by care of the mother and adoption for her baby. We have saved thousands of lives. We have sent word to the clinics, to the hospitals, and police stations: Please don't destroy the child; we will take the child." So we always have someone tell the mothers in trouble: "Come, we will take care of you, we will get a home for your child."

And we have a tremendous demand from couples who cannot have a child. But I never give a child to a couple who has done something not to have a child. Jesus said, "Anyone who receives a child in my name, receives me." By adopting a child, these couples receive Jesus, but by aborting a child, a couple refuses to receive Jesus.

Please don't kill the child. I want the child. Please give me the child. I am willing to accept any child who would be aborted, and to give that child to a married couple who will love the child, and be loved by the child. From our children's home in Calcutta alone, we have saved over 3,000 children from abortions. These children have brought such love and joy to their adopting parents, and have grown up so full of love and joy! I know that couples have to plan their family, and for that there is natural family planning. The way to plan the family is natural family planning, not contraception. In destroying the power of giving life, through contraception, a husband or wife is doing something to self. This turns the attention to self, and so it destroys the gift of love in him or her. In loving, the husband and wife must turn the attention to each other, as happens in natural family planning, and not to self, as happens in contraception. Once that living love is destroyed by contraception, abortion follows very easily.

The greatness of the poor

I also know that there are great problems in the world - that many spouses do not love each other enough to practice natural family planning. We cannot solve all the problems in the world, but let us never bring in the worst problem of all, and that is to destroy love. This is what happens when we tell people to practice contraception and abortion.

The poor are very great people. They can teach us so many beautiful things. Once one of them came to thank us for teaching them natural family planning, and said: "You people - who have practiced chastity - you are the best people to teach us natural family planning, because it is nothing more than self-control out of love for each other." And what this poor person said is very true. These poor people maybe have nothing to eat, maybe they have not a home to live in, but they can still be great people when they are spiritually rich. Those who are materially poor can be wonderful people. One evening we went out and we picked up four people from the street. And one of them was in a most terrible condition. I told the Sisters: "You take care of the other three; I will take care of the one who looks worse." So I did for her all that my love can do. I put her in bed, and there was a beautiful smile on her face. She took hold of my hand, and she said one thing only: "Thank you." Then she died.

I could not help but examine my conscience before her. I asked, "What would I say if I were in her place?" And my answer was very simple. I would have tried to draw a little attention to myself. I would have said, "I am hungry, I am dying, I am cold, I am in pain," or something like that. But she gave me much more - she gave me her grateful love. And she died with a smile on her face.

Then there was the man we picked up from the drain, half-eaten by worms. And after we had brought him to the home, he only said, "I have lived like an animal in the street, but am going to die as an angel, loved and cared for." Then, after we had removed all the worms from this body, all he said - with a big smile - was: "Sister, I am going home to God." And he died. It was so wonderful to see the greatness of that man, who could speak like that without blaming anybody, without comparing anything. Like an angel - this is the greatness of people who are spiritually rich, even when they are materially poor.

A sign of care

We are not social workers. We may be doing social work in the eyes of some people, but we must be contemplatives in the heart of the world. For we must bring that presence of God into your family, for the family that prays together, stays together. There is so much hatred, so much misery, and we with our prayer, with our sacrifice, are beginning at home. Love begins at home, and it is not how much we do, but how much love we put into what we do.

If we are contemplatives in the heart of the world with all its problems, these problems can never discourage us. We must always remember what God tells us in the Scripture: Even if the mother could forget the child in her womb - something that is impossible, but even if she could forget - I will never forget you. And so here I am talking with you. I want you to find the poor here, right in your own home first. And begin love there. Bear the good news to your own people first. And find out about your next-door neighbors. Do you know who they are?

I had the most extraordinary experience of love of a neighbor from a Hindu family. A gentleman came to our house and said, "Mother Teresa, there is a family who have not eaten for so long. Do something." So I took some rice and went there immediately. And I saw the children, their eyes shining with hunger. (I don't know if you have ever seen hunger, but I have seen it very often.) And the mother of the family took the rice I gave her, and went out. When she came back, I asked her, "Where did you go? What did you do?" And she gave me a very simple answer: "They are hungry also." What struck me was that she knew. And who were "they?" A Muslim family. And she knew. I didn't bring any more rice that evening, because I wanted them - Hindus and Muslims - to enjoy the joy of sharing.

But there were those children, radiating joy, sharing the joy and peace with their mother because she had the love to give until it hurts. And you see this is where love begins: at home in the family. God will never forget us, and there is something you and I can always do. We can keep the joy of loving Jesus in our hearts, and share that joy with all we come in contact with. Let us make that one point: that no child will be unwanted, unloved, uncared for, or killed and thrown away. And give until it hurts - with a smile.

Because I talk so much of giving with a smile, once a professor from the United States asked me, "Are you married?" And I said, "Yes, and I find it sometimes very difficult to smile at my spouse - Jesus - because he can be very demanding - sometimes this is really something true. And there is where love comes in - when it is demanding, and yet we can give it with joy.

One of the most demanding things for me is traveling everywhere, and with publicity. I have said to Jesus that if I don't go to heaven for anything else, I will be going to heaven for all the traveling with all the publicity, because it has purified me and sacrificed me and made me really ready to go to heaven. If we remember that God loves us, and that we can love others as he loves us, then America can become a sign of peace for the world. From here, a sign of care for the weakest of the weak - the unborn child - must go out to the world. If you become a burning light of justice and peace in the world, then really you will be true to what the founders of this country stood for. God bless you!

OPRAH WINFREY

INTRODUCTION

Oprah Winfrey was born on January 29, 1954, Kosciusko, Mississippi, U.S.A. American television personality, actress, and entrepreneur whose syndicated daily talk show was among the most popular of the genre. She became one of the richest and most influential women in the United States.

Winfrey moved to Milwaukee, Wisconsin, at age six to live with her mother. In her early teens she was sent to Nashville, Tennessee, to live with her father, who proved to be a positive influence in her life.

Winfrey excelled in the casual and personal talk-show format, and in 1984 she moved to Chicago to host the faltering talk show *AM Chicago*. Winfrey's honest and engaging personality quickly turned the program into a success, and in 1985 it was renamed *The Oprah Winfrey Show*. Syndicated nationally in 1986, the program became the highest-rated television talk show in America and earned several Emmy Awards.

In 1998 Winfrey expanded her media entertainment empire when she cofounded Oxygen Media, which operates a cable television network for women.

54th Annual EMMY Awards Famous Speech Oprah Winfrey Receives the first Bob Hope Humanitarian Award - September 22, 2002

"THANK YOU everybody. Thank you Tom, and Bob and Dolores, who are home watching I hope, thank you so much, and to everyone who voted for me.

There really is nothing more important to me than striving to be a good human being. So, to be here tonight and be acknowledged as the first to receive this honor is beyond expression in words for me. 'I am a human being, nothing human is alien to me.' Terence said that in 154 B.C. and when I first read it many years ago, I had no idea of the depth of that meaning.

I grew up in Nashville with a father who owned a barbershop, Winfrey's Barber Shop, he still does, I can't get him to retire. And every holiday, every holiday, all of the transients and the guys who I thought were just losers who hung out at the shop, and were always bumming haircuts from my father and borrowing money from my dad, all those guys always ended up at our dinner table. They were a cast of real characters—it was Fox and Shorty and Bootsy and Slim. And I would say, 'Bootsy, could you pass the peas please?' And I would often say to my father afterwards, 'Dad, why can't we just have regular people at our Christmas dinner?'—because I was looking for the Currier & Ives version. And my father said to me, 'They are regular people. They're just like you. They want the same thing you want.' And I would say, 'What?' And he'd say, 'To be fed.' And at the time, I just thought he was talking about dinner. But I have since learned how profound he really was, because we all are just regular people seeking the same thing. The guy on the street, the woman in the classroom, the Israeli, the Afghani, the Zuni, the Apache, the Irish, the Protestant, the Catholic, the gay, the straight, you, me—we all just want to know that we matter. We want validation. We want the same things. We want safety and we want to live a long life. We want to find somebody to love.

Stedman, thank you. We want to find somebody to laugh with and have the power and the place to cry with when necessary.

The greatest pain in life is to be invisible. What I've learned is that we all just want to be heard. And I thank all the people who continue to let me hear your stories, and by sharing your stories, you let other people see themselves and for a moment, glimpse the power to change and the power to triumph.

Maya Angelou said, 'When you learn, teach. When you get, give.' I want you to know that this award to me means that I will continue to strive to give back to the world what it has given to me, so that I might even be more worthy of tonight's honor.

Thank you."

PEARL BUCK

INTRODUCTION

Pearl Buck (1892-1973) was born in Hillsboro, West Virginia. She grew up in China, where her parents were missionaries, but was educated at Randolph-Macon Woman's College. After her graduation she returned to China and lived there until 1934 with the exception of a year spent at Cornell University, where she took an M.A. in 1926.

Pearl Buck began to write in the twenties; her first novel, *East Wind, West Wind,* appeared in 1930. It was followed by *The Good Earth* (1931), *Sons* (1932), and *A House Divided* (1935), together forming a trilogy on the saga of the family of Wang. *The Good Earth* stood on the American list of «best sellers» for a long time and earned her several awards, among them the Pulitzer Prize and the William Dean Howells Medal. She also published *The First Wife and Other Stories* (1933), *All Men are Brothers* (a translation of the Chinese novel *Shui Hu Chuan*) (1933), *The Mother* (1934), and *This Proud Heart* (1938). The biographies of her mother and father, *The Exile* and *Fighting Angel,* were published in 1936 and later brought out together under the title of *The Spirit and the Flesh* (1944). *The Time Is Now,* a fictionalized account of the author's emotional experiences, although written much earlier, did not appear in print until 1967. Pearl Buck has been active in many welfare organizations; in particular she set up an agency for the adoption of Asian-American children (Welcome House, Inc.) and has taken an active interest in retarded children *(The Child Who Never Grew, 1950).*

Nobel Lecture - The Chinese Novel Famous Speech December 12, 1938 Stockholm, Sweden

WHEN I came to consider what I should say today it seemed that it would be wrong not to speak of China. And this is none the less true because I am an American by birth and by ancestry and though I live now in my own country and shall live there, since there I belong. But it is the Chinese and not the American novel which has shaped my own efforts in writing. My earliest knowledge of story, of how to tell and write stories, came to me in China. It would be ingratitude on my part not to recognize this today. And yet it would be presumptuous to speak before you on the subject of the Chinese novel for a reason wholly personal. There is another reason why I feel that I may properly do so. It is that I believe the Chinese novel has an illumination for the Western novel and for the Western novelist.

When I say Chinese novel, I mean the indigenous Chinese novel, and not that hybrid product, the novels of modern Chinese writers who have been too strongly under foreign influence while they were yet ignorant of the riches of their own country.

The novel in China was never an art and was never so considered, nor did any Chinese novelist think of himself as an artist. The Chinese novel its history, its scope, its place in the life of the people, so vital a place, must be viewed in the strong light of this one fact. It is a fact no doubt strange to you, a company of modern Western scholars who today so generously recognize the novel.

But in China art and the novel have always been widely separated. There, literature as an art was the exclusive property of the scholars, an art they made and made for each other according to their own rules, and they found no place in it for the novel. And they held a powerful place, those Chinese scholars. Philosophy and religion and letters and literature, by arbitrary classical rules, they possessed them all, for they alone possessed the means of learning, since they alone knew how to read and write. They were powerful enough to be feared even by emperors, so that emperors devised a way of keeping them enslaved by their own learning, and made the official examinations the only means to political advancement, those incredibly difficult examinations which ate up a man's whole life and thought in preparing for them, and kept him too busy with memorizing and copying the dead and classical past to see the present and its wrongs. In that past the scholars found their rules of art. But the novel was not there, and they did not see it being created before their eyes, for the people created the novel, and what living people were doing did not interest those who thought of literature as an art. If scholars ignored the people, however, the people, in turn, laughed at the scholars. They made innumerable jokes about them, of which this is a fair sample: One day a company of wild beasts met on a hillside for a hunt. They bargained with each other to go out and hunt all day and meet again at the end of the day to share what they had killed. At the end of the day, only the tiger returned with nothing. When he was asked how this happened he replied very disconsolately, «At dawn I met a schoolboy, but he was, I feared, too callow for your tastes. I met no more until noon, when I found a priest. But I let him go, knowing him to be full of nothing but wind. The day went on and I grew desperate, for I passed no one. Then as dark came on I found a scholar. But I knew there was no use in bringing him back since he would be so dry and hard that he would break our teeth if we tried them on him.»

The scholar as a class has long been a figure of fun for the Chinese people. He is frequently to be found in their novels, and always he is the same, as indeed he is in life, for a long study of the same dead classics and their formal composition has really made all Chinese scholars look alike, as well as think alike. We have no class to parallel him in the West - individuals, perhaps, only. But in China he was a class. Here he is, composite, as the people see him: a small shrunken figure with a bulging forehead, a pursed mouth, a nose at once snub and pointed, small inconspicuous eyes behind spectacles, a high pedantic voice, always announcing rules that do not matter to anyone but himself, a boundless self-conceit, a complete scorn not only of the common people but of all other scholars, a figure in long shabby robes, moving with a swaying haughty walk, when he moved at all. He was not to be seen except at literary gatherings, for most of the time he spent reading dead literature and trying to write more like it. He hated anything fresh or original, for he could not catalogue it into any of the styles he knew. If he could not catalogue it, he was sure it was not great, and he was confident that only he was right. If he said, «Here is art», he was convinced it was not to be found anywhere else, for what he did not recognize did not exist. And as he could never catalogue the novel into what he called literature, so for him it did not exist as literature.

Yao Hai, one of the greatest of Chinese literary critics, in 1776 enumerated the kinds of writing which comprise the whole of literature. They are essays, government commentaries, biographies, epitaphs, epigrams, poetry, funeral eulogies, and histories. No novels, you perceive, although by that date the Chinese novel had already reached its glorious height, after centuries of development among the common Chinese people. Nor does that vast compilation of Chinese literature, SsuV Ku Chuen Shu, made in 1772 by the order of the great Emperor Ch'ien Lung, contain the novel in the encyclopedia of its literature proper.

No, happily for the Chinese novel, it was not considered by the scholars as literature. Happily, too, for the novelist! Man and book, they were free from the criticisms of those scholars and their requirements of art, their techniques of expression and their talk of literary significances and all that discussion of what is and is not art, as if art were an absolute and not the changing thing it is, fluctuating even within decades! The Chinese novel was free. It grew as it liked out of its own soil, the common people, nurtured by that heartiest of sunshine, popular approval, and untouched by the cold and frosty winds of the scholar's art. Emily Dickinson, an American poet, once wrote, «Nature is a haunted house, but art is a house that tries to be haunted». «Nature», she said,

Is what we see,

Nature is what we know

But have no art to say -

So impatient our wisdom is,

To her simplicity.

No, if the Chinese scholars ever knew of the growth of the novel, it was only to ignore it the more ostentatiously. Sometimes, unfortunately, they found themselves driven to take notice, because youthful emperors found novels pleasant to read. Then these poor scholars were hard put to it. But they discovered the phrase «social significance», and they wrote long literary treatises to prove that a novel was not a novel but a document of social significance. Social significance is a term recently discovered by the most modern of literary young men and women in the United States, but the old scholars of China knew it a thousand years ago, when they, too, demanded that the novel should have social significance, if it were to be recognized as an art.

But for the most part the old Chinese scholar reasoned thus about the novel:

Literature is art.

All art has social significance.

This book has no social significance.

Therefore it is not literature.

And so the novel in China was not literature.

In such a school was I trained. I grew up believing that the novel has nothing to do with pure literature. So I was taught by scholars. The art of literature, so I was taught, is something devised by men of learning. Out of the brains of scholars came rules to control the rush of genius, that wild fountain which has its source in deepest life. Genius, great or less, is the spring, and art is the sculptured shape, classical or modern, into which the waters must be forced, if scholars and critics were to be served. But the people of China did not so serve. The waters of the genius of story gushed out as they would, however the natural rocks allowed and the trees persuaded, and only common people came and drank and found rest and pleasure.

For the novel in China was the peculiar product of the common people. And it was solely their property. The very language of the novel was their own language, and not the classical Wen-li, which was the language of literature and the scholars. Wen-li bore somewhat the same resemblance to the language of the people as the ancient English of Chaucer does to the English of today, although ironically enough, at one time Wen-li, too, was a vernacular. But the scholars never kept pace with the living, changing speech of the people. They clung to an old vernacular until they had made it classic, while the running language of the people went on and left them far behind. Chinese novels, then, are in the «Pei Hua», or simple talk, of the people, and this in itself was offensive to the old scholars because it resulted in a style so full of easy flow and readability that it had no technique of expression in it, the scholars said.

I should pause to make an exception of certain scholars who came to China from India, bearing as their gift a new religion, Buddhism. In the West, Puritanism was for a long time the enemy of the novel. But in the Orient the Buddhists were wiser. When they came into China, they found literature already remote from the people and dying under the formalism of that period known in history as the Six Dynasties. The professional men of literature were even then absorbed not so much in what they had to say as in pairing into couplets the characters of their essays and their poems, and already they scorned all writing which did not conform to their own rules. Into this confined literary atmosphere came the Buddhist translators with their great treasures of the freed spirit. Some of them were Indian, but some were Chinese. They said frankly that their aim was not to conform to the ideas of style of the literary men, but to make clear and simple to common people what they had to teach. They put their religious teachings into the common language, the language which the novel used, and because the people loved story, they took story and made it a means of teaching. The preface of Fah Shu Ching, one of the most famous of Buddhist books, says, «When giving the words of gods, these words should be given forth simply.» This might be taken as the sole literary creed of the Chinese novelist, to whom, indeed, gods were men and men were gods.

For the Chinese novel was written primarily to amuse the common people. And when I say amuse I do not mean only to make them laugh, though laughter is also one of the aims of the Chinese novel. I mean amusement in the sense of absorbing and occupying the whole attention of the mind. I mean enlightening that mind by pictures of life and what that life means. I mean encouraging the spirit not by rule-of-thumb talk about art, but by stories about the people in every age, and thus presenting to people simply themselves. Even the

Buddhists who came to tell about gods found that people understood gods better if they saw them working through ordinary folk like themselves.

But the real reason why the Chinese novel was written in the vernacular was because the common people could not read and write and the novel had to be written so that when it was read aloud it could be understood by persons who could communicate only through spoken words. In a village of two hundred souls perhaps only one man could read. And on holidays or in the evening when the work was done he read aloud to the people from some story. The rise of the Chinese novel began in just this simple fashion. After a while people took up a collection of pennies in somebody's cap or in a farm wife's bowl because the reader needed tea to wet his throat, or perhaps to pay him for time he would otherwise have spent at his silk loom or his rush weaving. If the collections grew big enough he gave up some of his regular work and became a professional storyteller. And the stories he read were the beginnings of novels. There were not many such stories written down, not nearly enough to last year in and year out for people who had by nature, as the Chinese have, a strong love for dramatic story. So the storyteller began to increase his stock. He searched the dry annals of the history which the scholars had written, and with his fertile imagination, enriched by long acquaintance with common people, he clothed long-dead figures with new flesh and made them live again; he found stories of court life and intrigue and names of imperial favorites who had brought dynasties to ruin; he found, as he traveled from village to village, strange tales from his own times which he wrote down when he heard them. People told him of experiences they had had and he wrote these down, too, for other people. And he embellished them, but not with literary turns and phrases, for the people cared nothing for these. No, he kept his audiences always in mind and he found that the style which they loved best was one which flowed easily along, clearly and simply, in the short words which they themselves used every day, with no other technique than occasional bits of description, only enough to give vividness to a place or a person, and never enough to delay the story. Nothing must delay the story. Story was what they wanted.

And when I say story, I do not mean mere pointless activity, not crude action alone. The Chinese are too mature for that.

They have always demanded of their novel character above all else. Shui Hu Chuan they have considered one of their three greatest novels, not primarily because it is full of the flash and fire of action, but because it portrays so distinctly one hundred and eight characters that each is to be seen separate from the others. Often I have heard it said of that novel in tones of delight, «When anyone of the hundred and eight begins to speak, we do not need to be told his name. By the way the words come from his mouth we know who he is.» Vividness of character portrayal, then, is the first quality which the Chinese people have demanded of their novels, and after it, that such portrayal shall be by the character's own action and words rather than by the author's explanation.

Curiously enough, while the novel was beginning thus humbly in teahouses, in villages and lowly city streets out of stories told to the common people by a common and unlearned man among them, in imperial palaces it was beginning, too, and in much the same unlearned fashion. It was an old custom of emperors, particularly if the dynasty were a foreign one, to employ persons called «imperial ears», whose only duty was to come and go among the people in the streets of cities and villages and to sit among them in teahouses, disguised in common clothes and listen to what was talked about there. The original purpose of this was, of course, to hear of any discontent among the emperor's subjects, and more especially to find out if discontents were rising to the shape of those rebellions which preceded the fall of every dynasty.

But emperors were very human and they were not often learned scholars. More often, indeed, they were only spoiled and willful men. The «imperial ears. had opportunity to hear all sorts of strange and interesting stories, and they found that their royal masters were more frequently interested in these stories than they were in politics. So when they came back to make their reports, they flattered the emperor and sought to gain favor by telling him what he liked to hear, shut up as he was in the Forbidden City, away from life. They told him the strange and interesting things which common people did, who were free, and after a while they took to writing down what they heard in order to save memory. And I do not doubt that if messengers between the emperor and the people carried stories in one direction, they carried them in the other, too, and to the people they told stories about the emperor and what he said and did, and how he quarreled with the empress who bore him no sons, and how she intrigued with the chief eunuch to poison the favorite concubine, all of which delighted the Chinese because it proved to them, the most democratic of peoples, that their emperor was after all only a common fellow like themselves and that he, too, had his troubles, though he was the Son of Heaven. Thus there began another important source for the novel that was to develop with such form and force, though still always denied its right to exist by the professional man of letters.

From such humble and scattered beginnings, then, came the Chinese novel, written always in the vernacular, and dealing with all which interested the people, with legend and with myth, with love and intrigue, with brigands and wars, with everything, indeed, which went to make up the life of the people, high and low.

Nor was the novel in China shaped, as it was in the West, by a few great persons. In China the novel has always been more important than the novelist. There has been no Chinese Defoe, no Chinese Fielding or Smollett, no Austin or Brontë or Dickens or Thackeray, or Meredith or Hardy, any more than Balzac or Flaubert. But there were and are novels as great as the novels in any other country in the world, as great as any could have written, had he been born in China. Who then wrote these novels of China?

That is what the modern literary men of China now, centuries too late, are trying to discover. Within the last twenty-five years literary critics, trained in the universities of the West, have begun to discover their own neglected novels. But the novelists who wrote them they cannot discover. Did one man write Shui Hu Chuan, or did it grow to its present shape, added to, rearranged, deepened and developed by many minds and many a hand, in different centuries? Who can now tell? They are dead. They lived in their day and wrote what in their day they saw and heard, but of themselves they have told nothing. The author of The Dream ofthe Red Chamber in a far later century says in the preface to his book, «It is not necessary to know the times of Han and T'ang - it is necessary to tell only of my own times.»

They told of their own times and they lived in a blessed obscurity. They read no reviews of their novels, no treatises as to whether or not what they did was well done according to the rules of scholarship. It did not occur to them that they must reach the high thin air which scholars breathed nor - did they consider the stuff of which greatness is made, according to the scholars. They wrote as it pleased them to write and as they were able. Sometimes they wrote unwittingly well and sometimes unwittingly they wrote not so well. They died in the same happy obscurity and now they are lost in it and not all the scholars of China, gathered too late to do them honor, can raise them up again. They are long past the possibility of literary post-mortems. But what they did remains after them because it is the common people of China who keep alive the great novels, illiterate people who have passed the novel, not so often from hand to hand as from mouth to mouth.

In the preface to one of the later editions of Shui Hu Chuan, Shih Nai An, an author who had much to do with the making of that novel, writes, «What I speak of I wish people to understand easily. Whether the reader is good or evil, learned or unlearned, anyone can read this book. Whether or not the book is well done is not important enough to cause anyone to worry. Alas, I am born to die. How can I know what those who come after me who read my book will think of it? I cannot even know what I myself, born into another incarnation, will think of it. I do not know if I myself then can even read. Why therefore should I care?»

Strangely enough, there were certain scholars who envied the freedom of obscurity, and who, burdened with certain private sorrows which they dared not tell anyone, or who perhaps wanting only a holiday from th weariness of the sort of art they had themselves created, wrote novels, too under assumed and humbie names. And when they did so they put aside pedantry and wrote as simply and naturally as any common novelist.

For the novelist believed that he should not be conscious of techniques. He should write as his material demanded. If a novelist became known for a particular style or technique, to that extent he ceased to be a good novelist and became a literary technician.

A good novelist, or so I have been taught in China, should be above all else tse ran, that is, natural, unaffected, and so flexible and variable as to be wholly at the command of the material that flows through him. His whole duty is only to sort life as it flows through him, and in the vast fragmentariness of time and space and event to discover essential and inherent order and rhythm and shape. We should never be able, merely by reading pages, to know who wrote them, for when the style of a novelist becomes fixed, that style becomes his prison. The Chinese novelists varied their writing to accompany like music their chosen themes.

These Chinese novels are not perfect according to Western standards. They are not always planned from beginning to end, nor are they compact, any more than life is planned or compact. They are often too long, too full of incident, too crowded with character, a medley of fact and fiction as to material, and a medley of romance and realism as to method, so that an impossible event of magic or dream may be described with such exact semblance of detail that one is compelled to belief against all reason. The earliest novels are full of folklore, for the people of those times thought and dreamed in the ways of folklore. But no one can understand the mind of China today who has not read these novels, for the novels have shaped the present mind, too, and the folklore persists in spite of all that Chinese diplomats and Western-trained scholars would have us believe to the contrary. The essential mind of China is still that mind of which George Russell wrote when he said of the Irish mind, so strangely akin to the Chinese,« that mind which in its folk imagination believes anything. It creates ships of gold with masts of silver and white cities by the sea and rewards and faeries, and when that vast folk mind turns to politics it is ready to believe anything.»

Out of this folk mind, turned into stories and crowded with thousands of years of life, grew, literally, the Chinese novel. For these novels changed as they grew. If, as I have said, there are no single names attached beyond question to the great novels of China, it is because no one hand wrote them. From beginning as a mere tale, a story grew through succeeding versions, into a structure built by many hands. I might mention as an example the well-known story, The White Snake, or Pei She Chuan, first written in the T'ang dynasty by an unknown author. It was then a tale of the simple supernatural whose hero was a great white snake. In the next version in the following century, the snake has become a vampire woman who is an evil force. But the third version contains a more gentle and human touch. The vampire becomes a faithful wife who aids her husband and gives him a son. The story thus adds not only new character but new quality, and ends not as the supernatural tale it began but as a novel of human beings.

So in early periods of Chinese history, many books must be called not so much novels as source books for novels, the sort of books into which Shakespeare, had they been open to him, might have dipped with both hands to bring up pebbles to make into jewels. Many of these books have been lost, since they were not considered valuable. But not all - early stories of Han, written so vigorously that to this day it is said they run like galloping horses, and tales of the troubled dynasties following - not all were lost. Some have persisted. In the Ming dynasty, in one way or another, many of them were represented in the great collection known as T'ai P'ing Kuan Shi, wherein are tales of superstition and religion, of mercy and goodness and reward for evil and well doing, tales of dreams and miracles, of dragons and gods and goddesses and priests, of tigers and foxes and transmigration and resurrection from the dead. Most of these early stories had to do with supernatural events, of gods born of virgins, of men walking as gods, as the Buddhist influence grew strong. There are miracles and allegories, such as the pens of poor scholars bursting into flower, dreams leading men and women into strange and fantastic lands of Gulliver, or the magic wand that floated an altar made of iron. But stories mirrored each age. The stories of Han were vigorous and dealt often with the affairs of the nation, and centered on some great man or hero. Humor was strong in this golden age, a racy, earthy, lusty humor, such as was to be found, for instance, in a book of tales entitled Siao Ling, presumed to have been collected, if not partly written, by Han Tang Suan. And then the scenes changed, as that golden age faded, though it was never to be forgotten, so that to this day the Chinese like to call themselves sons of Han. With the succeeding weak and corrupt centuries, the very way the stories were written became honeyed and weak, and their subjects slight, or as the Chinese say, «In the days of the Six Dynasties, they wrote of small things, of a woman, a waterfall, or a bird.»

If the Han dynasty was golden, then the T'ang dynasty was silver, and silver were the love stories for which it was famous. It was an age of love, when a thousand stories clustered about the beautiful Yang Kuei Fei and her scarcely less beautiful predecessor in the emperor's favor, Mei Fei. These love stories of T'ang come very near sometimes to fulfilling in their unity and complexity the standards of the Western novel. There are rising action and crisis and dénouement, implicit if not expressed. The Chinese say, «We must read the stories of T'ang, because though they deal with small matters, yet they are written in so moving a manner that the tears come.

It is not surprising that most of these love stories deal not with love that ends in marriage or is contained in marriage, but with love outside the marriage relationship. Indeed, it is significant that when marriage is the theme the story nearly always ends in tragedy. Two famous stories, Pei Li Shi and Chiao Fang Chi, deal entirely with extramarital love, and are written apparently to show the superiority of the courtesans, who could read and write and sing and were clever and beautiful besides, beyond the ordinary wife who was, as the Chinese say even today, «a yellow-faced woman », and usually illiterate.

So strong did this tendency become that officialdom grew alarmed at the popularity of such stories among the common people, and they were denounced as revolutionary and dangerous because it was thought they attacked that foundation of Chinese civilization, the family system. A reactionary tendency was not lacking, such as is to be seen in Hui Chen Chi, one of the earlier forms of a famous later work, the story of the young scholar who loved the beautiful Ying Ying and who renounced her, saying prudently as he went away, «All extraordinary women are dangerous. They destroy themselves and others. They have ruined even emperors. I am not an emperor and I had better give her up » - which he did, to the admiration of all wise men. And to him the modest Ying Ying replied, «If you possess me and leave me, it is your right. I do not reproach you.» But five hundred years later the sentimentality of the Chinese popular heart comes forth and sets the thwarted romance right again. In this last version of the story the author makes Chang and Ying Ying husband and wife and says in closing, «This is in the hope that all the lovers of the world may be united in happy marriage.» And as time goes in China, five hundred years is not long to wait for a happy ending.

This story, by the way, is one of China's most famous. It was repeated in the Sung dynasty in a poetic form by Chao Teh Liang, under the title The Reluctant Butterfly, and again in the Yuan dynasty by Tung Chai-yuen as a drama to be sung, entitled Suh Hsi Hsiang. In the Ming dynasty, with two versions intervening, it appears as Li Reh Hua's Nan Hsi Hsiang Chi, written in the southern metrical form called «ts'e», and so to the last and most famous Hsi Hsiang Chi. Even children in China know the name of Chang Sen.

If I seem to emphasize the romances of the T'ang period, it is because romance between man and woman is the chief gift of T'ang to the novel, and not because there were no other stories. There were many novels of a humorous and satirical nature and one curious type of story which concerned itself with cockflghting, an important pastime of that age and particularly in favor at court. One of the best of these tales is Tung Chen Lao Fu Chuan, by Ch'en Hung, which tells how Chia Chang, a famous cockfighter, became so famous that he was loved by emperor and people alike.

But time and the stream pass on. The novel form really begins to be clear in the Sung dynasty, and in the Yuan dynasty it flowers into that height which was never again surpassed and only equalled, indeed, by the single novel Hung Lou Meng, or The Dream of the Red Chamber, in the Ts'ing dynasty. It is as though for centuries the novel had been developing unnoticed and from deep roots among the people, spreading into trunk and branch and twig and leaf to burst into this flowering in the Yuan dynasty, when the young Mongols brought into the old country they had conquered their vigorous, hungry, untutored minds and demanded to be fed. Such minds could not be fed with the husks of the old classical literature, and they turned therefore the more eagerly to the drama and the novel, and in this new life, in the sunshine of imperial favor, though still not with literary favor, there came two of China's three great novels, Shui Hu Chuan and San Kuo-Hung Lou Meng being the third.

I wish I could convey to you what these three novels mean and have meant to the Chinese people. But I can think of nothing comparable to them in Western literature. We have not in the history of our novel so clear a moment to which we can point and say, «There the novel is at its height.» These three are the vindication of that literature of the common people, the Chinese novel. They stand as completed monuments of that popular literature, if not of letters. They, too, were ignored by men of letters and banned by censors and damned in succeeding dynasties as dangerous, revolutionary, decadent. But they lived on, because people read them and told them as stories and sang them as songs and ballads and acted them as dramas, until at last grudgingly even the scholars were compelled to notice them and to begin to say they were not novels at all but allegories, and if they were allegories perhaps then they could be looked upon as literature after all, though the people paid no heed to such theories and never read the long treatises which scholars wrote to prove them. They rejoiced in the novels they had made as novels and for no purpose except for joy in story and in story through which they could express themselves.

And indeed the people had made them. Shui Hu Chuan, though the modern versions carry the name of Shi Nai An as author, was written by no one man. Out of a handful of tales centering in the Sung dynasty about a band of robbers there grew this great, structured novel. Its beginnings were in history. The original lair which the robbers held still exists in Shantung, or did until very recent times. Those times of the thirteenth century of our Western era were, in China, sadly distorted. The dynasty under the emperor Huei Chung was falling into decadence and disorder. The rich grew richer and the poor poorer and when none other came forth to set this right, these righteous robbers came forth.

I cannot here tell you fully of the long growth of this novel, nor of its changes at many hands. Shih Nai An, it is said, found it in rude form in an old book shop and took it home and rewrote it. After him the story was still told and re-told. Five or six versions of it today have importance, one with a hundred chapters entitled Chung I Shui Hu, one of a hundred and twenty-seven chapters, and one of a hundred chapters. The original version attributed to Shih Nai An, had a hundred and twenty chapters, but the one most used today has only seventy. This is the version arranged in the Ming dynasty by the famous Ching Shen T'an, who said that it was idle to forbid his son to read the book and therefore presented the lad with a copy revised by himself, knowing that no boy could ever refrain from reading it. There is also a version written under official command, when officials found that nothing could keep the people from reading Shui Hu. This official version is entitled Tung K'ou Chi, or, Laying Waste the Robbers, and it tells of the final defeat of the robbers by the state army and their destruction. But the common people of China are nothing if not independent. They have never adopted the official version, and their own form of the novel still stands. It is a struggle they know all too well, the struggle of everyday people against a corrupt officialdom.

I might add that Shui Hu Chuan is in partial translation in French under the title Les Chevaliers Chinois, and the seventy-chapter version is in complete English translation by myself under the title All Men Are Brothers. The original title, Shui Hu Chuan, in English is meaningless, denoting merely the watery margins of the famous marshy lake which was the robbers' lair. To Chinese the words invoke instant century-old memory, but not to us.

This novel has survived everything and in this new day in China has taken on an added significance. The Chinese Communists have printed their own edition of it with a preface by a famous Communist and have issued it anew as the first Communist literature of China. The proof of the novel's greatness is in this timelessness. It is as true today as it was dynasties ago. The people of China still march across its pages, priests and courtesans, merchants and scholars, women good and bad, old and young, and even naughty little boys. The only figure lacking is that of the modern scholar trained in the West, holding his Ph.D. diploma in his hand. But be sure that if he had been alive in China when the final hand laid down the brush upon the pages of that book, he, too, would have been there in all the pathos and humor of his new learning, so often useless and inadequate and laid like a patch too small upon an old robe.

The Chinese say «The young should not read Shui Hu and the old should not read San Kuo.» This is because the young might be charmed into being robbers and the old might be led into deeds too vigorous for their years. For if Shui Hu Chuan is the great social document of Chinese life, Sa Kuo is the document of wars and statesmanship, and in its turn Hung

Lou Meng is the document of family life and human love.

The history of the San Kuo or Three Kingdoms shows the same architectural structure and the same doubtful authorship as Shui Hu. The story begins with three friends swearing eternal brotherhood in the Han dynasty and ends ninety-seven years later in the succeeding period of the Six Dynasties. It is a novel rewritten in its final form by a man named Lo Kuan Chung, thought to be a pupil of Shih Nai An, and one who perhaps even shared with Shih Nai An in the writing, too, of Shui Hu Chuan. But this is a Chinese Baconand-Shakespeare controversy which has no end.

Lo Kuan Chung was born in the late Yuan dynasty and lived on into the Ming. He wrote many dramas, but he is more famous for his novels, of which San Kuo is easily the best. The version of this novel now most commonly used in China is the one revised in the time of K'ang Hsi by Mao Chen Kan, who revised as well as criticised the book. He changed, added and omitted material, as for example when he added the story of Suan Fu Ren, the wife of one of the chief characters. He altered even the style. If Shui Hu Chuan has importance today as a novel of the people in their struggle for liberty, San Kuo has importance because it gives in such detail the science and art of war as the Chinese conceive it, so differently, too, from our own. The guerillas, who are today China's most effective fighting units against Japan, are peasants who know San Kuo by heart, if not from their own reading, at least from hours spent in the idleness of winter days or long summer evenings when they sat listening to the storytellers describe how the warriors of the Three Kingdoms fought their battles. It is these ancient tactics of war which the guerillas trust today. What a warrior must be and how he must attack and retreat, how retreat when the enemy advances, how advance when the enemy retreats - all this had its source in this novel, so well known to every common man and boy of China.

Hung Lou Meng, or The Dream of the Red Chamber, the latest and most modern of these three greatest of Chinese novels, was written originally as an autobiographical novel by Ts'ao Hsüeh Ching, an official highly in favor during the Manchu regime and indeed considered by the Manchus as one of themselves. There were then eight military groups among the Manchus, and Tstao Hsüeh Ching belonged to them all. He never finished his novel, and the last forty chapters were added by another man, probably named Kao O. The thesis that Ts'ao Hsüeh Ching was telling the story of his own life has been in modern times elaborated by Hu Shih, and in earlier times by Yuan Mei. Be this as it may, the original title of the book was Shih T'ou Chi, and it came out of Peking about 1765 of the Western era, and in five or six years, an incredibly short time in China, it was famous everywhere. Printing was still expensive when it appeared, and the book became known by the method that is called in China, «You-lend-me-a-book-and-I-lend-you-a-book».

The story is simple in its theme but complex in implication, in character study and in its portrayal of human emotions. It is almost a pathological study, this story of a great house, once wealthy and high in imperial favor, so that indeed one of its members was an imperial concubine. But the great days are over when the book begins. The family is already declining. Its wealth is being dissipated and the last and only son, Chia Pao Yü, is being corrupted by the decadent influences within his own home, although the fact that he was a youth of exceptional quality at birth is established by the symbolism of a piece of jade found in his mouth. The preface begins, «Heaven was once broken and when it was mended, a bit was left unused, and this became the famous jade of Chia Pao Yü.» Thus does the interest in the supernatural persist in the Chinese people; it persists even today as a part of Chinese life.

This novel seized hold of the people primarily because it portrayed the problems of their own family system, the absolute power of women in the home, the too great power of the matriarchy, the grandmother, the mother, and even the bondmaids, so often young and beautiful and fatally dependent, who became too frequently the playthings of the sons of the house and ruined them and were ruined by them. Women reigned supreme in the Chinese house, and because they were wholly confined in its walls and often illiterate, they ruled to the hurt of all. They kept men children, and protected them from hardship and effort when they should not have been so protected. Such a one was Chia Pao Yü, and we follow him to his tragic end in Hung Lou Meng.

I cannot tell you to what lengths of allegory scholars went to explain away this novel when they found that again even the emperor was reading it and that its influence was so great everywhere among the people. I do not doubt that they were probably reading it themselves in secret. A great many popular jokes in China have to do with scholars reading novels privately and publicly pretending never to have heard of them. At any rate, scholars wrote treatises to prove that Hung Lou Meng was not a novel but a political allegory depicting the decline of China under the foreign rule of the Manchus, the word Red in the title signifying Manchu, and Ling Tai Yü, the young girl who dies, although she was the one destined to marry Pao Yü, signifying China, and Pao Ts'ai, her successful rival, who secures the jade in her place, standing for the foreigner, and so forth. The very name Chia signified, they said, falseness. But this was a farfetched explanation of what was written as a novel and stands as a novel and as such a powerful delineation, in the characteristic Chinese mixture of realism and romance, of a proud and powerful family in decline. Crowded with men and women of the several generations accustomed to living under one roof in China, it stands alone as an intimate description of that life.

In so emphasizing these three novels, I have merely done what the Chinese themselves do. When you say «novel», the average Chinese replies, « Shui Hu, San Kuo, Hung Lou Meng.» Yet this is not to say that there are not hundreds of other novels, for there are. I must mention Hsi Yü Chi, or Record of Travels in the West, almost as popular as these three. I might mention Feng Shen Chuan, the story of a deified warrior, the author unknown but said to be a writer in the time of Ming. I must mention Ru Ling Wai Shi, a satire upon the evils of the Tsing dynasty, particularly of the scholars, full of a double-edged though not malicious dialogue, rich with incident, pathetic and humorous. The fun here is made of the scholars who can do nothing practical, who are lost in the world of useful everyday things, who are so bound by convention that nothing original can come from them. The book, though long, has no central character. Each figure is linked to the next by the thread of incident, person and incident passing on together until, as Lu Hsün, the famous modern Chinese writer, has said, «they are like scraps of brilliant silk and satin sewed together.»

And there is Yea Shou Pei Yin, or An Old Hermit Talks in the Sun, written by a famous man disappointed in official preferment, Shia of Kiang-yin, and there is that strangest of books, Ching Hua Yuen, a fantasy of women, whose ruler was an empress, whose scholars were all women. It is designed to show that the wisdom of women is equal to that of men, although I must acknowledge that the book ends with a war between men and women in which the men are triumphant and the empress is supplanted by an emperor.

But I can mention only a small fraction of the hundreds of novels which delight the common people of China. And if those people knew of what I was speaking to you today, they would after all say «tell of the great three, and let us stand or fall by Shui Hu Chuan and San Kuo and Hùng Lou Meng.» In these three novels are the lives which the Chinese people lead and have long led, here are the songs they sing and the things at which they laugh and the things which they love to do. Into these novels they have put the generations of their being and to refresh that being they return to these novels again and again, and out of them they have made new songs and plays and other novels. Some of them have come to be almost as famous as the great originals, as for example Ching P'ing Mei, that classic of romantic physical love, taken from a single incident in Shui Hu Chuan.

But the important thing for me today is not the listing of novels. The aspect which I wish to stress is that all this profound and indeed sublime development of the imagination of a great democratic people was never in its own time and country called literature. The very name for story was «hsiao shuo », denoting something slight and valueless, and even a novel was only a «ts'ang p'ien hsiao shuo », or a longer something which was still slight and useless. No, the people of China forged their own literature apart from letters. And today this is what lives, to be part of what is to come, and all the formal literature, which was called art, is dead. The plots of these novels are often incomplete, the love interest is often not brought to solution, heroines are often not beautiful and heroes often are not brave. Nor has the story always an end; sometimes it merely stops, in the way life does, in the middle of it when death is not expected.

In this tradition of the novel have I been born and reared as a writer. My ambition, therefore, has not been trained toward the beauty of letters or the grace of art. It is, I believe, a sound teaching and, as I have said, illuminating for the novels of the West.

For here is the essence of the attitude of Chinese novelists - perhaps the result of the contempt in which they were held by those who considered themselves the priests of art. I put it thus in my own words, for none of them has done so.

The instinct which creates the arts is not the same as that which produces art. The creative instinct is, in its final analysis and in its simplest terms, an enormous extra vitality, a super-energy, born inexplicably in an individual, a vitality great beyond all the needs of his own living - an energy which no single life can consume. This energy consumes itself then in creating more life, in the form of music, painting, writing, or whatever is its most natural medium of expression. Nor can the individual keep himself from this process, because only by its full function is he relieved of the burden of this extra and peculiar energy - an energy at once physical and mental, so that all his senses are more alert and more profound than another man's, and all his brain more sensitive and quickened to that which his senses reveal to him in such abundance that actuality overfiows into imagination. It is a process proceeding from within. It is the heightened activity of every cell of his being, which sweeps not only himself, but all human life about him, or in him, in his dreams, into the circle of its activity.

From the product of this activity, art is deducted - but not by him. The process which creates is not the process which deduces the shapes of art. The defining of art, therefore, is a secondary and not a primary process. And when one born for the primary process of creation, as the novelist is, concerns himself with the secondary process, his activity becomes meaningless. When he begins to make shapes and styles and techniques and new schools, then he is like a ship stranded upon a reef whose propeller, whirl wildly as it will, cannot drive the ship onward. Not until the ship is in its element agam can lt regain its course.

And for the novelist the only element is human life as he finds it in himself or outside himsel# The sole test of his work is whether or not his energy is producing more of that life. Are his creatures alive? That is the only question. And who can tell him? Who but those living human beings, the people? Those people are not absorbed in what art is or how it is made-are not, indeed, absorbed in anything very lofty, however good it is. No, they are absorbed only in themselves, in their own hungers and despairs and joys and above all, perhaps, in their own dreams. These are the ones who can really judge the work of the novelist, for they judge by that single test of reality. And the standard of the test is not to be made by the device of art, but by the simple comparison of the reality of what they read, to their own reality.

I have been taught, therefore, that though the novelist may see art as cool and perfect shapes, he may only admire them as he admires marble statues standing aloof in a quiet and remote gallery; for his place is not with them. His place is in the street. He is happiest there. The street is noisy and the men and women are not perfect in the technique of their expression as the statues are. They are ugly and imperfect, incomplete even as human beings, and where they come from and where they go cannot be known. But they are people and therefore infinitely to be preferred to those who stand upon the pedestals of art.

And like the Chinese novelist, I have been taught to want to write for these people. If they are reading their magazines by the million, then I want my stories there rather than in magazines read only by a few. For story belongs to the people. They are sounder judges of it than anyone else, for their senses are unspoiled and their emotions are free. No, a novelist must not think of pure literature as his goal. He must not even know this field too well, because people, who are his material, are not there. He is a storyteller in a village tent, and by his stories he entices people into his tent. He need not raise his voice when a scholar passes. But he must beat all his drums when a band of poor pilgrims pass on their way up the mountain in search of gods. To them he must cry, «I, too, tell of gods!» And to farmers he must talk of their land, and to old men he must speak of peace, and to old women he must tell of their children, and to young men and women he must speak of each other. He must be satisfied if the common people hear him gladly. At least, so I have been taught in China.

PRINCESS DIANA

(Princess Of Wales and Anti-Landmine Activist)

INTRODUCTION

DIANA FRANCES SPENCER was born on July 1, 1961, in Norfolk, England, the third of the Lord and Lady Althorp's four children. She grew up at Park House, a mansion in Norfolk located next door to the royal family's Sandringham estate. One of Diana's playmates was Prince Andrew, Charles's brother.

Diana's mother, the Honorable Frances Shand-Kydd, is the daughter of a wealthy Anglo-Irish baron. Diana's father, the Viscount Althorp who became an earl in 1975, was a remote descendant of the Stuart kings and a direct descendant of King Charles II (1630-1685).

Prince Charles proposed to Diana at dinner in his Buckingham Palace apartment on February 3, 1981. Lady Diana Spencer began enchanting the public and international press shortly before July 29, 1981, wedding to Prince Charles of Wales, heir to the British throne, in a ceremony that was broadcast worldwide. On February 29, 1996, the Princess announced that she had agreed to a divorce.

On August 31, 1997, the paparazzi followed the couple after they dined at the Ritz Hotel in Paris (owned by Fayed's father). The combination of the pursuing paparazzi, driving at a high rate of speed, and having a drunk driver behind the wheel, all played into the automobile accident which claimed Princess Diana's life.

Responding To Landmines: A Modern Tragedy And It's Consequences Keynote Address at a one day seminar co-hosted by the Mines Advisory Group and the Landmine Survivors Network, London: June 12, 1997

LADIES and Gentlemen,

I must begin by saying how warmly I welcome this conference on landmines convened by the Mines Advisory Group and the Landmines Survivors' Network. It is so welcome because the world is too little aware of the waste of life, limb and land which anti-personnel landmines are causing among some of the poorest people on earth. Indeed, until my journey to Angola early this year - on which I am going to speak this morning - I was largely unaware of it too.

For the mine is a stealthy killer. Long after conflict is ended, its innocent victims die or are wounded singly, in countries of which we hear little. Their lonely fate is never reported. The world, with its many other preoccupations, remains largely unmoved by a death roll of something like 800 people every month - many of them women and children. Those who are not killed outright - and they number another 1,200 a month - suffer terrible injuries and are handicapped for life. I was in Angola in January with the British Red Cross - a country where there are 15 million landmines in a population, Ladies and Gentlemen, of 10 million - with the desire of drawing world attention to this vital, but hitherto largely neglected issue.

Some people chose to interpret my visit as a political statement. But it was not. I am not a political figure. As I said at the time, and I'd like to re-iterate now, my interests are humanitarian. That is why I felt drawn to this human tragedy. This is why I wanted to play down my part in working towards a world-wide ban on these weapons. During my days in Angola, I saw at first hand three aspects of this scourge. In the hospitals of Luanda, the capital, and Huambo, scene of bitter fighting not long ago, I visited some of the mine victims who had survived, and saw their injuries. I am not going to describe them, because in my experience it turns too many people away from the subject. Suffice to say, that when you look at the mangled bodies, some of them children, caught by these mines, you marvel at their survival. What is so cruel about these injuries, is that they are almost invariably suffered, where medical resources are scarce.

I observed for myself some of the obstacles to improving medical care in most of these hospitals. Often there is a chronic shortage of medicine, of pain killers, even of anaesthetics. Surgeons constantly engaged in amputating shattered limbs, never have all the facilities we would expect to see here. So the human pain that has to be borne is often beyond imagining. This emergency medical care, moreover, is only the first step back to a sort of life. For those whose living is the land, loss of an arm or leg, is an overwhelming handicap which lasts for life. I saw the fine work being done by the Red Cross and other agencies to replace lost limbs. But making prostheses is a costly as well as a complicated business. For example; a young child will need several different fittings as it grows older. Sometimes, the severity of the injury makes the fitting of an artificial limb impossible. There are never enough resources to replace all the limbs that are lost.

As the Red Cross have expressed it: "Each victim who survives, will incur lifetime expenses for surgery and prosthetic care totalling between 2,000 and 3,000."

That is an intolerable load for a handicapped person in a poor country. That is something to which the world should urgently turn its conscience.

In Angola, one in every 334 members of the population is an amputee! Angola has the highest rate of amputees in the world. How can countries which manufacture and trade in these weapons square their conscience with such human devastation?

My third main experience was to see what has been done, slowly and perilously, to get these mines out of the earth. In the Kuito and Huambo region I spent a morning with small team from Halo Trust, which is training Angolans to work on the pervasive minefields and supervising their work. I speak of "our team" because men of the Mines Advisory group - or, in this instance, the Halo Trust - who volunteer for this hazardous work are usually former members of our own Services. I take this opportunity to pay my tribute to the work these men do on our behalf - the perils they encounter are not just confined to mines. Two members of the Mines Advisory Group team in Cambodia, Chris Howes and Houn Horth, were kidnapped by the Khmer Rouge a year ago and their fate is uncertain. We can only pray for their safe return.

Much ingenuity has gone into making some of these mines. Many are designed to trap an unwary de-miner. Whenever such tricky mines appear, the de-miner will call in one of the supervising team, who will then take over. That is what keeps their lives perpetually at risk. It might be less hazardous, I reflected, after my visit to Angola, if some of the technical skills used in making mines had been applied to better methods of removing them. Many of these mines are relatively cheap - they can be bought for 5 apiece, or less. Tracing them, lifting them, and disposing of them, costs far more - sometimes as much as a hundred times more.

Angola, is full of refugees returning after a long war. They present another aspect of this tragedy. The refugee turns towards home, often ignorant of conditions in his homeland. He knows of mines, but homeward bound, eagerness to complete the journey gets the better of him. Or he finds mines on what was once his land, and attempts to clear them. There were many examples of that in Angola. These mines inflict most of their casualties on people who are trying to meet the elementary needs of life. They strike the wife, or the grandmother, gathering firewood for cooking - They ambush the child sent to collect water for the family

I was impressed to see the work being done by many of the world's agencies on "Mine Awareness"." If children can be taught at school, if adults can be helped to learn what to do, and what not to do in regions that have been mined, then lives can be saved and injuries reduced.

There are said to be around 110 million mines lurking somewhere in the world - and over a third of them are to be found in Africa! Angola is probably more heavily mined than anywhere else, because the war went on for such a long time, and it invaded so much of the country. So that country is going to be infested with mines, and will suffer many more victims. And this brings me to one of the main conclusions I reached after this experience.

Even if the world decided tomorrow to ban these weapons, this terrible legacy of mines already in the earth would continue to plague the poor nations of the Globe. "The evil that men do, lives after them "

And so, it seems to me, there rests a certain obligation upon the rest of us

One of my objectives in visiting Angola was to forward the cause of those, like the Red Cross, striving in the name of humanity to secure an international ban on these weapons. Since them, we are glad to see, some real progress has been made. There are signs of a change of heart - at least in some parts of the world. For that we should be cautiously grateful. If an international ban on mines can be secured it means, looking far ahead, that the world may be a safer place for this generation's grandchildren.

But for this generation in much of the developing world, there will be no relief, no relaxation The toll of deaths and injuries caused by mines already there, will continue.

This tracing and lifting of mines, as I saw in Angola, is a desperately slow business. So in my mind a central question remains. Should we not do more to quicken the de-miners' work, to help the injured back to some sort of life, to further our own contribution to aid and development?

The country is enriched by the work done by its overseas agencies and non-governmental organisations who work to help people in Africa and Asia to improve the quality of their lives. Yet mines cast a constant shadow over so much of this work. Resettlement of refugees is made more hazardous. Good land is put out of bounds. Recovery from war is delayed. Aid workers themselves are put at risk. I would like to see more done for those living in this "no man's land" which lies between the wrongs of yesterday and the urgent needs of today.

I think we owe it. I also think it would be of benefit to us, as well as to them. The more expeditiously we can end this plague on earth caused by the landmine, the more readily can we set about the constructive tasks to which so many give their hand in the cause of humanity.

SHEIKH HASINA

INTRODUCTION

Former Prime Minister of the of Bangladesh, Sheikh Hasina was born on September 28, 1947 at Tungipara. She is the eldest daughter of Bangabandhu Sheikh Mujibur Rahman. Her mother Begum Fazilatunnesa was widely respected as a tender hearted lady. In 1968, Sheikh Hasina was married to an eminent scientist of Bangladesh Mr. M. A. Wazed Miah.

Sheikh Hasina was unanimously elected the president of the Awami League in 1981 while she was still in exile. Ending six years in exile she returned home finally on May 17, 1981 to a tumultuous welcome by million of people when she declared, " I have nothing to lose. I pledge you to fight for restoration of the democratic rights of the people of my country." In 1982 she was the first to raise the voice of protest against an assumption of state-power through military coups d'etat.

In 1984 she was put under house arrest in February and then again in November. In March 1985, she was put under house arrest for three months at a stretch.

In the Elections of 1991 following the ouster of General Ershad she assumed the mantle of leader of the opposition. Under her leadership, the Awami League government was the first government to complete a full 5 year tenure. The 2001 elections saw Awami League losing the elections and once again becoming the largest opposition party. Hasina resigned on 5 August 2024, as large crowds of demonstrators surrounded the prime minister's residence.

Address on towards Partnership between Men and Women in Politics, held in New Delhi (February 15, 1997)

IN the Name of Allah, The Most Beneficent and the Most Merciful, Mr. President, Your Excellency Prime Minister, Excellencies, Ladies and Gentlemen,

I feel greatly privileged and honoured to have the opportunity to address such a distinguished gathering of parliamentarians and eminent persons from all over the world. May I at the outset thank the Prime Minister of India. His Excellency Mr. H.D. Deve Gowda, for his warm invitation to me. We recall with pleasure and satisfaction his recent visit to Bangladesh. It was an honour to welcome him in our midst. I also thank Mr. P.A. Sangma, the distinguished Speaker of the Loka Sabha and Mrs. Nazma Heptullah, Deputy President of the Rgjya Sabha for their kind invitation to me to attend the inaugural session of this important conference.

May I offer you, Mr. President, on behalf of myself and my delegation our heartiest congratulation on your election to this high office. I am confident that your wisdom, experience and diplomatic skill will help steer the conference to a successful conclusion. I would also like to avail of the opportunity to express my sincere appreciation to the Government of India for the warm reception and generous hospitality extended to us and for the excellent arrangements made for the conference. Personally, I cherish fond memories of my previous visits to this ancient and picturesque city and in particular, I recall my recent visit at the kind invitation of Prime Minister Deve Gowda when we signed the historic Treaty on the sharing of the Ganges Waters. It marked a new milestone in the streng the ning of friendship, cooperation and good neighbourly relations between our two countries.

The subject chosen for the conference is of vital importance for humankind. As the rebel poet of Bangladesh noted, though men and women have been equal partners in the development of civilizations, women were denied an equal status. Social and political institutions as well as the legal systems discriminated against them. Women's role in most societies was defined by household demands and largely limited to the private domain. Despite the sacrifices made by them and their contributions in building up the family as the nucleus of society and civilized life, they were relegated to an inferior position. Unequal opportunities in education and training, unequal access to health facilities, limited rights in owning wealth and assets and denial of the right to exercise political power condemned them to a subordinate status in most societies. The right of franchise was denied to them until recently even by liberal Western societies. Fortunately, the world has witnessed great changes in perceptions on the gender issue over the last two decades. Our deliberations are happily taking place at a time when age-old prejudices and gender-based inequities are finally giving way and we are drawing closer to our cherished goal of gender equality, harmonious development and lasting peace. Women no longer want to remain peripheral actors and want to play their rightful role in all spheres of life including economic and political life. The awakening that has been achieved since the Nairobi Conference on Women has led to basic changes in the thinking everywhere about their role in socio-political structure. The urgency of political empowerment of women is now widely recognized. However, the journey from Mexico to Beijing was a long one. This journey was marked by a sense of dedication and commitment on the part of both men and women who were determined to break the social, political, legal and psychological barriers and obstacles in ensuring genuine gender equality. The Beijing World Conference on Women not only proclaimed the rights of women in every aspect of life but it gave us a Platform for Action. The central thrust of this epoch-making document is in the domain of decision-making. Indeed one may say that a new era has dawned for women and significant progress has been achieved. Yet the full implementation of the Platform for Action is still a distant dream.

Please allow me to share my country's experience with the participants of this conference. South Asia a rich tradition of people's movements fighting for the right of self-determination, self-rule and human rights. The peasant movements of Bengal could be termed as a fore-runner of the struggles for self-rule, leading ultimately to our glorious War of Liberation. Women have actively participated in all such movements. The names of Pritilata Wadeddar, Kalpana Dutta, Ila Mitra, Matungini Hajera are just a few of the many women whose heroic deeds inspire us even today. In the present context, this region has seen women as heads of governments in four out of the seven SAARC countries. Here I would like to pay a special tribute to a great daughter of India. Sreemati Indira Gandhi, who set an example of dedicated service to the people of her country. For us in Bangladesh, Begum Rokeya Sakhwat Hossain stands unparalleled as a pioneer in social reform, champion of women's rights and an educationist. Her actions and writings have deeply influenced the movement for the emancipation of women of my country. While speaking about the contribution of great women in our history I would like to note the silent but important role played by my mother Begum Fazilatunnesa. Few people know her immense contributions in our struggle for independence. While my father inspired, mobilized and prepared the nation for the final struggle, it was my mother who, with quiet courage, looked after the family when he was in prison, stood by him through every trial and tribulation and gave him support and strength at critical moments in our history. I do not know if history will fully record her contributions but I believe her patience, sound judgement and above all, her courage entitles her to be ranked as one of the foremost freedom-fighters of Bangladesh.

It is a matter of deep concern that despite such examples of courage and leadership qualities, the vast majority of our women continue to be consigned to an inferior status. Indeed, society judges these women as exceptions. Political and economic life is still dominated by the privileged and powerful and therefore largely by men. Democratic politics has to include all the people regardless of gender and class. Where half of the population are women and the majority are poor, the participation of women and the poor in politics has to be integrated in such a manner as to make democracy truly meaningful. Age old traditions, social norms and values, economic dependence and illiteracy have contributed to the marginal position of women in the realm of power and decision-making at all levels. Their participation in politics is much less than their numbers would demand. Let me declare at this august assembly that my commitment, the commitment of my party, is to remedy this imbalance in the years ahead with unflinching determination.

The Constitution of Bangladesh, passed by the parliament during the stewardship of Bangabandhu Sheikh Mujibur Rahman, is a unique document which guarantees equal rights to the women of the country in every sphere of life. It provides for representation of women on terms of equality with men in political and public representative institutions such as the parliament and the local government bodies. At the same time, in order to ensure a minimum representation of women in the parliament the Father of the Nation took the far-sighted step of reserving seats for them to guarantee their participation in the highest law-making institution of the Republic. Articles 28 and 29 of our Constitution embody the fundamental rights relating to women. Article 122 guarantees the right to vote by both males and females without any discrimination. The legal framework for ending discrimination against women was strengthened when Bangladesh became a signatory to the Convention on Elimination of all forms of Discriminations against Women. The identified critical areas of concern for women of Bangladesh are gender equality, women's autonomy and women's paid work. The right to equal compensation for equal work is also being articulated.

Women's marginalized position in national politics especially electoral politics has gone through remarkable changes during the political and civil movements of the eighties and nineties. Women from all strata of society including housewives actively participated in these movements. The movement for the restoration of the right to vote freely under a neutral caretaker government received universal support from the nation. The record number of women who cast their vote in the June 12, 1996 general election is eloquent testimony to their deep interest in playing an active part in shaping the destiny of the nation. It is also a matter of satisfaction that women politicians in different political parties have emerged in their own rights as frontline leaders. This is an encouraging development. Whereas only one women was elected to the second parliament in 1979-82, there are as many as 7 women in the current parliament who have been directly elected from non-reserved constituencies. In our cabinet, in addition to myself, two ministers and one deputy minister are women. We know that we have still a long way to go but we have certainly made a start in right earnest.

How can we fully integrate women in the social, economic and political life of the nation? Local government seems to be an excellent starting point. My government is about to place a local government till in the parliament which will not only decentralize the administration but involve women even in the rural areas with the institutions envisaged in the bill. Women in all the tiers of the local government will be directly elected. We believe this will be the forerunner towards true equality in participation by both men and women in the politics and decision-making process of the country. But this is not all. Apart from the 10 per cent reserved seats in the parliament, there are quotas for women in government services. The government's efforts at empowering women have been significantly supplemented by the initiatives of the private and non-governmental organizations. Their activities at the grassroot level have started to change the attitudes of the rural women who are beginning to yearn for a change from their subordinate status. Income-generating activities in the rural areas supported by successful micro-credit schemes and the induction of a large number of women into the garment industry have also made their impact in changing the social environment. Last but not least, we have intensified our efforts towards boosting women's access to education, which we feel is the only sure means of ensuring that women can secure their rights. It is ineffectual to merely legislate equality and provide women with various legal safeguards if women are unable to fully appreciate their rights or lack the knowledge and skills to defend them.

This important conference will, I hope deal with the following key issues confronted by women all over the world but especially in the developing world:

(i) Women in parliament at the national level,

(ii) Women in the political process as participants in party politics,

(iii) Gender-based discrimination, as it is reflected in political systems and practices, and

(iv) Women in higher administration and national and local economic management areas. Effective partnership, one hardly needs to emphasize, between men and women in politics will remain an unfulfilled objective unless the right steps are

taken for the empowerment of women politically. We must find ways to reach out to women in order to make them politically more aware and conscious. Coordination and cooperation of both government and civil society comprising private voluntary organisations are necessary to achieve this goal.

The United Nations deserves our thanks for having organised in recent years global conferences in a number of fields of highest priority for the international community. The Rio Earth Summit (1992), the Population and Development Conference held in Cairo (1994) and the World Social Development Summit in Copenhagen (1995) and a number of other global conferences attached highest priority to the rights of women and children. Against the backdrop of global acknowledgement of these basic rights we must search for the answers to the complex multidimensional issues standing in the way of women's political empowerment. The latent potentials of women must be realized. The constraints that do not allow the realization of these potentials must be identified and removed. As we step into the next millennium just three years from now, we have to plan for a more dynamic and comprehensive role for women. This calls for major shifts not only in the thought process, but the entire socio-political agenda that we might want to adopt individually and collectively.

Before I conclude, I would like to convey my best wishes to you, Mr. Speaker, the sponsors and to all the delegates for a successful conference. My thanks and gratitude go out to the organisers of the Conference for inviting me and giving me this opportunity to share my thoughts with you on the important subject that has been set for our deliberations. Thank you Mr. President, Distinguished Delegates, Excellencies, Ladies and Gentlemen.

Khoda Hafez. Joi Bangla, Joi Bangabandhu.

Long Live Bangladesh.

SHIRLEY CHISHOLM

INTRODUCTION

Shirley St. Hill Chisholm was born on November 30, 1924 in Brooklyn, New York to Charles and Ruby St. Hill. Her father was from British Guiana and her mother was from Barbados. In 1927, Shirley was sent to Barbados to live with her maternal grandmother. She received a good education from the British school system, which she later credited with providing her with a strong academic background.

In 1934, she rejoined her parents in New York. Shirley excelled in academics at Girls High School in Brooklyn from which she graduated in 1942.

In 1949, she married Conrad Chisholm, a Jamaican who worked as a private investigator. Shirley and her husband participated in local politics, helping form the Bedford-Stuyvesant political League. In addition to participating in politics, Chisholm worked in the field of day care until 1959. In 1960, she started the Unity Democratic Club. The Unity Club was instrumental in mobilizing black and Hispanic voters.

In 1964 Chisholm ran for a state assembly seat. She won and served in the New York General Assembly from 1964 to 1968.

She has received many honorary degrees, and her awards include Alumna of the Year, Brooklyn College; Key Woman of the Year; Outstanding Work in the Field of Child Welfare; and Woman of Achievement. Shirley Chisholm passed away on January 1, 2005.

Equal Rights For Women Famous Speech Address To The United States House Of Representatives, Washington, DC: May 21, 1969

MR. SPEAKER, when a young woman graduates from college and starts looking for a job, she is likely to have a frustrating and even demeaning experience ahead of her. If she walks into an office for an interview, the first question she will be asked is, "Do you type?"

There is a calculated system of prejudice that lies unspoken behind that question. Why is it acceptable for women to be secretaries, librarians, and teachers, but totally unacceptable for them to be managers, administrators, doctors, lawyers, and Members of Congress.

The unspoken assumption is that women are different. They do not have executive ability orderly minds, stability, leadership skills, and they are too emotional.

It has been observed before, that society for a long time, discriminated against another minority, the blacks, on the same basis - that they were different and inferior. The happy little homemaker and the contented "old darkey" on the plantation were both produced by prejudice.

As a black person, I am no stranger to race prejudice. But the truth is that in the political world I have been far oftener discriminated against because I am a woman than because I am black.

Prejudice against blacks is becoming unacceptable although it will take years to eliminate it. But it is doomed because, slowly, white America is beginning to admit that it exists.

Prejudice against women is still acceptable. There is very little understanding yet of the immorality involved in double pay scales and the classification of most of the better jobs as "for men only."

More than half of the population of the United States is female. But women occupy only 2 percent of the managerial positions. They have not even reached the level of tokenism yet No women sit on the AFL-CIO council or Supreme Court There have been only two women who have held Cabinet rank, and at present there are none. Only two women now hold ambassadorial rank in the diplomatic corps. In Congress, we are down to one Senator and 10 Representatives.

Considering that there are about 3 1/2 million more women in the United States than men, this situation is outrageous.

It is true that part of the problem has been that women have not been aggressive in demanding their rights. This was also true of the black population for many years. They submitted to oppression and even cooperated with it. Women have done the same thing. But now there is an awareness of this situation particularly among the younger segment of the population.

As in the field of equal rights for blacks, Spanish-Americans, the Indians, and other groups, laws will not change such deep-seated problems overnight But they can be used to provide protection for those who are most abused, and to begin the process of evolutionary change by compelling the insensitive majority to reexamine it's unconscious attitudes.

It is for this reason that I wish to introduce today a proposal that has been before every Congress for the last 40 years and that sooner or later must become part of the basic law of the land – the equal rights amendment.

Let me note and try to refute two of the commonest arguments that are offered against this amendment. One is that women are already protected under the law and do not need legislation. Existing laws are not adequate to secure equal rights for women. Sufficient proof of this is the concentration of women in lower paying, menial, unrewarding jobs and their incredible scarcity in the upper level jobs. If women are already equal, why is it such an event whenever one happens to be elected to Congress?

It is obvious that discrimination exists. Women do not have the opportunities that men do. And women that do not conform to the system, who try to break with the accepted patterns, are stigmatized as ''odd'' and "unfeminine." The fact is that a woman who aspires to be chairman of the board, or a Member of the House, does so for exactly the same reasons as any man. Basically, these are that she thinks she can do the job and she wants to try.

A second argument often heard against the equal rights amendment is that is would eliminate legislation that many States and the Federal Government have enacted giving special protection to women and that it would throw the marriage and divorce laws into chaos.

As for the marriage laws, they are due for a sweeping reform, and an excellent beginning would be to wipe the existing ones off the books. Regarding special protection for working women, I cannot understand why it should be needed. Women need no protection that men do not need. What we need are laws to protect working people, to guarantee them fair pay, safe working conditions, protection against sickness and layoffs, and provision for dignified, comfortable retirement. Men and women need these things equally. That one sex needs protection more than the other is a male supremacist myth as ridiculous and unworthy of respect as the white supremacist myths that society is trying to cure itself of at this time.

~~~
~~~